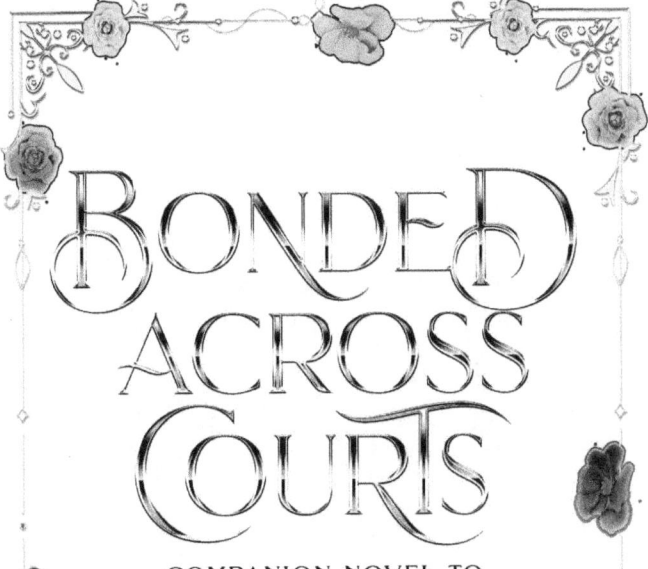

BONDED ACROSS COURTS

COMPANION NOVEL TO
THE FAE KING DUOLOGY

TM GOODKEY

Credit

Cover Designer: Emcat Designs

Editor: Delanie Prins

Contents

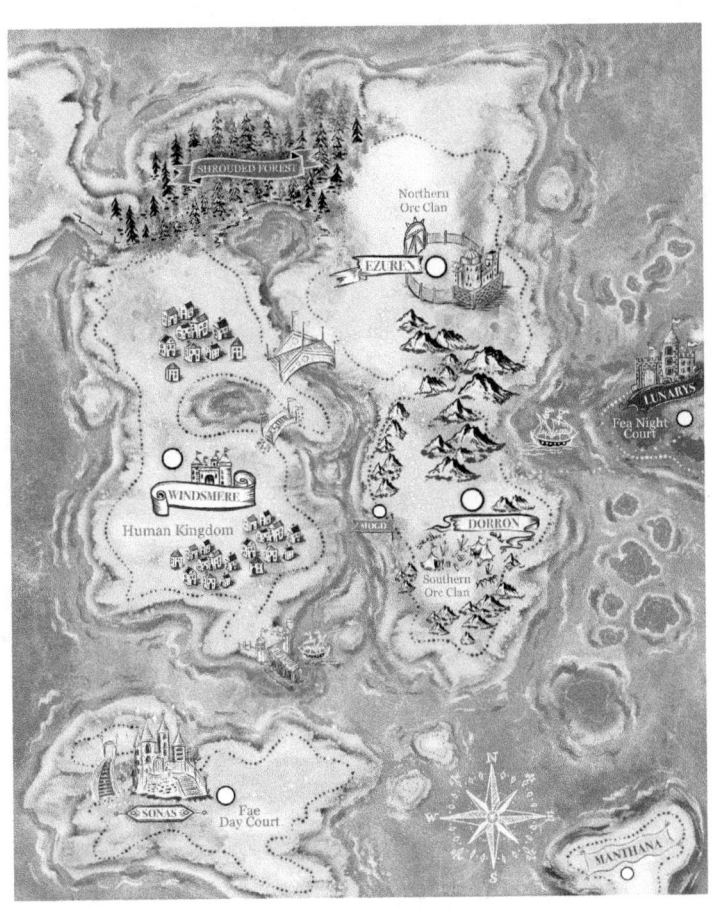

This story is for every single person who took a chance on this series and wanted more.

Author Note

Well it's finally finished! The Fae King Series has reached its conclusion with book four—Milori's story.

Take one last trip into this world and adventure with our charming and funny Captain of the guard.

Enjoy!

TM

PLEASE NOTE!

I am Canadian and write in Canadian English, if you think it is spelt wrong it may just be spelt in Canadian English. Please feel free to email me at authortmgoodkey@outlook.com for any grammatical mistakes.

Chapter 1

Nesi

The darkness has always called to me more than the glittering court. I smile as people pass by, completely oblivious to my presence in the shadows. The new Night Court halls gleam with an iridescent glow giving it a bluish hue. The shadows swirl around me as I glide past, the guards unaware of my passing. I prefer the shadows and darkness, where I can avoid the annoyance of other people. Here I can observe and gather information undisturbed.

"The Queen has requested your presence." Jasmine speaks into the darkness, leaning casually against a large marble column. The nearby guard glances around frantically, searching for whoever she's addressing. She smirks in my direction though I know she can't fully see me, and I can't help but return her smile. She has always had an uncanny ability to spot me, which proved invaluable when I delivered information to Neeve.

Deciding to put the guard out of his paranoid misery, I step out from the shadows. The chandeliers cast a warmer glow, a contrast to the colder moonlight that streams in. Like every other time someone sees me materialize from the darkness, the guard's eyes go wide and his skin pales.

"Rather late at night, isn't it, to be looking for my–" I quickly glance at the guard who swallows hard–"presence?" Jasmine straightens from her leaning position, amusement dancing in her eyes. I walk with deliberate and concise purpose, each step silent even in this large hall, while Jasmine's heels echo off the empty walls. We leave the frightened guard behind, heading toward Neeve's wing.

"You find far too much enjoyment in scaring the guards." she says barely containing her own enjoyment.

"They are going to fear me no matter what I do. I might as well enjoy it." I allow myself a moment of satisfaction at others' discomfort with my presence. When I was far younger and much more influenced by other people's opinions, it did hurt having everyone fear me and my powers, but much time has passed now and those insecurities no longer consume me. I am content with who I am, even if others do not care for me.

Jasmine huffs out a laugh, her long dark brown hair swaying behind her as she shakes her head, the light shining off the embellishments in her hair. "You know it might do you some good to smile and befriend the court instead of scaring them. And if you're lucky, you can talk one of the less scared men into taking you out! How long has it been since you've gone out to have some fun?"

I turn my head to look at her, eyebrow raised, but she doesn't face me because she knows the idea does not interest me in the slightest, especially spending time with a male. They are just an inconvenience I can not tolerate if I want to get the job done. Does the twinge of desire to find someone still linger? Yes, but it is easily ignored.

"Tell me, when do I have time to have 'fun' when I can't even slink around in the darkness without being summoned?" The look of sympathy covers her face and I avert my gaze. I do not want or need anyone's sympathy. I have resolved myself to this current life, and I have found a sense of purpose in it, though it wouldn't have been something I would have originally chosen for myself had I been given the choice.

"I'm—" She begins but I put up my hand softly to stave off the apologize I know is coming.

"I don't need an apology, Jasmine. This role is one I accept willingly. Our people still need someone with my abilities, and as long as Neeve requires my service, I will follow her commands to ensure our people never again fall under a tyrant's rule or face exile in that cursed forest." I hear her sigh, but I keep my gaze fixed ahead, unwilling to see the pity in her eyes.

Before King Oberon summoned me to become his enforcer, I was content in my solitude, happy when others simply looked past me. I should have known such peace wouldn't last. After King Maegren's assassination, I knew my quiet life was forfeit. Oberon had always known what I was—a shadow walker, an ability so rare it hadn't manifested in nobility for centuries. The entire royal family knew of my power, though only Oberon saw its true potential for his twisted purposes.

Fear had ruled me then, but Oberon was neither patient nor understanding. The guilt of what I did in his service weighs heavy on my soul: the lives I took, the terror I was forced to inflict. Even now, the memories threaten to overwhelm me, but I can't afford to dwell on things that were beyond my control. Not anymore.

"Don't do that," Jasmine whispers, her voice barely carrying even in the empty hall. A guard we pass takes in our presence, but when he meets my gaze, he quickly looks away.

"Do what?" Irritation rises within me. I have no desire to continue this conversation.

"Act as if being a weapon—or shield, if you prefer—is all you're good for." I look over at her, finding both sadness and determination etched in her features. "Oberon may have used you as his sword, but protecting this court from future threats isn't solely your burden to bear. Many here would die for Neeve, just as you would. Don't condemn yourself to a life of self-sacrifice, throwing away any hope of the future you truly desire."

Her gaze holds mine, unwavering. It's been so long since I've allowed myself to imagine a future beyond protecting Neeve and our people. Such dreams feel distant and unreachable.

"Perhaps when there's more stability, I can consider that future." It's a half-hearted commitment, but she seems to recognize my attempt at sincerity. Maybe someday. Just not today.

"Better than nothing, I suppose," she mutters, and I can't help the slight smile that pulls at my lips. Though I wouldn't call us close, I'm not sure anyone truly knows me, but Jasmine has proven herself a good friend, one of the few people I truly trust.

The glittering opulence of the main halls fades into a more subdued and practical wing of the palace. Though construction of the new Night Court Palace continues, Neeve has never been one to indulge in the extravagance of court life, preferring to keep her personal wing simple and unadorned. Eventually, certain appearances must be maintained, regardless of her preferences, but for now, King Timas' gifts and financial support barely cover the essential foundations—both for the palace's construction and establishing the trade routes that will help the Night Court regain its independence.

As we approach Neeve's private chambers, two guards stand vigilant at her doors, their faces stoic, but alert. They straighten as we near.

"This is where I leave you," Jasmine says, pausing a few steps from the guards. She turns to me, fatigue evident in the slope of her shoulders. "Whatever task the Queen has for you...I hope it's not one that pulls you further from finding your own path." Her words carry a weight of concern that makes me uncomfortable.

"Get some rest, Jasmine," is all I can offer her. Her lips press into a thin line. She recognizes the deflection for what it is, but she nods and turns away, her footsteps fading into the quiet of the night.

I approach the doors, and the guards move to open them without a word. They know better than to question my presence at this hour. Being Neeve's spy master I am often summoned at all hours. My duty to Neeve will always be my priority and for that reason I will do whatever she needs. It's not the future Jasmine hopes for me, but it's the one I've chosen. At least for now.

I slip through the doors into Neeve's chambers, the warmth from the hearth chases away the evening's chill. The sitting room, like its occupant, maintains an elegant simplicity: comfortable chairs in deep blues gather around the fireplace, their rich fabric one of the few concessions to luxury. Moonlight streams through tall windows, casting long shadows across the polished wooden floor.

To my right, the partially open door reveals a glimpse at the bedchamber, as austere as one might expect from a queen who spent years in exile. But it's the left side of the sitting room that draws my attention—her personal library, a testament to her relentless pursuit of understanding. Shelves line the walls from floor to ceiling, filled with ancient texts and scrolls salvaged from the Shrouded Forest. Papers and open books cover every available surface, some marked with her neat handwriting as she pieces together our people's fractured history.

Neeve stands at one of the tables, her dark hair pulled back loosely as she leans over what appears to be a centuries-old manuscript. She's been consumed by this research since our return from exile, determined to understand how the Night and Day Courts—once unified in purpose and power—became so deeply divided over the millennia. The answers, she believes, lie somewhere in these yellowed pages and faded ink.

She doesn't look up as I enter, but I know she's aware of my presence. I wait silently, watching as she finishes making notes in the margins of her current document.

I wander closer to the library, and Neeve finally looks up, the dark circles under her eyes betraying months of sleepless nights.

"Thank you for coming so late." She straightens to her full height, her elegant dress wrinkled from a long day of running the court.

"Of course, my Queen." The formality feels appropriate, though I know how she bristles at the title.

"Nesi, if you cannot address me as Neeve, at least call me something else." I raise an eyebrow, fighting back amusement at her exasperation.

"You are, in fact, my Queen." I don't mean to be disrespectful, but perhaps I need this formality when I'm about to be assigned something undoubtedly dangerous. She runs her hand through her hair, destroying what remains of her neat appearance and dislodging the tie completely. Without another word, she walks past me to a small cabinet housing some of the finest Fae wine available—one of her few indulgences.

"Nesi, I don't have the patience to argue with you tonight, so I won't." She pauses, and I can sense the weight of what's coming. "I've received new information about the rebels causing problems on the mainland. It seems they're not merely upset with our alliance with the Day Court. They're recruiting allies, hoping to destabilize both Courts."

My heart pounds against my ribs.

"How could they possibly think causing dissent in both Courts will get them what they want? Is freedom from that horrid forest not worth celebrating? They're acting like spoiled children!" Neeve tips her glass back, draining its contents before turning to face me.

"It's rare to see such emotion from you, cousin." My chest rises and falls rapidly, but I can't begin to comprehend their twisted logic.

"I'm not emotionless, but emotions rarely serve any purpose beyond distracting from a goal. Since I currently lack an objective, I can risk being annoyed." The word is wholly inadequate, but it's all I'm willing to show right now. "If their aim was simply to free the Night Court from Day Court influence, I could understand that sentiment. But destabilizing both Courts? It makes no sense. To what end? Why weaken both Courts if their supposed goal is to strengthen the Night Court's power? None of this adds up." I begin to run through possible reasons for their behaviour, but Neeve interrupts my thoughts.

"I don't believe they want to see the Night Court gain independence from Day Court influence. I believe they simply want power for themselves." Neeve's expression darkens. "My spies have returned. They've discovered that Soren is leading the rebel group."

Bile rises in my throat at the mere mention of his name. That vile, despicable man haunts many of my nightmares. Though not Oberon's right hand, he held a place in the inner circle, tasked with ensuring I completed my assignments, even as I wept through their execution.

"What does he want?" The anger I hold for that man is nothing less than an unleashed war. He deserves death, and I find myself hoping Neeve will name me his executioner.

"From what I can tell, he wants power. All of it. He's gathering recruits by spreading lies throughout the remote islands. He's exploiting the anger some islanders harbor toward King Timas and his human Queen. His followers grow by the day, and if he continues, we'll face not only an uprising in the Night Court, but King Timas will confront one far larger within the Day Court." Neeve's voice carries the weight of command. "I need you to go to Sonas and report this to King Timas. Then you'll request permission to visit an island called Manthana. Our latest intelligence suggests it's Soren's next target. You need to discover who they're recruiting, and what they're searching for on that island."

Her authority as Queen is inspiring. She truly represents the best possible future for our people.

"What do you mean? What are they searching for?" I ask.

She exhales and returns to her papers. I follow, curious. She hands me a worn sheet covered in ancient Fae script, dominated by an image of a prism. "What is this?"

"I fear this is the objective they are looking for. I found it in an old tome filled with Fae mysteries. The author supposedly lost his mind in the forest, which eventually claimed his life. His writings are mostly indecipherable ramblings in the old Fae tongue. But this..." She pauses, gesturing to the paper. "This intrigued me, so I looked into it a bit more. I had heard of the island while I was hiding from Oberon. It's far from the other Fae islands, known for agriculture and strange occurrences. Visitors speak of a heavy, mystical presence that locals seem immune to. When asked about it most locals can't even feel the heaviness. I believe it's old magic, and I want you to investigate."

The text means nothing to me. Only the image of a bird loosely wrapped in some sort of fabric. The image takes up half the page and it makes me think that it is somehow being bound. Interesting. "Should I share this with King Timas?"

Neeve pauses, crafting her response with political cunning. "This is merely speculation. Without concrete evidence of Soren's objectives, I see no reason to involve King Timas. We need access to that island, and I want you to handle it. Don't be seen. Fade into the shadows, observe, and report back."

She wants the shadow walker, and she'll have it. "I'll leave at first light." I place the paper down and turn toward the door.

"Nesi..." I look back over my shoulder to see the weight of leadership bearing down on her. "Be safe. If you don't retur n...well, I would hate to have to kill so many for harming my cousin." I don't suppress my smile. She is truly fierce.

I nod and exit her suite. While I don't plan on dying, if I get the chance to kill Soren, I won't hesitate.

Chapter 2

Milori

These early morning meetings usually don't bother me, but after a restless night, I'm in no mood for pleasantries. My boots strike sharp against the marble floors, each step only feeding my agitation. It isn't just the lack of sleep that's getting to me. I've been having the same dream for weeks. A dream about a shadow that was so breathtaking it left me gasping. By the sun, I must be losing my mind. Perhaps Garrick slipped something into my drink last night, because there's no other explanation for why I woke in a panic, questioning my sanity over a dream. A shadow. I've found many women attractive, but never have I sunk so low as to find the very darkness alluring. I need to see a healer.

I rub my temple, exhaling sharply. The last thing I need is for today's meeting to add to my already throbbing headache.

The grand windows lining the hall spill warm sunlight into the corridor, and though I usually welcome the heat, today it grates on me.

Some part of me longs for the cool embrace of the darkness. To find a quiet place away from everything and everyone. Maybe

I'm still stuck on the lingering bitterness from my wasted journey to Manthana last month. The memory still stings. I travelled all that way after receiving information from my agents that my mother was ill, so much so that she might not survive, only to arrive and find her conveniently absent. "She's been called away suddenly," Father had explained, his eyes not quite meeting mine. "She hasn't been well, but it's...manageable." I hadn't even waited to see when she would return. I booked passage back on the same boat I had arrived on. Jalnor had witnessed the whole humiliating scene, his attempts to convince me to stay falling on deaf ears. If Mother couldn't be bothered to be at home getting better for the sake of no one other than my father then it wasn't worth staying. She did what she always does best: be absent and keep secrets.

Now, to add to all of that, I've got dreams and irritability as constant companions. Dreams of a shadow that feels more real than anything I've experienced before. Dreams that leave me gasping for air and questioning my sanity. Is this what real madness feels like? To be attracted to the darkness itself?

I'm starting to sound like Emilia. She's been skipping morning training, citing some persistent illness, yet I caught her raiding the kitchens at midnight last week, inhaling an entire loaf of fresh bread and three honey cakes. Even Timas had no explanation when she requested pickled fish with her breakfast yesterday. A strange human sickness, no doubt. At least she has an excuse for her odd behaviour. Me? I'm unravelling over a dream. A dream shadow. An infuriatingly attractive dream shadow.

I definitely need that healer.

The heavy wooden doors of the command room come into view, with a lone guard stationed at his post.

"Farlin," I greet, as he snaps to attention, offering a curt nod.

"Sir. All quiet."

Not that I expected anything else, but it's still a relief.

"Good. Reports will begin shortly. Show the guards in when they arrive."

I push open the door to what is officially my office, though I refuse to treat it as such. The idea of a private space separating me from my men never sat well with me. My mother may have been noble, but my father was a farmer, and I grew up on an island where titles meant little. Walls and ranks only serve to isolate. The irony of befriending the heir to the throne didn't help my standing either. Timas and I understood each other too well, both of us out of place in a world obsessed with bloodlines and power. So when I earned my command, I made sure my office served as a hub for all my men, rather than a sanctuary of solitude.

A massive round table dominates the room, maps and reports scattered across its surface. I take my usual seat, positioned to watch the entrance—an old habit I've never shaken. The walls are adorned with the palace's proud history, none more imposing than the portrait of Timas' father. The old king's stern gaze still makes me straighten my posture, a lingering reflex from years of lectures on "proper noble conduct."

Lieutenant Roran and Kerris enter both with a serious expression on their face. "Captain, western islands remain quiet. Trade routes are secure. However..." Roran recites wasting no time but he drums his fingers once against his sword hilt, a subtle tell. "The locals seem...hesitant. Less willing to engage with our patrols."

Not unheard of, but concerning. Before I can press further, Lieutenant Kerris shifts uncomfortably beside him.

"Eastern routes?" I prompt.

She hesitates—unusual for her. "Same, sir. No direct threats, but something feels... off."

The door opens once more, this time revealing a gate guard carrying a message orb tinged with the deep blue of the Night Court. My body tenses on instinct. Despite our recent alliance with Queen Neeve, old habits die hard.

"From Queen Neeve, Captain." The guard places the orb on the table, bows, and withdraws.

Once alone, I activate the orb. Magic flares to life, and the Queen's voice fills the room.

"Captain Milori, I require your immediate attention. I am sending my most trusted agent to brief you on a matter of growing concern. Please extend her every courtesy, and arrange an audience with the King upon her arrival in one day."

The orb dims, leaving me with more questions than answers. Vague messages, wary locals, and increasing tensions all point to something brewing beneath the surface. I should reach out to my contacts, though intelligence from the Night Court has been... unreliable since their recent restoration.

I'll need to brief Timas, but that can wait until after lunch. Emilia's arranged a lunch for our little makeshift family, and they deserve their peace. Besides, I have rounds to make, and an endless pile of reports to sign. The joys of command. Some battles come with swords, others with ink.

The mountain of paperwork leaves me more irritable than before. I need something beyond signing my name and sifting through dry reports. The lunch in the conservatory calls, and while I typically enjoy its warmth, today even that seems unlikely to soothe me.

The grand staircase stretches before me, the ascent offering a momentary reprieve from my frustrations. Guards nod in acknowledgement as I pass, while noblewomen whisper behind their fans. I ignore them, focused only on reaching my destination.

The conservatory doors swing open at my approach, sunlight streaming through in golden waves, it still does nothing to my sour mood.

"Look what the cat dragged in," Garrick drawls, feet propped irreverently on one of Emilia's prized plant stands. "You look like you've been wrestling mountain trolls."

"Paperwork," I correct, dropping into my usual seat—one with a clear view of both entrances. "Though I'd take the trolls at this point."

Alette arches a brow. "You're brooding more than usual. What aren't you telling us?"

Seven months married to Garrick and the woman has become annoyingly perceptive. Before I can deflect, the doors open again. Timas enters with Emilia tucked against his side, her usual brightness dimmed by dark circles under her eyes and exhaustion. He helps her into her chair with excessive care.

"Still buried in reports?" Timas asks, smirking. "I recall ordering you to take an actual break."

"I'm here, aren't I?" I spread my arms. "Though if we're discussing rest, perhaps you'd like to explain why your wife was raiding the kitchens at midnight again?"

Emilia flushes, shifting in her seat. "I—I have no idea what you're talking about."

"Three honey cakes," I remind her. "And an entire loaf of bread."

Laughter rings around the table, a familiar comfort. Yet beneath it, the weight of Queen Neeve's message lingers in my mind. Unrest in the islands, vague warnings, an incoming agent. Whatever is coming, it won't be simple.

"Milori." Timas' voice sharpens, pulling me back. "What is it? And don't charm your way out of it—I know that look."

I glance around at the others before plastering on my most winning smile. "Can't a man have a headache without being accused of conspiracy? Besides," I turn to Emilia with perhaps too much enthusiasm, "I believe someone promised us news that doesn't involve trade routes or border patrols."

Timas narrows his eyes at my obvious deflection, but Emilia practically glows as she straightens in her chair. "Well, since you asked so nicely..." She reaches for Timas' hand. "We're having a baby!"

Garrick and Alette burst from their chairs with exclamations of joy, while I sit here feeling like the most oblivious captain in Fae history. The midnight kitchen raids, the morning illness, Timas' protective hovering. By the sun, I've been so distracted I missed what was right in front of my face. Some spymaster I am. I blame the shadow dream. And the headache. And possibly that questionable wine Garrick insisted I try last week.

I rise from my chair, a genuine smile replacing my earlier forced one. "This is wonderful news! When is the little one due?"

"In six months, give or take a few. That's at least what the healers are predicating anyways." Emilia beams, her hand still clasped in Timas'.

"Six months?" The words come out more accusatory than intended as I look between them. "You've managed to keep this secret for three months?"

Emilia's laugh fills the conservatory. "It wasn't easy, especially with your supposedly keen observation skills." Her teasing only highlights how distracted I've been lately.

"The mighty Captain Milori, outsmarted by morning sickness and honey cakes." Garrick's grin is insufferable. "Perhaps we should revise those intelligence reports of yours."

I ignore him, moving to embrace Timas first. My oldest friend returns the hug fiercely, and I can feel the barely contained joy radiating from him. When I pull back, his eyes are suspiciously bright. "Congratulations, my friend." The words feel inadequate for the magnitude of this moment.

Turning to Emilia, I bow with exaggerated formality. "My Queen, I formally request permission to spoil this child absolutely rotten."

She rolls her eyes but accepts my hug when I straighten. "As if you needed permission. Though," she adds quietly enough that only I can hear, "you might want to practice your shadowing skills if you plan to keep up with a half-Fae child."

The word *shadow* sends an unwanted shiver down my spine, that ridiculous dream threatening to surface again. I cover my momentary discomfort with a laugh. "I'll have you know I'm excellent with children. They find me charming and engaging!" An obnoxious laugh behind me forces me to turn and glare at its source.

Garrick clenches his stomach with laughter. "Charming! Engaging! I saw a child stomp on your foot and glare at you when you offered to play with him and his friends in the lower city!" My brows dip even further as my glare becomes fire.

"I'll have you know that child was an oddity, I am loved by all fae children! How can't they love me? I'm amazing!" I gesture in an exaggerated way to myself to make my point clear, but he continues to chuckle as Emilia smacks him in the shoulder.

"Well, I think you will be an amazing godfather to the baby," Emilia says as she side-eyes Garrick.

Godfather. To a sweet little child. My throat constricts with emotion completely overcome with gratitude. These people are everything to me, my family.

"Godfather?" The word comes out barely above a whisper as I look between Timas and Emilia. A first in my life, I'm utterly speechless. Timas' smile radiates pure joy, while Emilia's holds such profound trust it makes my chest ache.

"Yes, my friend. We want you to be the godfather to the little one." Timas pulls Emilia closer to his side, and the sight of them—my dearest friend and his queen, offering me this piece of their future—makes my throat close with emotion.

"Did you break him?" Garrick's voice comes from beside me, his big chunky finger pokes at my face, which is enough to get my emotions under control. Swatting his hand away, I look at my truest friend, and the woman that created this new family of ours.

"I am beyond grateful." Bowing deep and straightening to my full height. "This honour means more to me than I can explain. This child will be obscenely loved. Thank you."

Looking around at our little group, I see the love we have all grown to have for one another. Timas finding his spirit bond with Emilia and Garrick finding his soul bond in Alette. I can't control the twinge of jealousy that threatens to surface, but I take a moment to really look at the love we all share for each other. Even if my deepest desire is to find my perfect other half, I will not throw away this family we have made together.

"Oh this is such a beautiful moment," Alette whispers, which breaks the tense emotional moment. Thank goodness, as I would hate to actually cry right now.

"I had special cakes made just for this!" Emilia squeaks as she motions to a server standing by the door. "Specially made with moss root." I look over at Timas with concern, and his restraint tells me these are not going to be very good, but I paste a smile on my face anyway. The server comes and places a suspiciously brown cake-like structure on the table.

"Oh I haven't had one of these in months!" Garrick excitedly grabs one, popping the entire thing in his mouth.

"Seriously, Garrick! Have some class. At least take a smaller bite," I chastise as I pick up the suspicious baked good. Garrick just grunts in response.

"I have been craving them non-stop for weeks. Thank goodness we could get a shipment of moss root from the southern tribes, or else we would have had to celebrate with those overly sweet cakes." Emilia says, picking up her own brown blob. Timas, Alette, and I have obvious forced smiles on while we tentatively take a bite of the concerning excuse for a cake. Meanwhile, Emilia and Garrick mumble appreciatively over how much they miss Orc food, looking for all the world like they're eating something actually edible. I cover a shiver of disgust as I take a small bite. A burst of earthy flavour coats my mouth—no, assaults it—with a hit of what can only be described as fresh grave dirt mixed with mould. The three of us catch each other's desperate glances and try to discreetly toss our cakes into the garden while Garrick and Emilia continue their enthusiastic praise. Some threats, it seems, come in the form of celebratory desserts. I'm not sure I'm going to be able to forget the taste of that anytime soon, or forgive Timas for not warning me.

The conversation flows easily after that, everyone talking over each other with plans and wild ideas. I let myself sink into their joy, into this moment of perfect belonging. But Queen Neeve's message keeps nagging at the back of my mind, I can't seem to ignore the feeling of doom that stirs every time I think about this. Whatever her agent brings tomorrow could ruin all of this. These moments of peace—this family we've built—have been hard-won, and I'll reduce to ash anyone who dares threaten them.

A shadow passes briefly across the conservatory's windows, and my heart inexplicably races. Cursing silently, I force my attention back to Alette's elaborate plans for a celebration, but my hand instinctively rests where my blade should be.

"Well, my flower, I must return to my duties but I will be back later." Timas leans over to kiss Emilia on the cheek. Emilia smiles, knowing this is part of being married to the King. "Milori, with me." He stands, and as his captain, I stand as well, saying goodbye to everyone as we leave.

The conservatory falls away behind us as we head towards the throne room.

"Explain." Timas' no-argument tone reminds me of his terrifying power and authority. No room for messing around.

"We have had some disturbing reports from the trade routes on the outer islands. It seems that there is some discontent brewing. The reports state that our patrols are being avoided, people going into their homes and locking their doors—some even have refused service to our patrols." Unease twists in my stomach. Timas glances at me but continues to maintain his pace.

"What aren't you telling me?" It takes me a moment to respond, not because I desire to hide any information, just so I can't fully explain or understand what makes me feel so concerned.

"The reports are an indication of something bigger going on. I have sent out some scouts to see what can be gleaned but I won't hear back from them for a while. But that's not what is most concerning." We turn the corner and take the side stairs down to the main level where the throne room is. "I received a message from Queen Neeve this morning."

Timas stops dead in his tracks. His eyes sweep over my stance—shoulders rigid, hands clasped behind my back, chin high. Without a word, he motions to the side room off the great hall. I follow him inside, the heavy door closing us off from prying ears.

"In all our years, you've never held back information about the Day Court." Timas' voice is quiet but firm. "Yet for weeks now, I've watched you stare into nothing, lost in thoughts you won't share. The outer islands are restless, Queen Neeve is making moves, and my Captain—my friend—is keeping secrets." He steps closer, his eyes never leaving mine. "I trust you with my life, Milori, but I won't stand by while you sacrifice yourself over some misguided sense of duty. Tell me what's really going on."

I run a hand through my hair, trying to organize my scattered thoughts. "Something feels...wrong. Not just with the court, but with me." The words taste strange on my tongue. "Watching you find your spirit bond with Emilia, seeing Garrick with his soul bond—" I wave my hand dismissively, uncomfortable with this level of honesty. "I never thought I'd be the one distracted by such things."

Timas waits, patient as ever. I can't help but pace.

"Then there's this ridiculous dream that won't leave me alone. A shadow, of all things. Not a threat, not an attack, just...a shadow that—" I stop, realizing how absurd this sounds. "I woke up gasping for air, like some lovesick fool. Me, attracted to darkness itself. I should probably see a healer."

Timas' expression remains carefully neutral, which somehow makes this worse.

"And now the outer islands are showing signs of unrest. All of this would be upsetting, yes, but it was the message from Queen Neeve that has put me on edge. She is sending an agent to the palace tomorrow and has requested an audience with you. The entire situation is causing me a great deal of unease. The timing of it all... my intelligence from the Night Court has been questionable since their restoration, but this message, combined with the unrest—" I meet Timas' gaze. "Something is brewing, my friend, and I can't shake the feeling that my dream and these events are somehow connected."

Timas is quiet for a long moment, his expression thoughtful as he studies me. Finally, a small smile tugs at the corner of his mouth. "Only you would manage to make yourself sick with worry over both matters of state and matters of the heart at the same time."

I scoff, though there's no real heat behind it. "I am not sick with worry. I'm being prudent."

"Of course you are." He clasps my shoulder, his grip warm and reassuring. "And you're right—something isn't adding up. But we won't know more until your scouts return, and Queen Neeve's agent arrives tomorrow." His eyes sparkle with sudden mischief. "Though I must say, finding yourself attracted to a shadow is a new level of dedication to your work. Perhaps you should take some time off. When was the last time you actually relaxed?"

"I relaxed just this morning," I protest, gesturing vaguely toward the conservatory. "There was cake. Terrible, terrible cake, which you could have warned me about, by the way."

"That wasn't relaxing, that was you pretending to relax while probably cataloguing every person who walked past the windows." He shakes his head, amused. "Your spirit bond is out there somewhere, my friend. But you won't find her if you're too busy staring at reports to notice them walk by." He pauses, glancing at a shadowy corner of the room with exaggerated interest. "Unless, of course, your true love really is lurking in dark corners. In which case, I highly recommend that healer visit. Immediately."

"Very funny," I mutter, but I can't help the slight smile that breaks through. "I'll have you know that shadow was very attractive. Mysterious. Graceful, even."

"Now I'm definitely worried." Timas laughs, steering me toward the door. "Come on, let's get back to work before you start composing poetry about the elegant way shadows dance across walls."

I follow him out, my spirits somewhat lifted despite the weight of everything else. Still, I can't resist one last glance at the corner he'd pointed out, just to be sure.

Chapter 3

Nesi

The sky bleeds amber and crimson as the ferry docks of Carraig Cove, a small inlet nestled between weathered cliffs on the eastern side of the Day Court's main island. I chose this landing deliberately. It's far from the watchful eyes of Sonas and its busy harbour. Information flows more freely where people don't expect to be observed, and I need to understand what's happening beyond the polished reports that reach Neeve.

A chill runs through me as memories surface like unwelcome ghosts from a past I've tried to forget. This isn't the first time I have landed on these shores, but last time it was under the command of Oberon. The intent was to destabilize the city of Sonas and cause unease within the population. I arrived with a couple other assassins intent on doing one thing: kill. Though this is the first time I feel like I can actually look around and take in what this island has to offer.

Salt-laden air fills my lungs as I disembark, my boots landing silently on worn planks that groan beneath other passengers. The shadows here are different, sharper and more defined in the harsh sunlight that characterizes the Day Court. They offer less cover than the velvet darkness of home, but they're still mine to command. I pull my hood lower, obscuring my features from curious glances as I blend into the small crowd dispersing from the ferry.

The dock workers glance at me, likely taking in my foreign appearance, but to them I am nothing more than a passing traveller, so their attention quickly returns to securing the vessel and unloading cargo. Their casual banter carries on the breeze—complaints about long hours, talk of recent storms, whispers about mainland politics. I linger just within earshot, hoping to understand the current temperature of the land.

"—third ferry this week with half-empty cargo holds," a burly man grunts, heaving a crate onto a waiting cart. "Trade's drying up faster than puddles in high summer."

His companion nods, wiping sweat from his brow. "Heard Eastmarsh refused to load their grain shipment. Said they're keeping their stores for winter."

"Winter? It's barely past midsummer."

"Strange times." The second man lowers his voice, twisting his hands as he survey's the area. "My cousin in Lochdale says there's been talk. People gathering after dark, speaking of how things were better before the Courts reunited." He lowers his voice further. "Some are even saying a human has no place as queen. That she will only produce a half-fae heir with no power."

The other man's eyes widen as he nervously looks around and hisses, "Are you mad? Keep that kind of talk to yourself. The

King may be kind at times but he is far from forgiving when it comes to the Queen!"

"I'm just telling you what I heard," the first man mutters defensively, becoming very interested in the knots on his rope.

I stiffen, careful to keep my expression neutral as I adjust my small travel bag. This is worse than Neeve anticipated. Discontent isn't just brewing in remote territories, but here on the main island as well, at the heart of Timas' court. And targeting the human queen? This is no longer on the outskirts of the courts like Neeve originally reported.

Moving away from the docks, I follow a dusty path into the small settlement of Carraig. Unlike the grandeur of Sonas, with its gleaming spires and magical embellishments, this village embraces simplicity. Stone cottages with thatched roofs cluster around a central square, where a modest market operates. Merchants call out their wares: fresh fish, woven baskets, herbs bundled with twine. The scene appears peaceful, ordinary. Sometimes it makes me jealous to see such simple things when we, the Night Court, have just come back to civilization.

There are subtle signs of unease as I watch the townsfolk. Guards patrol in pairs rather than alone. Villagers speak in hushed tones, conversations halting when uniformed soldiers pass. Children are quickly ushered indoors despite the pleasant weather.

Several locals eye me with obvious suspicion, which isn't all that surprising. The Night Court fae have stronger facial features, with hard lines where the Day Court fae are softer and rounder. Is the difference between us due to our time in exile? Potentially, but what I know for sure is that most people at a glance can tell I am from the Night Court. The reunification of Courts hasn't translated to true integration, at least not yet. It will take more time, potentially decades, for the fear and hatred the Day Court fae have for the Night Court to fade away.

I approach a weathered stable at the edge of the square, where an elderly Fae woman brushes down a dappled mare. She straightens as she senses my approach, her movements betraying the fluid grace that all Fae possess regardless of age.

"Need something?" she asks without looking up, her hands never pausing in their rhythmic strokes.

"A horse," I reply simply. "I need to reach Sonas by nightfall."

Now she turns, her amber eyes narrowing as they take in my hooded form. "Don't get many Night Court folk asking for mounts, though I guess there have been a few of you passing through the past couple months." There's no hostility in her voice, merely observation.

Lowering my hood, I let my navy blue hair fall to the side. Many Day Court fae have light blonde hair or shades that mimic the sun whereas Night Court fae typically have dark hair with a subtle sheen. Their hair coloration ranges from deep black to dark brown, often appearing to reflect minimal light similar to the night sky. Honestly it's rather odd that King Timas has such black hair, but my own thoughts on that are unimportant.

"Is that a problem?" I ask.

The woman shrugs, returning to her grooming. "Your coin spends the same as anyone's. But the road to Sonas isn't as friendly as it once was, especially for lone travelers." She glances at me again. "Particularly those from your Court."

"I can handle myself." I don't feel like I need to argue the point but I state it in a matter of fact way that grabs the woman's attention.

The woman studies me, eyes narrowing as they take in what little she can at a simple glance. "A slim thing like you traveling alone? These aren't peaceful times anymore." She lets out a dry chuckle. "Though I don't doubt you've got some fight in you. You have that look about you—all you Night Court folk do. Something in the eyes." She has no idea of my noble blood or the power I can wield but she isn't wrong. The Night Court has fought to survive, each one of us has a fight that we needed to simply exist. Even when Oberon was in control we fought back. We lost many to his tyranny.

She sets down her brush and disappears into the stable, emerging moments later with a sleek black gelding. "This is Midnight. Fast and steady, doesn't spook easy. Fifteen silver for the day, another five if you want him fed and stabled in Sonas."

I count out twenty silver pieces, placing them in her weathered palm. "Has there been trouble on the roads?"

The woman pockets the coins before answering. "Not the kind you're thinking of. No bandits or thieves. King Timas keeps the main routes well-patrolled." She lowers her voice. "It's the patrols themselves that have folk nervous. Too many questions, too many searches. On a couple of occasions townsfolk have disappeared for a night or two. They return shaken, unwilling to talk about where they've been."

This doesn't align with what I know of how King Timas runs his court. From Neeve's accounts and my own limited observations during diplomatic visits, he's fair-minded and progressive, not the type to authorize intimidation tactics or allow his men to do whatever they want.

"When did this start?" I ask, accepting Midnight's reins.

"A few months ago. Subtle at first..." She seems to pause and think twice about who she is talking to, but continues anyway. "Not sure I should really be telling you this but...these are unsettling times. There are whispers that not all who wear the royal insignia truly serve the king." Her eyes meet mine, sharp with meaning.

Interesting. Infiltration. If true, this is worse than we thought, going much deeper than originally reported. I need to send a message back to Neeve, but it will have to wait.

"Thank you for the warning," I say, mounting the horse with practiced ease. The woman nods, her eyes still studying me with uncomfortable intensity.

"You're no ordinary traveller," she observes. "Whatever brings you here, watch your back. Shadows have eyes these days."

The irony of that statement almost brings a smile to my lips. "Shadows are exactly what I'm counting on." I pull my hood back up, more comfortable under its cover.

I guide Midnight away from the stables, across the square, and onto the main road leading inland. The landscape unfolds before me: rolling hills dotted with farms and orchards, forest-covered ridges in the distance, all bathed in the warm glow of late afternoon sun. It's beautiful in its own way, though too bright and exposed for my comfort.

Having grown up in the Shrouded Forest during our exile, I find myself longing for deeper shadows. Strange how a place of such burden and angry magic—a prison for our people—could become so ingrained in me. The twisted trees, the perpetual twilight, the dangerous mystical fog that kept us contained, all of it terrible, yet familiar. It didn't seem to affect me like the others, which always scared everyone. Many would say I was a child of the forest or that the forest was going to use me to punish them further. Not exactly what I wanted to be known for but eventually people just ignored me and left me alone when I did nothing to them. Until Oberon that is.

Everyone celebrated escaping its boundaries, but part of me still finds comfort in darkness, in places where others fear to tread. Perhaps that's why the shadow magic chose me.

As the horse settles into a steady trot, I allow my thoughts to organize the information I've gathered so far. Declining trade. Villagers fearful of their own guards. Possible infiltration of the king's forces. An artefact hidden on Manthana. All of this leads me to believe an organized rebellion is underway and if rumours are true, led by Soren.

Two hours into the journey I come up to a crossroads marked by a weathered stone pillar, I pause to grab a drink from the saddle bag, and I can't help but look around. Something is making me feel uneasy. Midnight stamps impatiently beneath me, sensing my unease. A movement in the periphery of my vision catches my attention—figures on horseback emerging from a side trail, six of them wearing the unmistakable uniform of the Day Court.

I have nothing to hide. Queen Neeve's diplomatic seal will grant me passage anywhere in the allied territories, but instinct keeps me from drawing too much attention to myself. I nudge Midnight into motion again, continuing along the main road keeping an eye on the patrol.

They follow, maintaining a distance that might seem coincidental to less observant travellers. Their pursuit is subtle but deliberate, tracking rather than intercepting. I could lose them easily in the shadows, but perhaps I have become too paranoid so I maintain my pace, appearing oblivious to their surveillance.

When we reach a dense stretch of forest where the road narrows between ancient trees, I decide to test their intentions as they continue to follow me. I slow Midnight to a walk, pretending to adjust my saddle strap. The patrol closes the distance but still doesn't approach, instead dividing to flank the road ahead. A standard manoeuvre to cut off escape routes.

I guide Midnight forward again, acting as if nothing is wrong while I simultaneously map the shadows that collect on the forest floor. Each twirl of darkness is a call to my powers. Fighting would be a tactical misstep, but I won't allow anything to stop me from my objective, though if they are with Soren I wouldn't mind seeing him again, with no restraints this time. For now it's better to evade and observe. Their behaviour tells me more about what's happening here than any confrontation would.

After another mile, the forest grows denser, the ancient trees forming a canopy that blocks much of the fading sunlight. *Perfect*. I slow Midnight, taking in the forest, playing the part of a visitor. The patrol hangs back at a distance, still watching, still waiting. I don't appreciate being followed, so disappearing will hopefully show me some information about their intentions while also causing them distress, and I am feeling particularly annoyed so having some fun is in order.

I stroke Midnight's neck, his soft fur soothing under my palm. While whispering soothing words I begin to pull at the shadows beneath the trees. They respond eagerly to my call, coiling around my ankles like affectionate creatures. I draw them to me, the dark cloud moving elegantly around our legs as the darkness begins to take hold even in the day time. Even with the glances from the patrol I know they must be having a difficult time seeing us, a haze at first until a deep darkness covers us and they squint trying to decipher where we went.

Midnight tenses initially, but doesn't bolt. The stable keeper was right about his temperament. With one fluid motion, I lead him through the darkness, off the path and into the undergrowth, the darkness following us and concealing our tracks.

From the shelter of the trees, I watch the patrol advance cautiously to where I'd stood moments before. Midnight nips at my cloak as my body tenses. Their confusion is evident as they scan the area, hands on weapons, voices low and urgent. One signals to split up and search, but their eyes pass right over us, unable to penetrate the veil I've drawn around us.

"She can't have vanished," a guard hisses, frustration evident in his jerky movements. "Search the area. She has to be hiding."

The other shakes his head. "This feels wrong. No one just disappears." His voice holds a touch of fear. "You heard what he said. The Night Court Queen has a shadow-walker at her command. Perhaps this is her."

Their leader silences them with a sharp gesture. "Spread out. Find her. Our orders are clear. Any Night Court Fae are to be isolated and questioned."

This has to be Soren's doing, though I can't be certain. The signs are there, however, the positioning of his people in important roles within the Day Court is concerning.

I remain perfectly still, one hand on Midnight's muzzle to keep him quiet as the patrol searches fruitlessly. The darkness embraces us completely, any time one of the soldiers touches the edge of my shadows they practically recoil from it. Just like the forest, my shadows weigh heavy and incite fear. After several minutes of desperate searching, they reluctantly regroup.

"We'll report back," the leader decides. "She's likely heading to Sonas. Alert those in the city patrol to watch for her."

They mount and ride back toward the main road, frustration evident in their rigid postures. Only when they're well out of sight do I release my hold on the shadows, though I keep enough darkness draped around us to remain concealed.

Midnight nickers softly as I mount him again, seemingly unbothered by our shadow-cloaked state. I guide him deeper into the forest, following a game trail that runs parallel to the main road. My knowledge of these paths comes from unwelcome memories, routes I once used when Oberon sent me to spy on Timas' kingdom, but I push those thoughts away.

For nearly an hour we travel in silence, the sounds of rustling leaves and a distant owl calling our only companion. Thankfully the sun has set and the night has covered the land.

When the lights of Sonas finally appear in the distance, I feel a sense of relief but it's clouded with everything that I have learned. It doesn't help that a nagging feeling pulls at me, like it did when I was Oberon's agent. It's an unsettling feeling, like I lost something here. Shaking my head I try to push it out of my mind. I need to get to the palace, meet with the Captain of the Guard and with any luck meet with the King tonight. Then set out on the next part of my mission. The strings of this conspiracy pull at me. With the threat to the Night Court I need to find answers so my Queen can protect our people.

I guide Midnight toward the city gates, the city lights up the darkening sky, a beacon for anyone to see. Quickly I check to ensure I have the paper's with Neeve's seal in my bag which will ensure I can enter the upper city with no issue. The guards at the lower city barely glance my way, which leaves me with a mix of emotions. If the patrol that followed me were speaking truthfully then someone should be watching for me, but perhaps they don't have the influence I originally thought.

The lower city is bustling with activity after a long day's work. Laughter and conversations fill the streets. The sound of music flows down the street from the tavern and from what I remember it is always full. The higher I climb, the more the city changes from simple Day Court buildings to extravagant buildings with stained glass windows that shout money and importance. I control the disgust I feel as I judge these people for holding all the money from those who work so hard in the lower city.

The towering walls that surround the palace come into view, and the intricate arched gates sit as a prominent statement of power. The tall spires that seem to float in the sky make me wonder about what our old capitol would have looked like before we were exiled. Only stories and some drawings show that part of our history but they are few and many have never seen them to know what it used to be like.

Several royal guards stand at attention in front of the gate, on the wall, and I am sure in places that cannot be easily seen. The guard on the left steps forward, hand on his sword, as I come into view. I guide Midnight over to him.

"State your business in Sonas," he demands, his voice carrying the practiced authority of someone who expects immediate compliance.

I don't lower my hood, but I do reveal the page with Queen Neeve's seal, its enchanted surface glimmering with authenticity that cannot be counterfeited. "Official business with Captain Milori, by request of Queen Neeve of the Night Court."

Their expressions shift from suspicion to surprise, then to a carefully constructed neutrality. He looks back at the other guard before stepping back and giving me a quick nod. "We've been expecting you. Proceed directly to the palace courtyard. An escort will meet you to take you to the throne room."

"Thank you." I state. He thinks for a moment longer, an assessing eye cataloguing everything. A traitor perhaps? "Your name, sir?" He pauses unsure if he should answer me. "I merely want to know who has treated me with kindness this evening." I hope the comment will relax him and it seems to do the job.

"Therion Xaltheon," passes from his mouth and I try to smile, further putting him at ease.

"Thank you, Therion." His disposition changes as I move my body in such a way that welcomes his attention. He adjusts his stance again and steps back allowing me to proceed. I feel the guards' eyes track my movement long after I pass.

The enchanted lanterns illuminating the path to the palace's innermost sanctum radiate a warmth unlike any I've known—a welcoming glow that feels foreign to my nature, yet stirs something surprisingly pleasant within me.

The sound of Midnight's hooves clop on the stone path, echoing off the walls. The main courtyard comes into view where a large statue sits in the centre to welcome all visitors. The statue is of two fae in a dance or battle, depending on who is looking at it. One is a woman holding a sceptre thrust into the air, the dark onyx stone a symbol of the night court. The other is a man holding a staff, also thrust into the air a yellow sapphire, brighter symbolizing the Day Court. Water floats around them frozen in mid air. The writing around the bottom is ancient fae script. "Thalas un'voren nys durath, seph'ira vyl'thani su'mara eth'ernal. Bound in stillness we endure, divided power ensures peace eternal."

Many cannot read the ancient words, but they stand here as a testament to the time we once were unified as a people.

A man wearing a longer dark blue robe that reaches his knees and the posture of someone in service to the King descends the stairs. Swinging my leg over Midnight, I land on my feet and rub his neck in gratitude.

"Good job." I whisper to the beast, as someone comes out from the side to guide Midnight to the stables.

"Welcome to the Day Court. I hope your journey wasn't unpleasant." His kind smile is welcoming.

"Uneventful," I say with a smile adjusting my bag. Did I lie? Yes, but I don't know who to trust in this place, so I will reserve my thoughts for the moment. The man gestures to someone who comes walking out from a side door and offers to take my bag.

"I am fine to carry it. Thank you." It's a small bag with few belongings. I don't need much and what I don't have I can either find or buy. The man is taken off guard for a moment before

fixing his surprised features and smiling in that pleasant way
again.

"Of course. Please follow me. King Timas and Captain Milori
await you in the throne room." With a quick bow he turns to
head up the stairs as I follow behind him. I guess I won't have to
wait to meet the King after all. If I meet them tonight I can also
leave and head to Manthana tonight. I know of a boat captain
on the south end of the island who will take me discreetly.

The glamorous halls pass in a blur. They are all the same to
me. Large intricate doors open as we walk down the main hall
leading to the throne room. Warm light from the lanterns cast a
glow, illuminating the artistic design of the palace, emphasizing
the nature of the sun and how it brings growth. This is high-
lighted by the growing plants that live among the paintings.

The throne room opens up before us, its greatness a testament to King Timas and his strength. Sitting upon the throne
is none other than the King himself. Long black hair cascading
down his shoulders, a contrast to the blue and white robes he
wears, but then a sea of green grabs my attention.

That feeling of missing something suddenly crashes over me,
a tidal wave of emotion that makes my stomach lurch and my vision swim. Disbelief floods through me as unwelcome warmth
spreads across my chest—this can't possibly be happening. Not
here. Not now. My heart hammers against my ribs as the impossible truth takes shape—my spirit bond. Standing beside the
King is *my* spirit bond. I almost laugh at the cruel timing of it
all. After years of secretly wondering if such a connection would

ever find me, it appears now? When I'm carrying vital intelligence for my Queen? When rebellion threatens both Courts? The shadows around me pulse in response to my agitation, and I force myself to breathe. This connection is a liability, a distraction I never accounted for in my carefully laid plans. By the darkness, what am I supposed to do with this complication?

Chapter 4

Milori

The throne room hums with tense energy as we await. Queen Neeve's agent takes their time getting here. Timas sits on his throne, somehow managing to look both regal and completely annoyed, a talent I've never understood, but that's why he is the King and I am not. Meanwhile, I'm pacing around, unable to shake this strange feeling crawling beneath my skin. It's been building all day, a vibration deep in my chest that makes it impossible to stand still. Maybe it's those dreams. I had another one again last night. This time it seemed to swirl around me like a warning, giving me a foreboding feeling that set me on edge, while also simultaneously making me think "how does one ask a shadow out on a date?" *Get it together Milori*! I grip the roots of my hair and roughly tug it back, frustrated I can't seem to stay focused.

"I'm starting to get concerned, Milori. I haven't seen you this rattled in...well, ever. Except perhaps that time your parents announced their visit." Timas shivers dramatically. "I should have developed a sudden diplomatic emergency that night."

I stop pacing and glare at my dearest friend. "Oh please, because eating dinner with your parents was equally as comfortable. It's not my fault my father hasn't figured out how to act in a courtly setting, even after being married to my mother for centuries." I pinch the bridge of my nose at the memory. "Just be glad he didn't start singing. He's a favourite at the local tavern." I release a heavy sigh, straightening my posture in hopes of relieving the tension coursing through my body.

"Yes, well, his overly flirtatious remarks with the serving staff certainly made for exciting noble gossip for months." Timas winces at the same time I do.

"I told you, it's friendly to do that with the serving staff on Manthana...he just somehow forgot he was in the palace of the King of the Day Court and not a run-down, mead-smelling bar," I mutter.

"So then what is the issue?" Timas leans back slightly in his throne, relaxing as we wait.

"I don't know, I just have this feeling. I can't explain why, but I know whatever we find out tonight will clear up whatever this is." I wave at myself to indicate what I can't describe. "This look isn't good for me. I'm supposed to be the pretty one, not getting stress lines on my head for no reason at all." I mutter.

"The Night Court emissary will be here shortly,"Timas calmly says. "It's just past sundown. But if the emissary takes much longer they will have to wait to meet me tomorrow. I will be going to Emilia. She has barely kept anything down all day." He shakes his head. "I thought all that sickness ended after three months." Timas flops against his throne, the concern for Emilia transforming him from fearsome King to doting spirit bond in an instant.

"That's not always the case," I inform him with perhaps too much pleasure. "Some women are sick their entire pregnancy."

Timas shoots up, sitting straight on his seat. "What?! I was never told this! I insisted the healers tell me everything she could experience, and they did not share *that*!" His voice rises with each word.

I turn my body to face him fully, hands planted on my hips as I stare down my friend. "And were you acting rationally when you spoke to them? Talking calmly with kindness and respect as they delivered the report of how this child of yours is going to completely change your spirit bond's entire body, both mentally and physically? How it will cause her pain and how they aren't entirely sure how this pregnancy will go because she is human and you are Fae?"

Timas springs to his feet, his skin going a shade paler as his eyes dart anxiously around my face. "Of course I did!"

I cock an eyebrow at him as he clenches his hands.

"Well, I tried," he admits, "but then they explained how the baby would come out and used words like tearing, and pain, and screaming and well..." He doesn't need to finish. I know exactly what happened. I was the one who had to smooth things over with the terrified staff.

"Yes, well, suffice it to say when you destroyed the examination room in your 'fear,'" I make air quotes with my fingers,

"You weren't exactly acting stable. After Emilia calmed your ridiculous self down, she and I returned the next day to get a full report. The healers knew I could tell you what was going to happen without risking the furniture." I flash him a grin. "They think you won't hurt me, but I know better. I can take your royal temper tantrums."

He glares at me with enough intensity to set a lesser man ablaze, which only makes my smile widen.

"You will tell me everything, Milori, and Emilia is getting a stern talking to after this." He grumbles and sits back on his throne as I nearly topple over in laughter.

"You couldn't possibly give Emilia a stern talking to. You can barely give her a stern glare!" I straighten, chuckling. "I, on the other hand, need to dodge rogue bolts of lightning when I remotely annoy you."

"Careful, I may have enough time to toss you out that window before the emissary gets here." The reminder of the Night Court emissary snuffs out our laughter like a candle in a storm. My amusement dies in my throat as the massive doors at the end of the throne room creak open, and everything in me shifts.

My body reacts before my mind processes. My muscles tense and my breathing picks up, every sense painfully alert. The hair at the back of my neck rises as if I'm standing too close to lightning.

"By the sun," I whisper. Timas glances at me sharply, but I can't explain. I don't understand it myself.

Kaelith, the seneschal, enters first, his composure perfect as always. "Your Majesty. Captain Milori," he begins with a formal bow. "The envoy from Queen Neeve has arrived."

And then she steps into the room.

The hooded figure moves with fluid grace, each step deliberate, yet effortless. Even with her face partially concealed, there's something about her that draws my eye. No, not something. Everything. My heart pounds against my ribs as a strange heat rushes through my veins, and I know without question what this means.

I hear her inhale sharply, a barely audible sound that nonetheless reaches me across the room. It's as if her soul reaches out to mine, as if drawn by the pull of an unseen thread. She feels it too.

"Welcome to Sonas," Timas says, completely oblivious to my internal crisis. "I trust your journey was without incident?"

The woman lowers her hood, revealing striking features framed by midnight navy blue hair that has been delicately braided over her shoulder. It catches the light and the stray pieces shine like that of a raven's wing. Her dark brown eyes scan the room, locking onto me with unsettling intensity before shifting to Timas.

"King Timas," she acknowledges with a bow, her voice controlled but with an undercurrent I can't quite place. "The journey was educational." She walks further into the throne room coming to stand a few feet away and my body buzzes with anticipation. It takes all my restraint not to rush to her and touch her delicate hands.

Pushing the cloak to the side, I can see what she's wearing—a simple dress with a black corset that covers nearly all her skin, as if she can hide her true self beneath layers of fabric. Not that it matters. She is, without question, the most beautiful woman I've ever seen. She pulls a paper from her bag, Queen Neeve's insignia shining in the light of the throne room.

"I bring urgent intelligence from Queen Neeve. She believes a threat is developing that could endanger both Courts." The throne attendant receives the paper and passes it to Timas but my eyes never leave her, memorizing every movement, every facial feature, everything about her.

Timas gestures toward me as the attendant walks back to his place. "This is Captain Milori, my second-in-command and head of security. Anything you share with me can be shared with him."

I step forward, take the steps as delicately as possible but my legs feel like they're moving through honey and I am sure I look like I don't know how to walk. My heart hammers against my ribs as the realization crashes over me in waves. Her. It's really her. The one I've been waiting for my entire life. My spirit bond.

"You're—" I start, then stop, my mouth hanging open in a way that's definitely not befitting for the King's captain. "I'm Milori," I manage, extending my hand, watching it tremble slightly. "It's a pleasure to meet you."

She hesitates before slowly reaching out. The moment our fingers touch, the world explodes in colour and sensation, a surge of energy so powerful it feels like being struck by lightning. My body pulls instantly towards her but I try not to fall into the feeling, something in her eyes—fear maybe, or dread—tells me this is a lot for her.

"By the sun," I breathe, unable to contain my wonder. "It's you." She smells amazing, like the cool air on a winter night and frosted sweets.

Her eyes widen as that earlier fear surfaces, only to be replaced by a steely resolve. She withdraws her hand quickly, though the connection lingers like a phantom touch. My heart squeezes in pain by how quickly she retreats from our connection.

"Nesi," she says, her voice steady despite the tension radiating from her. "Queen Neeve's spymaster."

I can't help the smile that spreads across my face. "Nesi," I repeat, savouring the name, but the title of her position within the Night Court piques my interest. I have not heard who Queen Neeve's spymaster is, only that they are very effective.

"You have information about rebel recruitment?" I ask instead of trying to dissect why I know nothing about this spymaster. I try desperately to focus on why she's actually here, and not the fact she is my spirit bond, or that my own network of spies missed this information.

Nesi straightens, her professional mask firmly in place, despite the faint tremor I notice in her hands. "Yes. We've identified a former advisor to Oberon named Soren who is gathering followers, primarily targeting remote islands where discontent with Court unity is strongest."

I try to focus on her words, I really do, but all I can think about is how her eyes sparkle under the lights in the throne room. I have to actually shake my head to refocus on what she is saying. The confused look on her face and the look of concern on Timas' tells me I am not being as subtle as I thought.

"I'm sorry," I say, running a hand through my hair when I realize I've missed part of what she's said. "Could you repeat that last part?"

Timas shoots me a pointed look. "Captain, are you...ill?" Timas knows I'm not, but he doesn't know what is going on. Well, neither do I. In my mind, when I met my spirit bond, we would run towards one another in joyous celebration of what we'd found, but instead I'm standing here, utterly lost in her presence.

"Yes. No! My apologies, Your Majesty. I'm fine." I straighten, forcing myself to concentrate. "Rebel recruitment. Soren. Remote islands. I'm listening."

Nesi's mouth tightens. "As I was saying, this isn't just about dissatisfaction with the alliance between Courts. Soren appears to be stoking broader resentment—targeting those who dislike your Queen because she is human, those who feel trade has favoured one Court over another, and those who resent noble privilege."

At the mention of people disliking Emilia, Timas' entire demeanour shifts. The walls begin to tremble as the roll of his power begins to move. I've seen my friend angry many times. This time is no exception, but even still the controlled fury radiating from him makes even me want to step back.

"They dare to criticize my Queen?" His voice is deadly quiet, like the stillness before a storm. "Because she is human?"

I force myself to tear my eyes away from Nesi—a struggle in itself—and step in front of her to intercept my friend's gaze. Lightning crackles at the edge of his eyes, a storm brewing within him, and I try to pull him back from the brink of his anger."

"Perhaps we should finish hearing what she has to say before we do anything...drastic." My voice is calm so as to not further aggravate him.

A muscle jumps in his jaw, but he gives a short nod. I step back to the side and turn to Nesi, hoping I can form a coherent thought when our eyes meet. With Timas this agitated, I need to maintain my own composure—for all our sakes.

"We've encountered similar reports about some unrest in the outer islands but we have not heard about all of these issues, which is concerning and something I will be looking into." I say refocusing the conversation.

"You might also want to investigate your forces." she says calmly, her gaze direct and unwavering.

"What?" Timas leans forward, alarm evident in his posture.

Something about her composed demeanour intrigues me almost as much as the fire in her eyes when she speaks. I wonder if she's always this controlled, this measured. I want to know everything about her—what makes her smile, what foods she enjoys, what her laugh sounds like. *Focus, Milori!*

Nesi turns to him. "I was followed on my journey here by six of your guards. They were specifically watching for Night Court Fae, with orders to isolate and question them. When I...evaded them, they mentioned reporting to 'him,' not to you or the captain."

A protective heat flares in my chest at the thought of her being in danger. "They tried to intercept you?" I demand, my voice sharper than intended.

"Did they see your face?" I ask, concern overriding everything else. "Would they recognize you now?"

A ghost of a smile graces her lips. "They never saw me clearly."

"How did you evade six armed guards?" I ask, unable to contain my curiosity and admiration.

She pauses, studying me with those penetrating eyes. "I have...certain abilities that make me difficult to track."

"Abilities?" I prompt.

"Not relevant to the current discussion," she counters firmly, turning back to Timas. "What's important is that there are those within your guard reporting to someone other than their rightful king."

I feel a sting of rejection at how deliberately she's steering away from anything personal, but I push past it. She's right. The mission comes first, even if all I want to do is learn everything about the woman fate has connected me to.

"Your Queen mentioned an island called Manthana in her message," Timas says, glancing my way with sudden interest. "Captain Milori's home island. What significance does it hold?"

I feel a jolt of shock at hearing my homeland mentioned, my eyes meeting Timas' in a silent exchange. He knows the wound is still fresh. It's only been a month since I have returned from Manthana. I had no intention of returning to Manthana for a long while but now that very well might change.

"Queen Neeve believes it may be Soren's next target for recruitment," Nesi says carefully. "The island has strategic importance due to its location and the isolation of its population. Ideal conditions for building a rebel movement away from scrutiny."

She holds Timas' gaze which is a feat in his current state, but I don't miss the slight shift in her posture—there's more she isn't saying. I've spent enough time in court to recognize when someone is providing only part of the truth.

Her eyes shift to me, studying my reaction. "You're from Manthana?"

"Yes," I confirm, emotions churning within me—a blend of pain and the desperate urge to forget. "I know every inch of that island." I pause, studying her intently. "It's a farming community—isolated, yes—but there's nothing strategic about it, hardly worth a rebel leader's attention."

A flicker of something—perhaps annoyance, or maybe respect—crosses her face. "Nevertheless, that is where Queen

Neeve believes we should focus our investigation. I would like to formally request access to the island if it suits Your Majesty."

Timas remains quiet for a moment as he contemplates this information while I gawk at the beautiful woman before me.

"You have my permission to go and investigate." Nesi seems to relax at his order, but just as I am about to encourage I go with her, Timas continues, "and Milori will accompany you."

"I beg your reconsideration King Timas. Queen Neeve has tasked me with travelling to Manthana," she continues. "I should go alone. No one knows me there, and a Night Court Fae operating independently can move through shadows where a Day Court captain would draw attention. Especially one who might be recognized by locals." Her eyes flick to me briefly. "The mission requires subtlety."

Relief fills me at Timas suggestion, but it continues to hurt that Nesi is trying to leave me behind in this mission.

Timas leans forward on his throne. "While I appreciate your orders, I will not allow you to be the only one to investigate this seeing as my Queen is being threatened. I am sending Milori whether you approve or not." Timas stands, his command final. "You will leave at first light. If you will excuse me I must find my spirit bond before I destroy something again," he mutters and walks out of the room leaving Nesi and I behind in the throne room.

The air between us seems charged with unspoken words. I can't help but take a step toward her, drawn by an instinct more powerful than conscious thought.

"So..." I begin, searching for something witty or profound to say and coming up embarrassingly short. "Spirit bonds. That's...unexpected."

Nesi takes a deliberate step backward, maintaining the distance between us. "I don't have time for this," she states, her voice crisp and final.

"Don't have time for what?" I ask, unable to keep the hurt from my voice. "For acknowledging what just happened between us?"

"What happened," she says, each word carefully measured, "was a physical response. Nothing more. I have a mission to complete, and I will not be distracted by this."

I blink, genuinely stunned. "This? That's what you are calling it?" I gesture between us. "Nesi, a spirit bond is the rarest, most sacred connection our people can experience. It's not just some inconvenient physical reaction."

Her eyes flash with something—anger? Fear? Frustration? "What I think," she says coldly, "is that we have a duty to our monarchs. Queen Neeve has entrusted me with this mission, and I will not fail her because of some...mythical bond."

The dismissal stings more than I care to admit. "Mythical bond?" I echo, unable to keep the incredulity from my voice. "You felt it too. I know you did."

For a fraction of a second, her mask slips, and I glimpse something vulnerable in her expression before she closes it up. "What I felt or didn't feel is irrelevant. We leave for Manthana at dawn. I suggest you prepare accordingly, Captain." With a curt nod, she turns to leave.

"Nesi, wait—" I reach for her hand, unable to stop myself.

She freezes at my touch, not looking back. "Don't," she says, her voice barely above a whisper. "Please."

There's something in that single word—a crack in her armour, a glimpse of the turmoil beneath her controlled exterior. I slowly withdraw my hand, respecting her boundary despite every instinct screaming at me to pull her close.

"I'll meet you at the eastern gate at first light," I say quietly. "We can talk about the mission then."

She doesn't respond, simply walks away with the same fluid grace she entered with. I watch her go, feeling like part of me is being pulled away with her.

When the massive doors close behind her, I sink onto the steps of the throne, running my hands through my hair. By the sun, what just happened? In the span of a few minutes, I found my spirit bond and had her reject me in the same breath. The pain in my chest feels physical, as if someone has reached in and squeezed my heart so tightly it is about to break into a million pieces.

But beneath the hurt, I can't shake the feeling that there's more to Nesi's rejection than simple denial. The plea in her voice when she said "don't"—there was genuine fear there. Not of me, but of something else.

I won't let her push away one of the greatest gifts this life has to offer. If she wants to focus on the mission, fine, but I will find out what she is and I will show her that this is worth taking a chance on. Perhaps she has never been wooed before. Well, I am the master of wooing! I will show her I am worth it.

Pushing up I walk with determination to the royal guard office. Before I leave tomorrow I will need more information, and seeing as I won't be sleeping tonight I might as well work.

Chapter 5

Nesi

The sun is about to crest over the horizon as I head to the gate where Milori said to meet. The air carries a subtle chill, untouched by daylight's warmth. I savour the sting against my skin, grounding myself as thoughts churn in my mind. Sleep evaded me entirely last night—my carefully laid plans to accomplish this mission swiftly and discreetly now shattered by the forced company of Milori, my spirit bond. Nothing could have prepared me for meeting *him*. Those sea green eyes pulled me in so completely I nearly lost my focus...nearly.

Spirit bond. The words echo in my mind though I'm still uncertain if they're a curse or a blessing. Every Fae grows up hearing the stories of spirit bonds, how the old magic finds two perfect souls and binds them together, strengthening both and bringing a peace that only such profound love can create. Most Fae search for centuries for their other half, yet mine appears now, precisely when this mission could alter everything for my court.

I'm not emotionless. Sleepless nights often found me in the Shrouded Forest, gazing at the milky sky barely visible through the canopy, dreaming of the one who might bring the joy I've secretly longed for. Even as we fought to survive, we girls would whisper about this rare and powerful love—a spirit bond. Once, old magic matched souls, weaving their destinies together seamlessly. But over the millennia, such bonds have grown scarce. Some say they were strongest when our courts stood united, yet those tales now linger only in fragments.

The eastern courtyard comes into view, bathed in the soft glow of dawn. I've arrived early, hoping to collect my thoughts before seeing him again. The memory of his face full of hurt from my rejection lingers. I didn't want to cause him pain, but I can't allow myself to be distracted from my duty to Neeve. Not now, when the future of both Courts hangs in the balance. But his hurt expression has haunted me and for the first time in years I let a tear fall from my eye.

Stupid fates.

My fingers absently trace the necklace that hangs around my neck that my mother gave to me when I was a small child. An obsidian fang engraved with an intricate symbol, the symbol swirls with a silver mist, always mesmerizing me. Something about it draws me in as if it's calling to me. Mother often said it would lead me to true strength, but that was just something she said to help me become more confident. If only she could see me now holding the strength she so wished I had as a young fae.

I push away these old thoughts, the mission ahead must be my priority, I need to focus on this artifact. Who knows what it could be or what it could do to my people. Either way I need to distance myself from Milori while I accomplish this task and then maybe I can consider the implications of a spirit bond to a day court Captain. Oh, the fates have a sense of humour.

"You're early."

The voice—his voice—sends an involuntary shiver down my spine. I turn to face him, steeling myself against the inevitable pull. Captain Milori stands several paces away, looking far too alert and composed for this hour. The golden light of dawn catches in his blonde hair, giving him an almost ethereal appearance that makes my heart stutter traitorously in my chest. This is going to be very annoying.

"I prefer to be punctual," I respond, keeping my voice neutral and dropping my hand from my necklace. Milori doesn't miss the movement, which makes me more annoyed I couldn't control my own actions. "The sooner we depart, the sooner we can complete this mission."

He studies me for a moment, those perceptive eyes seeing more than I'm comfortable with. "Did you sleep well?" The question carries genuine concern rather than the flirtation I expected. Difficult. This is going to be very difficult.

"Well enough." The lie falls easily from my lips. In truth, I spent most of the night pacing, torn between wanting to flee Sonas entirely and the inexplicable urge to seek him out. "Are the travel arrangements complete?"

"Yes." A smile tugs at the corner of his mouth. "Follow me."

I fall into step beside him, careful to maintain distance between us. Every fiber of my being seems attuned to his presence—the rhythm of his breathing, the subtle shift of his posture as we walk. It's maddening, this awareness. I force my gaze forward, focusing on the mission ahead rather than the strikingly handsome man beside me. He's far too distracting, and I silently berate myself for letting it show.

We make our way through the city in relative silence. The city is starting to come to life with people talking, laughing and making deals. It's normal and mundane and I can't help but think about what a normal life might look like for me if I ever choose it. Yet even amid this activity, I remain acutely conscious of him. There is a buzzing beneath my skin at his proximity and I desperately want to itch it hoping it will relieve this incessant feeling.

"You didn't tell Timas everything last night," he says suddenly, his voice low enough that only I can hear as we walk by the locals.

I tense, my pace faltering. I take a moment before I respond. "I told him what he needed to know." There's no sense lying. I have a feeling if I am aware of him he is likely just as aware of me.

"But not everything that Queen Neeve told you." It's not a question, and his keen observations make me uncomfortable.

"My Queen's information is shared at her discretion," I reply carefully. "There are aspects of this investigation that remain...speculative."

He nods, seeming unsurprised by my answer. "Fair enough. I have secrets of my own."

This catches me off guard. "About Manthana?"

A shadow crosses his face, something haunted and vulnerable that makes me want to reach for him despite my better judgment. "I was just there a month ago, actually. First time in decades." He pauses, his expression darkening. "It didn't go well."

The admission intrigues me more than it should. Before I can stop myself, I ask, "What happened?"

He meets my gaze, the intensity in his eyes making my breath catch. "Let's just say some places leave marks on you that never quite heal. Marks that serve as reminders to be careful who you let in." He looks away. "I went back because my mother was supposedly ill, but she wasn't even there when I arrived. I didn't stay long after that." There's raw honesty in his voice, a willingness to show vulnerability that I find both foreign and compelling.

We turn down a narrow street leading toward the harbor, and I force myself to refocus.

"I still believe I should conduct this investigation alone. Your presence will draw attention." I try to keep the frustration out of my voice but fail.

""Probably," he agrees, his earlier haunted look gone, replaced with a far easier expression, which is not what I expected. "But I know Manthana—the people, the terrain, the hidden paths. I know which farmers harbor old grudges and which village elders still remember the ancient stories. That knowledge might prove useful. Besides, I'm good at making distractions, that in and of itself is helpful." He has a cheeky grin on his face that makes me want to roll my eyes, but I focus straight ahead instead.

I can't argue with his logic, but the last thing I need is to spend days in close proximity to my spirit bond who makes things very difficult to process. The stories to explain it well, this pull is beyond distracting and that concerns me.

"Besides," he adds with a hint of his earlier charm, "I also have excellent taste in ships."

As we crest the hill overlooking the harbor, I understand what he means. Docked at the furthest pier is a vessel that can only be described as excessive: a gleaming private ship with elegant lines and billowing white sails, at least three times larger than would be necessary for two passengers.

"That's our transportation?" I ask, unable to keep the disbelief from my voice.

"The Sunfire," he confirms, looking entirely too pleased with himself. "Fastest ship in the merchant company."

"It's ridiculous." I stop walking, crossing my arms. "We're supposed to be conducting a discreet investigation, not arriving like visiting dignitaries. This might as well be a floating announcement of our presence."

"Actually, it's the perfect cover." He gestures toward the harbor. "Several wealthy merchants use similar vessels to transport high-value goods between islands. Another luxury ship will raise no eyebrows. Certainly less than two Fae from opposing Courts traveling together on a common transport. It also helps that Monstil, a prominent merchant, had already planned a trip to the outer islands. I just needed to persuade him to move up his timeline."

"And how did you do that?" I ask incredulously.

"With my charm of course." His wicked grin makes him look far too good.

I hate that his reasoning and cover makes sense. "We could have taken a smaller merchant vessel and it still would have accomplished the same goal and been more discreet." I can't help but emphasize the last bit.

"We could have," he agrees cheerfully, "if you wanted to spend four days at sea instead of two, possibly sharing cramped quarters with curious sailors who would recognize me instantly."

The thought of spending four days in close quarters with him sends a jolt of both anticipation and dread through me. Two days is already testing my resolve.

"The Sunfire has private cabins on opposite ends of the ship," he adds, as if reading my thoughts. "And a crew I trust implicitly. Your privacy will be respected." It sounds like it pains him to put distance between us, but it also makes my heart skip a beat that he considered my comfort. How irritating.

I examine the ship with a practical eye. It's well-built. The craftsmanship is obvious even from here. Intricate carvings line the hull, and the tall mast with its crows nest stands clear against the sky. Two days at sea instead of four. Simple math.

"Fine," I concede, keeping my voice flat. "But we maintain our focus on the mission. This isn't a pleasure cruise."

"I wouldn't dream of suggesting otherwise." His smile returns and my heart skips a beat... again. "Though there's no rule against enjoying the journey, is there?"

I don't bother responding. Instead I head down the hill toward the harbor. The sooner we board, the sooner this will be over.

The ship looks even better up close. The polished wooden structure is accented with gold and crisp sails ready to catch wind. The crew works efficiently, preparing to depart. A man in expensive clothing approaches as we reach the gangplank.

"Captain Milori," he greets with a nod. "We're ready to sail. I hope you are ready for a voyage of a lifetime! This ship will make you wish it sailed in the Royal Fleet!" He laughs, clearly pleased with himself.

"I'm looking forward to it! Might be just what we need to add to our fleet. This will give me a good understanding so I can report back to the King." Milori's voice changes slightly, and I can see the mask slide into place. Another face for another purpose. I wonder how many he has.

"Well, I can get you a great price if you need superior vessels such as this! I'm always willing to use my negotiating skills for the King." They laugh together like old friends playing the same game. I file this moment away. Milori adapts himself to whatever the situation needs. It's a useful skill and a dangerous habit. Either way, it's not my problem. Keeping my distance is all that matters while I complete this mission.

"This is Nesi, of the Night Court. She'll be joining us on this voyage." Milori gestures to me, stepping slightly to the side so the merchant can see me better. He maintains a welcoming expression, but I can see the dilation in his eyes when the Night Court is mentioned.

"Welcome aboard, my lady. Your cabin has been prepared, I hope you will find the accommodations suitable." He bows slightly which is surprising and kind.

"After you," Milori says, gesturing toward the gangplank with an exaggerated flourish that would be annoying if it weren't so cute. No! Not cute. Annoying.

I step onto the ship, feeling it sway beneath my feet. The deck is immaculate, gleaming in the morning sun. Several crew members pause in their duties to observe us before quickly returning to work. No doubt rumors will be flying before midday about the Captain of the Guard traveling with a mysterious Night Court woman. This much attention makes me very uncomfortable. I yearn to melt into the shadows and become invisible.

"Allow me to show you to your cabin," Milori offers, stepping beside me. "Unless you'd prefer to remain on deck for departure?"

The question is innocuous enough, but something in his expression makes me suspect this is a test to see if I'll retreat immediately or face this journey head-on. I straighten my shoulders, meeting his gaze directly.

"I'll stay for departure," I decide. "It would be rude to disappear below deck immediately." Not to mention cowardly, though I don't say this aloud.

His smile widens, genuine pleasure lighting his features. "Excellent choice. The view as we leave Sonas is quite spectacular." He gestures toward the bow. "Shall we?"

As we move toward the front of the ship, I feel the pull between us intensify, like gravity shifting, drawing me inexorably toward him. This is going to be the longest two days of my life. I have sworn my loyalty to Neeve, committed my life to protecting the Night Court. I cannot allow myself to be distracted by this connection, no matter how compelling it feels.

Yet as the crew calls out orders and the sails catch the morning breeze, I can't help but steal glances at the man beside me, wondering what might have been under different circumstances.

Chapter 6

Nesi

The gentle swaying of the ship is far nicer than the rough rocking I normally experience on lesser vessels while traveling. The cabin is excessive with a comfortable bed, a writing desk secured to the floor, and a small window offering a view of the ocean. The sun reflects off its surface painting the sea in beautiful colours, welcoming though it holds many dangers. The merchant spared no expense in outfitting this vessel, which makes me wonder what exactly he transports that earns such profits.

I've spent most of the day avoiding Milori, taking meals in my cabin and exploring only when I knew he was occupied elsewhere. The crew has respected my privacy, though I catch their curious glances whenever I emerge. A Night Court Fae is still a rarity to most, add to that traveling with the second most influential person within the Day Court I'm sure it brings up many questions.

Spreading the documents Neeve sent with me out on the desk I study them again for the hundredth time. Just like before there is no new information to be gleaned from them. The ancient text still means nothing to me. I am not as familiar with the language as Neeve is. The extent of my knowledge is the statue from the Day Court and a few other phrases taught to us growing up. The language itself has been lost to our people for millennia.

The image of a bird loosely wrapped in some sort of fabric puzzles me most. The image takes up half the page and it makes me think that it is being bound. The ancient text surrounding it remains frustratingly cryptic. Fragments of the old Fae language cover the page, some of the words I recognize while the majority mean nothing.

"What are you?" I murmur, tracing the outline of the bound bird with my finger. Whatever this artifact is, Soren wants it badly enough to build a rebellion. And Neeve clearly fears what might happen if he finds it, but it brings up so many questions. Why a bird? Does it symbolize the artifact, or is it the artifact? And where did it come from?

I lift the second page, which contains notes in Neeve's elegant handwriting, the reports about Manthana and the comments about a "heavy mystical presence," as well as theories about why Soren might target such an unremarkable island. She never explained how she gathered this information on the island, and her deliberate vagueness troubles me. Neeve doesn't withhold information without reason.

A knock at the door breaks my concentration, and I instantly sweep the documents into a hidden pocket of my bag. "Yes?" I call, composing my features into a neutral mask.

"It's Milori," comes the voice from the other side, and despite my best efforts, my heart quickens at the sound. My body immediately demands I get up to greet him. "May I come in?"

I hesitate, weighing my options. Refusing would only delay the inevitable. This ship isn't large enough to avoid him indefinitely. "Enter," I say finally, rising from my seat.

The door opens, and there he stands. His perpetually tousled hair adds to his easygoing presence, though something tells me he is not as gentle as he appears. Of course he's not. I've heard many stories of the King's Guard Captain, and he is not someone to trifle with. That makes me feel a sense of pride I have no right feeling. He's changed from his formal uniform into a casual white shirt and dark trousers. The sight of him causes that now-familiar pull in my chest, and I force myself to look past him rather than meet his gaze directly.

"I hope I'm not interrupting," he says, remaining in the doorway, as if understanding my need for space. His eyes briefly scan the room, noting my bag where I've just hidden the documents.

"Was there something you needed, Captain?" I ask, keeping my voice carefully neutral.

"Dinner," he says with a smile that reaches his eyes. "Our host has invited us to dine in his quarters. Apparently, he's quite proud of his chef."

The thought of spending an evening making polite conversation with Monstil while pretending not to feel this connection with Milori sounds like pure torture. "Please extend my regrets to the merchant. I prefer to dine alone."

Milori doesn't seem surprised by my refusal. In fact, he almost looks pleased, which immediately puts me on guard.

"I thought you might say that," he admits. "Which is why I made alternative arrangements." His eyes sparkle with mischief, and I find myself both suspicious and intrigued.

"Alternative arrangements?" I echo, crossing my arms. "I'm not sure I like the sound of that."

"Nothing scandalous, I assure you." He holds up his hands in mock surrender. "Just dinner in a location where we won't be disturbed by curious ears or prying eyes. Somewhere we can get to know each other a bit better."

The suggestion makes my pulse quicken, though I fight not to show it. "And where might that be?" I ask, skepticism evident in my voice.

His smile widens. "The crow's nest."

"The top of the mast?" I can't hide my surprise. "You want us to climb up there to eat?"

"We could fly, but I figured the others might grow envious at the sight of our wings," he says with a slight smirk.

His assumption about my noble birth doesn't surprise me. Most would expect Queen Neeve's spymaster to possess abilities beyond the common Fae. The divide between noble and common Fae is already a wound Soren seems eager to exploit. No sense in making it worse over something as trivial as convenience.

"Besides, if we aren't going to participate in the age-old tradition of making nice with the owner of this vessel, then we might as well enjoy the vessel. It's got the best view on the ship," he says with undisguised enthusiasm. "No one to bother us, fresh air, and a sunset that would make even the most hardened Night Court spy admit there's beauty in the daylight." He pauses, studying my reaction. "Unless heights are a concern?"

The challenge in his voice is clear and I raise an eyebrow at his obvious antagonistic comment. "Heights don't bother me," I respond coolly. But my heart pounds wickedly at the prospect of being so isolated with Milori. I clench my hands as I try to remain composed under his scrutinizing gaze.

"Good. I've already had food sent up." He steps back from the doorway, giving me space to exit. "Shall we?"

I weigh my options. I could easily refuse, and I know based on what little I know of Milori that he would respect my decision and leave. But that little nagging feeling in that annoying part of my chest wants to talk with him. Against my better judgment, I suck in a breath, which is a massive mistake because his scent lingers around me. He smells like sun-warmed earth and a spice I can't place. I drop my shoulders in defeat as I make what is likely a huge mistake.

"Lead the way, Captain," I say, stepping into the corridor and carefully maintaining a respectable distance between us.

He offers a slight bow that somehow manages to be both respectful and teasing at once. "After you."

We make our way through the ship, passing crew members who nod in acknowledgment. The vessel is larger than it appeared from shore, with multiple decks and passageways leading to various cabins and storage areas. Milori navigates confident-ly, occasionally pointing out features—the galley, the captain's quarters, the map room—as we pass. His knowledge of ships, not just this one, seems extensive.

"You spend a lot of time at sea?" I ask, curiosity getting the better of me.

"When I can," he replies, his expression softening. "There's a freedom on the water I've never found on land. The sky has its own kind of exhilaration, but sailing lets me embrace the unknown. When I fly, I have to stay focused—one mistake, and I'm plummeting. But on a ship, I can let go, feel the breeze and the salt in the air, and trust the Captain to guide us wherever we're meant to go."

The wistful way he speaks makes me think he carries a great deal of weight on top of those very nice looking shoulders. No! Shoulders. Just shoulders. *Nesi, pull it together.* He must feel the burden of serving the crown not that he doesn't have nice shoulders. This was a mistake.

We reach the main deck just as the sun begins to dip below the water, painting the sky in brilliant oranges and pinks. Milori leads me to the base of the mainmast, where a rope ladder ex-tends upward to the crow's nest high above.

"After you?" he offers with a grin.

I eye the swaying ladder skeptically. Of course, I'm wearing fitted leggings beneath my dress. I'd never risk mobility for the sake of fashion, especially on a mission. A spy who can't climb when needed isn't much of a spy.

"Strategic positioning, or just wanting to ensure I don't es-cape?" I counter, already grasping the first rung.

"Both," he admits without shame. "Though mostly I'm hop-ing the view at the top will convince you this was worth leaving your cabin for."

I begin my ascent, appreciating that he had the sense not to suggest I go second. Though I doubt he'd be so obvious as to look up my dress, the crew might not be so respectful. I don't particularly care what they think, but unnecessary attention is a liability in my line of work.

The ship's motion makes the climb more challenging than it would be on land, but I find my rhythm quickly. The wind grows stronger as I climb higher, whipping my braided hair around my face. Below, I hear Milori following, his movements as sure and graceful as mine.

When I reach the crow's nest, I'm momentarily taken aback. The circular platform, usually a simple lookout post, has been transformed. A thick blanket covers the wooden floor, and atop it sits a basket filled with food. Two lanterns hang from hooks, not yet lit but ready for when darkness falls. Cushions provide comfortable seating, and a bottle of wine rests in a bucket of ice.

It's thoughtful. No one has ever done something so consid-erate and...romantic.

Milori pulls himself up beside me, and the small space sud-denly feels even smaller. The temperature seems to rise despite the cold wind whipping around us. He watches my reaction with barely concealed anticipation, those sea-green eyes tracking every subtle shift in my expression.

"Do you approve?" he asks, sounding genuinely concerned about my opinion.

Against my better judgment, I feel a smile forming—genuine, unplanned, dangerous.

"Thank you," I say quietly, keeping my voice neutral despite the unfamiliar warmth spreading through my chest. Gratitude isn't a currency I trade in often. I turn my attention back to the horizon, using the spectacle of color and light to anchor myself against the pull of his presence beside me.

"It's acceptable," I say, though we both know it's more than that.

His smile returns, bright enough to rival the sunset. "High praise indeed from the Queen's spymaster." He gestures to the cushions. "Please, make yourself comfortable."

I settle onto one of the cushions, careful to maintain some distance between us. Milori sits across from me, opening the basket to reveal an assortment of fresh breads, cheeses, sliced fruits, and some kind of roasted meat.

"I wasn't sure what you'd prefer," he admits, arranging plates. "So I requested a variety."

The consideration behind this gesture is another unexpected layer to this man. "Thank you," I whisper, accepting the plate he offers. "This is thoughtful."

He looks pleased at the acknowledgment. "Wine?" he asks, reaching for the bottle.

I nod, watching as he pours two glasses. When he hands me mine, our fingers brush briefly, and the now-familiar spark of connection surges between us. I pull back quickly, but not before noticing his sharp intake of breath. He feels it too, every time. It's not surprising, yet every time I'm surprised. This connection goes beyond logic and understanding, which is something I have clung to these past several years.

For a few minutes, we eat in silence, the tension between us both uncomfortable, yet not unpleasant. The food is fresh and flavorful, likely the best the merchant's chef could prepare.

"So," Milori says finally, leaning back against the curved wall of the crow's nest. "Tell me about yourself, Nesi. Beyond being Queen Neeve's spymaster."

I regard him warily. "There's not much to tell."

"I doubt that very much," he says, his eyes studying me with genuine interest. "Everyone has a story."

I take a sip of wine, considering my response. "My story isn't particularly interesting. I serve my Queen and my Court."

"Before that, though," he presses gently. "What did you do in the Shrouded Forest? What were you like as a child?"

The questions feel surprisingly intimate, though they shouldn't. "I was quiet," I admit after a moment. "I preferred to be alone, even then. The shadows...they always seemed to find me."

"The shadows?" he asks, leaning forward, interest piqued in his expression.

I hesitate, weighing how much to reveal. But he's accompanying me on this mission and he is my spirit bond. Even if I don't want to act on this connection right now, at some point maybe it will be an option. "I'm a shadow walker," I say finally, watching his reaction carefully.

His eyes widen a fraction, but not as much as I would expect for someone just hearing about my abilities. "You're...you're a shadow walker," he says, running a hand through his hair, a smile and a look of relief on his face. "Well, that explains the dreams. Here I was, ready to blame questionable wine and possible head trauma for being attracted to actual darkness, when all along it was just..." He trails off, color rising to his cheeks as he realizes what he's admitting.

I arch an eyebrow, the ghost of amusement playing at my lips. "Just what, exactly?"

"Nothing. Absolutely nothing. I was merely having a temporary bout of insanity that happened to involve shadows. Very normal. It happens to everyone." He waves his hand dismissively, though the flush creeping up his neck betrays him.

"Does it now?" My voice carries that dry tone I reserve for particularly absurd statements. "So you regularly find yourself drawn to shadows?"

"Only the particularly attractive ones," he blurts out before he can stop himself. "I mean—that's not—by the sun, can we pretend I didn't say any of that?"

I pull a shadow from the edge of the nest, coaxing it into a delicate spiral around the hand he's leaning on. The darkness responds eagerly, curling like smoke through my fingers before wrapping around his wrist.

"This isn't happening. I swear this is how the dream began." He whispers, and something breaks loose inside me. A laugh erupts, genuine and unfamiliar. I can't remember the last time I laughed like this. Perhaps I never have.

"Fine, laugh it up," he says, watching the shadow caress his skin with fascination rather than fear. "I won't be ashamed of my attraction to the most dark and delicious shadow walker to grace this realm."

His words pull me back to reality, though I can't quite banish the smile lingering on my lips. "Well, that is not how people normally react to my abilities." The admission quiets something in me, my smile fading as I recall countless faces contorted with terror, bodies recoiling at my approach.

I withdraw my gaze to the horizon, where the last traces of sunlight have surrendered to the rising moon. Its silver light spills across the water, creating new shadows for me to find comfort in. The darkness has always been my ally, even when it made me an outsider.

"Their loss," Milori says quietly, and when I look back, his expression holds no pity, only understanding.

Memories surfacing that I rarely allow myself to revisit. "When I was very young. It frightened the other children. And many of the adults." I pause, surprised by my own willingness to share this. "They thought the forest was using me somehow. That I was tainted by it."

His expression softens with understanding. "It's never easy to be different. Especially when that difference frightens others around you."

Something in his tone makes me think he's speaking from experience. "You know something about that, don't you?"

The ghost of something crosses his face. "I do. On Manthana, I was...too powerful for rural life and by the time I got to Sonas I had the wrong background for court life." He smiles, but it doesn't reach his eyes. "I believe 'walking disaster' was the term most commonly used. 'Doesn't fit in' was another way to describe my existence in both the island I grew up on and the court I currently serve."

"What do you mean?" The question slips out before I can stop it, drawn by this glimpse of vulnerability.

He stands and with his hand open summons a flame to his palm. He lights the two hanging lanterns and returns to his seat.

"Fire magic is common enough among Day Court nobles," he says, a familiar tension tightening around his eyes. "But mine was different. More intense than it should have been. The first time it manifested, I was playing with my childhood friend, Jalnor, near the eastern fields. Something startled me and suddenly—" He spreads his fingers, mimicking an explosion–"fire erupted from my hands. It consumed an entire field of grain in seconds. Cost that farmer nearly a year's wages."

He glances away, the memory clearly uncomfortable. "My mother had mentioned I might inherit abilities—she's noble-born while my father is just a farmer. But what emerged was..." He shakes his head. "My ability to wield fire is far stronger than anyone has seen in centuries. It rivals Timas' power, though don't tell him I said that." His attempt at humor falls flat, and when his eyes meet mine, I can see the raw pain he's trying to mask. "Everyone feared me after that. Too unpredictable, too much a noble for an island of farmers. I imagine your shadows earned you similar treatment."

The parallel strikes me more deeply than I expect. All my life, I've thought of my shadow-walking as a singular burden, something no one else could truly understand. Yet here he sits, carrying his own version of the same weight.

"Does it still make people uncomfortable?" I ask.

He shrugs, a casual gesture at odds with the significance of the conversation. "It doesn't really matter anymore. Having the position I have makes it so that if someone was intimidated by my power they won't say so because I now also wield the power of the King. Which puts a different kind of wedge between me and everyone else." I can see the exhaustion on his face as if the many faces he wears are to protect himself from the rejection of others.

The admission creates an unexpected bond between us, beyond the spirit bond, beyond our mission. For the first time, I feel a genuine connection to him as a person, not just the irritating pull of fate.

"Your turn," he says, his voice lighter now. "Tell me something about yourself that would surprise me."

I consider the question, weighing what is safe to share. "I collect herbs," I offer finally. "Medicinal ones, mostly."

His eyebrows rise in genuine surprise. "Herbalism? I wouldn't have guessed that."

"Why not?"

"I don't know," he admits. "You just seem so practical. Focused on duty."

"Herbs are practical," I counter, feeling strangely defensive. "They can heal wounds, ease pain, or end a life if needed. There's power in knowing each plant's purpose."

He smiles, a warm, genuine smile that makes something flutter in my chest. "I stand corrected. Though now I'm curious. What kinds do you favor?"

"Shadow-blooms, night fern, mist lichen. Plants that thrive in the darkness of the Forest." I pause, then find myself continuing despite my better judgment. "And the flowers. Even in the darkest corners of the Shrouded Forest, somehow flowers always found a way to bloom."

His expression softens, and I immediately regret my candor.

"The luminous bell-blooms were my favorite," I whisper, unable to stop now. "They'd glow faintly blue at midnight, just enough to guide your way. When everything else was terrible, they were a small reminder that beauty could exist, even in our prison."

I look away, uncomfortable with how much I've revealed. "It's just a practical interest. Knowing which plants can help or harm."

"A revealing one," he observes, his gaze gentle in the fading light. "You found light worth cherishing, even while embracing the shadows that are part of you." An uncomfortable feeling threatens to overcome me, so I change the topic.

"Tell me about King Timas," I say, seeking safer ground. "You've known him a long time?"

Milori settles back, a fond expression crossing his face. "Since we were children. My mother arranged for me to train at court, hoping I'd learn to control my abilities better. Timas and I were paired as sparring partners. He knocked me down, I set his practice sword on fire. Somehow, we became friends."

The affection in his voice when he speaks of the King is unmistakable. "He trusts you completely," I observe.

"As I do him," Milori confirms. "We've saved each other's lives more times than I can count. And now he's having a child." A soft smile plays at his lips. "I'm to be the godfather."

The news that the King and Queen is expecting is shocking, if for no other reason than because it has not been officially announced yet, but he shared that information with me. A spy from the Night Court.

"You'll be good at it," I find myself saying, the words surprising me as much as him.

"What makes you say that?" he asks, clearly pleased, but curious.

I consider the question, trying to articulate what I've observed about him in our brief time together. "You pay attention.

Notice details. And you care, perhaps too much, but that's better than the alternative."

He blinks, surprise flickering across his face. "Thank you," he murmurs. "That's one of the kindest things anyone has said to me in a long time. Most people either seek favour with the King through me or hope to secure a marriage alliance with a powerful noble."

Something sharp and unexpected twists in my chest at the mention of marriage prospects. I picture faceless Day Court noblewomen with their perfect manners and bright, sunny dispositions—everything I am not—vying for his attention. The thought bothers me more than it should.

"How tiresome for you," I say, my voice coming out cooler than intended. "All those admirers to fend off."

He studies me for a moment, a smile slowly spreading across his face. "Why, Nesi of the Night Court, do I detect a hint of jealousy?"

"Don't be absurd," I reply too quickly, feeling heat creep up my neck.

"If it helps," he says, leaning slightly closer, "I find their transparent attempts at courtship far less interesting than a single genuine observation from someone who sees the world as clearly as you do."

The genuine gratitude in his voice makes me uncomfortable. I'm not used to giving compliments, or having them received with such sincerity. I look away, focusing on the darkening horizon to hide the conflicting emotions crossing my face.

We fall into silence, the gentle rocking of the ship and distant calls of seabirds filling the space between us. The quiet isn't uncomfortable. There's something peaceful in merely existing in the same moment, without the pressure to fill it with words.

"What about you?" he asks finally, his voice gentle. "Do you have family, beyond Queen Neeve?"

The question touches on old pain, but I find myself answering anyway. "No. My parents died during the early years in the forest. Many did." I keep my voice matter-of-fact, though the memories still ache. "Neeve's family took me in. We're distant cousins, technically. But she's the only family that matters now."

His hand moves across the space between us, coming to rest lightly on mine. The touch is gentle and comforting, rather than intrusive. "I'm sorry," he says simply.

I should pull away. I know I should. But the warmth of his hand, the sincere empathy in his eyes, they anchor me in a way I didn't know I needed. For a moment, we sit in silence, connected by this simple touch and the shared understanding of loss.

The ship sways beneath us, and he shifts slightly to maintain his balance. The movement brings him closer, his face now only inches from mine. In the lantern light, his eyes appear deeper, more complex—not just green, but flecked with gold and amber, like sunlight through leaves.

"Nesi," he says, my name barely more than a breath on his lips.

I know what's about to happen. I can feel the pull between us intensifying, drawing us together. His gaze drops to my lips, then back to my eyes, a question in them, seeking permission, not presuming.

Part of me wants to allow it, to discover if his kiss would feel like the completion I've secretly longed for. The connection of our spirit bond thrums between us, urging me forward.

But the larger part—the careful, controlled part that has kept me alive and effective—pulls me back. I turn my face away, withdrawing my hand from beneath his.

"It's getting late," I say, my voice sounding strained even to my own ears. "We should go back down."

Disappointment flickers across his features, but he doesn't argue or try to persuade me. "Of course," he says, moving back to give me space. The respect in that simple action nearly makes me want to reconsider, but I hold firm.

We pack up the remains of our meal in silence, the easy connection from moments before replaced by a tension that's both familiar and different, charged now with what almost happened, what still might.

As we prepare to descend, Milori pauses. "Nesi, I—"

"Don't," I interrupt, not quite meeting his eyes. "Please."

He studies me for a moment, then nods. "I'll go first," he says simply. "To make sure the ladder is stable."

As he disappears over the edge, I take a deep breath, trying to center myself. This mission is too important for distractions, no matter how compelling. I need to focus on finding the artifact before Soren does, not on the way Milori's hand felt against mine, or how his voice softened when he spoke my name.

By the time I reach the deck, I've composed myself again, my walls firmly back in place. Milori waits at a respectful distance, his expression carefully neutral.

"Thank you for dinner," I say formally. "It was...pleasant."

A small smile touches his lips. "High praise," he remarks, echoing his earlier comment. "Perhaps we can do it again tomorrow night."

The invitation hangs between us, weighted with possibility. "Perhaps," I answer noncommittally. "Goodnight, Captain."

"Goodnight, Nesi," he replies softly. "Sleep well."

I turn and walk away before I can change my mind, before the pull between us can draw me back. Yet as I close my cabin door behind me, I find my hand lifting to my lips, wondering what might have happened if I'd stayed just a moment longer.

Duty, I remind myself firmly. I am here for duty, not desire.

Chapter 7

Milori

The harsh wind is a welcome feeling against my face, offering a distraction from last night's disappointment. Nothing went as planned. I'd thought my little romantic gesture in the crow's nest would sweep her off her feet. Instead, she remained as guarded as ever. Maybe Garrick is right—maybe I really am too much for people. I let out a frustrated sigh. He'd love to hear me admit it, but that's never happening. He already thinks he's smarter than me, and I've spent far too much time trying to prove otherwise.

The Sunfire's bow cuts through the water at impressive speeds—I can see why Monstil has been lobbying so enthusiastically for these vessels to join the royal fleet. But even this marvel of Fae ingenuity can't distract me from thoughts of Nesi and those dark, captivating eyes.

The stories never mention someone actively fighting against a spirit bond. I know Garrick initially resisted his connection to Alette, but he's an idiot. Nesi isn't. She seems…lost. Trapped in a world she believes is the only option for her. I suppose I understand her loyalty to Neeve. By the sun, if anyone understands loyalty to a monarch, it's me. But for such a rare gift, I'd hoped she might at least be willing to explore what this connection could mean.

Though I know better, I can't help but fall into the familiar pattern of feeling like I'm not worth the effort. It wouldn't hurt so much if my spirit bond weren't rejecting me.

No. I will not allow my thoughts to spiral into self-pity. I did enough of that in my youth. I'm older now. Wiser! I'll continue proving to her that I can be her partner in this mission, and show her that loving someone isn't a weakness. It's far braver to love without restraint.

"Captain Milori!" the merchant's booming voice interrupts my thoughts. Monstil approaches with his usual excessive enthusiasm, clapping a hand on my shoulder. "You're up early! Enjoying another perfect day aboard the finest vessel in the Day Court?"

I straighten, slipping effortlessly into the persona he expects—charming, slightly arrogant, suitably impressed by his wealth. "The Sunfire continues to exceed my expectations. The King will be very interested in my report."

His chest puffs with pride. "I knew you'd appreciate superior craftsmanship! The sooner we arrive in Manthana, the sooner you can send that glowing recommendation to King Timas!"

I hide my smile at his transparency. Monstil is many things—successful, shrewd, exhaustingly boastful—but subtle isn't among them. "Speaking of our arrival, how's our progress?"

"That's actually why I sought you out." He gestures toward the stern where Captain Vaelin stands at the helm. "We've caught favorable winds all night. Vaelin believes we'll make land by nightfall—a full half-day earlier than expected!" You can hear the pride in his voice and the news sends a jolt of both anticipation and dread through me. Sooner to Manthana means sooner to face the island I've avoided for nearly a century, and sooner to confront whatever memories and ghosts await me there. But it also means less time alone with Nesi on this ship, where the boundaries between us feel somehow more fragile. It's easier to talk with her when we are waiting for our arrival and are unable to do anything.

"Excellent news," I say, forcing enthusiasm into my voice. "I should speak with the captain myself. Thank you, Monstil."

He nods, clearly pleased to be the bearer of good tidings. "Your Night Court companion—will she be joining us for breakfast? The chef has prepared something special."

"I doubt it," I reply honestly. "Lady Nesi prefers to dine privately."

Monstil nods his head and smiles. "Of course! We want her to feel comfortable on the Sunfire!"

Monstil bows slightly and departs, no doubt to oversee some unnecessary adjustment to the already perfect arrangement of his breakfast table. I make my way toward the helm, nodding to crew members as I pass. Having only boarded yesterday the crew has become accustomed to my presence, no longer stiffening formally when I approach.

Captain Vaelin stands tall at the wheel, his weathered face creased with the permanent squint of someone who has spent decades staring at horizons. Unlike Monstil, Vaelin wastes no words on needless flattery.

"Captain," I greet him, receiving a gruff nod in return.

"We've made good time," he says without preamble, his eyes never leaving the stretch of ocean before us. "Wind's been with us since we left port. Should see Manthana's eastern cliffs by late afternoon, dock before sunset."

"So I heard." I move to stand beside him, gazing out at the endless blue. "The crew performed admirably."

Vaelin grunts, accepting the compliment without comment. We stand in comfortable silence for a moment, two men who understand that not every space needs to be filled with words.

"Been to Manthana before?" he finally asks, adjusting our course slightly.

"I grew up there," I admit, the words tasting strange on my tongue after so long avoiding the subject. "Though it's been a while since my last visit."

"Family still there?"

"My parents." I shift uncomfortably, guilt pricking at me for the years of deliberate distance. "They write occasionally."

Vaelin's eyes flick to me briefly, then back to the horizon. "Complicated, then."

I laugh despite myself. "That's one way to put it."

"Usually is with family." He adjusts our course again, his movements precise from years of practice. "Got three sons myself. Haven't spoken to the eldest in eight years. Stubborn fool thinks being a sailor is beneath him. Went and became a scribe in Sonas."

"And the other two?" I ask, grateful for the shift away from my own family complications.

Pride crosses his weathered face. "Both serving under me. Good lads. Know the value of the sea."

I nod, recognizing the simple contentment in his voice. "It's a worthy calling."

"Better than pushing papers at court," he says with the faintest hint of a smile, clearly referencing my official position.

"Sometimes," I concede. "Though the company at court has its advantages."

He snorts. "So I've heard. Monstil hasn't stopped talking about how the great Captain Milori graces his ship. Thinks you'll convince the King to order a fleet of these floating palaces."

I can't help but chuckle. "He may be disappointed. The royal treasury has other priorities at the moment."

"Figured as much." Vaelin adjusts our heading again. "Still, one of the finest vessels I've commanded. Fast, responsive. Almost makes Monstil's endless boasting tolerable." He pauses. "Almost."

We share a knowing look, and I find myself appreciating the captain's straightforward manner. He reminds me somewhat of my father—a man of few words, but those he chooses carry weight.

"Captain, do you have a carrier bird aboard?" I ask, the idea forming as I think about our early arrival. "I'd like to send word ahead to Manthana."

"Aye. Got three trained birds in the aft cabin. Small messages only, mind. Weight affects their range."

"Perfect. I'd like to inform a friend of our arrival."

Vaelin nods. "Speak to Hallen. He tends the birds."

"Thank you." I turn to leave, then pause. "And Captain? Impressive work, making this time. I'll be sure Monstil knows whose skill is truly responsible."

He offers a rare, genuine smile. "Appreciate that, Captain Milori."

I make my way to the aft cabin, where a young sailor, dirty from work on the ship, greets me enthusiastically. "Captain Milori! How may I help you, sir?"

"I need to send a message to Manthana," I explain. "Captain Vaelin said you could help."

"Certainly, sir!" Hallen beams, leading me to a small, windowed alcove where three carrier birds rest in ornate cages. "These beauties can reach any island in the archipelago within hours."

He hands me a small piece of parchment and a tiny charcoal stick. "Keep it brief, sir. The lighter the message, the faster they fly."

I nod, considering what to write. It's been nearly eight decades since I last saw Jalnor, though we write fairly often. He was to meet us tomorrow so it shouldn't be too difficult to keep it short.

Jalnor, Change of plans. Arriving in Manthana tonight with companion. —Milori

I roll the tiny parchment tightly and hand it to Hallen, who attaches it to the leg of the most robust-looking bird. "This one's our strongest flyer," he explains proudly. "Manthana, eastern settlement?"

"Yes. To a man named Jalnor Timris. Lives near the main square. Has a brewery."

"Perfect!" Hallen carries the bird to the small window and whispers something to it before releasing it into the open air. We watch as it circles once, then darts away toward the horizon. "He'll find your friend, sir. These birds never fail."

"Thank you, Hallen." I press a silver coin into his palm, earning a large smile before I depart.

Back on deck, I find myself drawn again to the railing, watching the endless stretch of ocean that separates me from my past. Manthana. Even the name conjures complicated emotions—childhood memories tangled with the pain of never quite belonging, of being both too much and not enough. My mother with her distant affection and mysterious errands. My father with his quiet resignation and gentle encouragement that never quite filled the void left by her absences. You would think two centuries would heal these wounds, but the marks of childhood hold onto us as adults, and no matter how hard we try to move on, it rears its ugly head to make an appearance.

I shake my head, tipping it back to look at the sky. Now I'm bringing Nesi here, my spirit bond who doesn't want to be my spirit bond, to the very place that shaped some of my greatest insecurities. I lower my gaze to the horizon. There goes my plan of being a heroic figure to the woman I hope to spend the rest of my life with. The cruelty of it all. I can't help but smile at how fate works and plays with us all.

Speaking of Nesi, she's nowhere to be seen. She's probably still in her cabin, avoiding me after last night's almost-kiss. Not that I can blame her. The mission comes first. She made that abundantly clear. And yet...

By the sun, I can still feel the ghost of her hand beneath mine, the way her eyes softened when she spoke of finding flowers in the darkness. The connection between us pulses like a second heartbeat, impossible to ignore no matter how hard she tries.

We have an adventure ahead of us and I will be by her side while we figure all of this out, even if it does require us to return to the one place I would prefer never to step foot on again.

The sun is sinking in the sky, and I can see the island of Manthana in the distance. It won't be much longer now. I make my way down towards Nesi's cabin and stop at the door to straighten my jacket before knocking. After last night's almost-kiss and her hasty retreat, I've barely seen her today. Only a brief sighting at dawn when she emerged to watch the sunrise before disappearing again.

"Nesi?" I call, knocking firmly. "We're approaching Manthana. You can see the island from the bow."

Silence greets me for several seconds before I hear movement inside. The door opens to reveal her fully dressed and ready, bag already packed beside her. No hint of awkwardness when she looks at me, only a composed expression.

"I know," she says simply. "I've been watching our approach from my window."

My lip ticks up in a smile at her quick response and observations. Nothing gets by her it would seem.

"Captain Vaelin says we'll dock within the hour," I inform her, trying not to stare at how the golden afternoon light catches in her navy hair. "I've arranged for someone to meet us—an old friend who can help us navigate the island discreetly."

Her eyebrow arches slightly. "You sent word ahead? I thought we were trying to keep a low profile?" She picks her words carefully, but I can tell she is not pleased I am sharing our arrival with anyone.

"Only to one person I trust implicitly," I assure her. "Jalnor won't betray our presence, and having a local guide will draw far less attention than us wandering around asking questions."

She studies me for a moment, those dark eyes revealing nothing of her thoughts. "Jalnor, the one from your story last night." I can't help but smile bigger. She referenced our meal! Even that small mention makes me happy, but I don't want to make it awkward so I just nod. "Very well," she says finally. "Though I'm perfectly capable of moving unseen when necessary."

"I don't doubt it," I respond with a smile she doesn't return. "But Manthana's unique. Outsiders are noticed, no matter how stealthily they move."

I step back, giving her space to exit the cabin. To my surprise, she doesn't immediately move past me but pauses in the doorway.

"Last night," she begins, her voice carefully neutral. "I—"

"Think nothing of it," I interrupt, saving her the awkwardness of whatever rejection she's formulating. "The mission comes first. I understand."

Something flickers across her face—relief? disappointment? Sadness? longing?—before she nods. "Yes. Exactly."

"Come," I say, gesturing toward the deck. "I'd like to point out some landmarks before we arrive. They might be useful in understanding the island's layout."

She follows me to the bow, maintaining a careful distance that feels both deliberate and painful. The crew members we pass offer respectful nods, though I notice several casting curious glances at Nesi. Her presence has been the subject of much speculation these past two days, despite her efforts to remain unnoticed.

At the railing, I point toward the approaching island. "There—the eastern cliffs. They run almost the entire length of this side, making the harbor one of the only safe approaches." I trace the outline with my finger. "Behind those trees at the top is the oldest settlement on the island. Most trading happens there."

Nesi absorbs this information with a nod, her gaze intent as she studies the landscape. "And where would rebels likely gather? Places away from authority, where people might speak freely."

The directness of her question doesn't surprise me. "The island isn't large, but there are secluded areas. Old quarries to the north, abandoned temples in the west. Places locals avoid because of old superstitions."

"Superstitions?" She seems particularly interested in this detail.

"Nothing specific. Just a general unease. Some places on the island have always felt... eerie, somehow. Most locals avoid them out of habit."

Nesi's attention sharpens at this. "Do any of the locals normally visit them? Or is it strictly off limits." Her question makes me stop to think of an appropriate response. There really is no sense hiding this especially since she is my spirit bond.

"My mother would spend time there, studying. She is a scholar of sorts. She has been studying the island for centuries but never really finished. It takes up a lot of her time." The last bit sounds bitter to my own ears, but it was the reality of my childhood.

"Did she ever tell you what she was studying?" I look over at Nesi as she listens intently to what I have to say.

"No." I shake my head. "She spent days away from Father and me, dropped in again for a while before repeating the same thing over and over again. I asked her once what she was studying, but she changed the subject and simply stated it was for the protection of the Kingdom. To this day after spending hours researching in the capital I have no idea what she is studying." Anger and resentment twist in my chest. I always felt like a nuisance to her and it didn't help the one person on the entire island that could understand me, understand my powers wouldn't spend the time to teach and train me.

"You know what's ironic?" My lips twist in a humorless smile. "I actually set foot on this island just last month. After years away, I finally returned because an agent reported my mother might be dying." I shake my head, the wound still fresh. "But when I arrived at that house—the same one I grew up feeling invisible in—she wasn't even there. My father stammered through excuses, unable to meet my eyes. Just urgent business, he said. Essential research. The same priorities that always mattered more than her own son."

I turn away briefly, composing myself. "I left on the same ship that brought me. Jalnor tried to convince me to stay, but what was the point? If she was truly ill, she chose her research over recovery—over my father who worships the ground she walks on, over her own health. That stung the most. That whatever this research is, it's worth risking everything, even her life." I clench my jaw, the familiar hurt turning to anger. "Two centuries, and nothing has changed. Some mysterious purpose still matters more than anything—or anyone—else."

"Did you reach out after you left?" she asks, her perceptive eyes studying my face.

"No." The single word hangs between us. "What would be the point? Another unanswered message? Another reply from my father making excuses for her absence?" Her facial expression doesn't change from the neutral one she wears, but I can see her mind at work behind her eyes.

"Do you want to visit them?" This feels more like she is worried about my desires and not the mission at hand, perhaps last night did shift something.

"If we can avoid it I would prefer that but I have a sinking feeling we will need to talk to them at some point." I say resignedly. Something inside tells me whatever is happening here, my mother will know the reason why.

She nods her head and looks out on the horizon. I wish I knew what she was thinking, what she is planning. I know she isn't telling me everything which is hard to accept but if I am patient she may just come to me willingly.

Captain Vaelin calls from the helm just then, "Preparing to dock! All hands to stations!" which breaks the silence around us.

The ship comes alive as everyone takes their positions. The Sunfire glides smoothly into the harbor, its approach slowing as the crew prepares to secure us to the dock.

I take a deep breath of the familiar air. Salt mingled with pine from the forests above, hints of smoke from cooking fires and the subtle sweetness of the moonberries that grow wild along the cliffs. My body remembers this place, even if my mind has tried to distance itself.

"We should gather our things," I tell Nesi, turning away from the railing. "Best to disembark quickly and without drawing attention."

She nods, already scanning the growing crowd of dockworkers and merchants gathering to greet the impressive vessel. "I'll meet you at the gangplank in five minutes."

We separate to retrieve our belongings, and I take a moment alone in my cabin to compose myself. I straighten my collar, checking that I've packed everything of importance. The fine clothes I brought would immediately mark me as court nobility, so I've changed into simpler attire—sturdy trousers, a plain shirt, and a practical jacket that won't draw attention. I look like any other reasonably successful trader now.

When I emerge, Nesi is already waiting, similarly dressed in understated clothing to help her blend in. The ship has docked, and Monstil is supervising the unloading of several crates—legitimate trade goods that were his actual reason for this journey, beyond accommodating my request.

"Ready?" I ask, approaching Nesi.

She nods, eyes constantly moving, cataloging everything around us. "Your friend is here."

I follow her gaze to the end of the dock where a broad-shoul-dered figure stands apart from the curious onlookers. Even at this distance, I'd recognize Jalnor anywhere—he's even larger than I remember, his massive frame standing out among the typically slender Fae folk around him. I used to joke that he had Orc blood in his family with how large he is. In reality, he ate his protein growing up, unlike most fae kids, who ate vegetables instead.

"That's him," I confirm, unable to keep a smile from spreading across my face. "Come on."

We thank Monstil for his hospitality, before finally making our way down the gangplank to the weathered wooden dock. The familiar scents and sounds of Manthana wrap around me. Mooring ropes creak as fishermen call out their day's catch, and in the distance, music drifts from the harbor tavern."

As we approach Jalnor, his bearded face breaks into a wide grin. He stands there, arms crossed over his massive chest, look-ing for all the world like he could snap a mast in half without breaking a sweat.

"Well, look what the tide washed in," he calls as we draw near. "The missing son returns again so soon! What's it been, a month since you stormed off the island?" I try to give him my most scathing look but it's no use.

"Jalnor," I say, my voice thick with unexpected emotion as I clasp his outstretched arm. We didn't get to really talk last I was here. It was about getting to my parents, and then well, I left. "You got fat."

He roars with laughter, pulling me into a bone-crushing hug that lifts me clear off the ground. "And you're still a scrawny court peacock! Though I see you've tried to dress the part of a common man this time." He sets me down, holding me at arm's length to inspect me properly. "Doesn't suit you. You've gone soft living in that palace."

"And you've clearly been sampling too much of your father's mead," I retort, grinning despite myself. "How many barrels did you steal this season?"

"Steal? I'll have you know I'm a respectable businessman now!" He pats his substantial belly proudly. "The meadery is mine, inherited fair and square when Father retired to the southern shores last year."

We grin at each other, the tension of my last visit—with him trying to convince me to stay after finding my mother conveniently absent—falling away in an instant. This is what I've missed most—the easy banter, the friendship that requires no pretense or careful calculation. Jalnor has always seen me exactly as I am, never feared my power or coveted my position.

Remembering my manners, I turn to Nesi, who watches our reunion with carefully concealed interest. "Jalnor, this is Lady Nesi of the Night Court. She's here on official business for Queen Neeve."

Jalnor studies her with undisguised curiosity before offering a surprisingly graceful bow. "Welcome to Manthana, my lady. Any friend of this troublemaker is welcome at my table, even if she does come from the mysterious Night Court."

Something that might almost be amusement flickers in Nesi's eyes. "Thank you for meeting us. We are hoping for discretion if at all possible."

"Aye, so his message said." Jalnor glances around the busy dock, then lowers his voice. "We'd best be moving along. Harbor gossip spreads faster than wildfire, and you two make an interesting pair."

He gestures for us to follow, leading us away from the docks toward a narrow path that winds toward the settlement above.

"I didn't know you knew how to bow." I can't help but tease as we walk.

"I may be an outer island fae with no courtly know-how, but I know how to make a good impression on my good friend's," He looks over his shoulder at me then her with a raised eyebrow. "Lady friend." His smile is huge and the laugh that follows makes me smile in turn. Meanwhile Nesi's composed face doesn't shift, but I can see red creeping up her neck, which gives me far too much pleasure.

"The old mill finally collapsed. They replaced it with a new one up on Baker's Ridge. Fishing's been good this season, though the western routes have been strangely quiet. Oh, and Ferren's daughter married that trader from Easthold. Big celebration. Went on for three days."

I listen with half an ear, my attention divided between Jalnor's updates and Nesi's reactions to my homeland. She walks slightly behind us, her perceptive eyes missing nothing. She catches the way islanders glance curiously at our small group before returning to their business.

"I've arranged lodging for you," Jalnor continues as we reach the edge of the settlement. Instead of turning toward the main square with its busy tavern and shops, he leads us along a less-traveled path that skirts the village outskirts. "Not at the inn, too many curious ears there. I've got a small cottage at the edge of my property that I built a couple years ago. Should suit your needs."

"Thank you," I say sincerely. "We appreciate the hospitality."

Jalnor waves off the gratitude. "Least I could do after you saved my hide from that rock drake all those years ago. Though," he adds with a curious glance, "No thought to stay with your parents? Maybe your mother would be there, and you know..."

I stiffen slightly, the familiar tension returning. "You know that's not a good idea, Jal."

He sighs, patting my shoulder. "Aye, I do. Still, a lot has changed in a month. Maybe it would be good to see if that bridge can be mended."

"Perhaps," I say noncommittally. "But this visit isn't about family reconciliation. We're here on official business."

"So mysterious," Jalnor teases, but he doesn't press further. Instead, he glances back at Nesi. "And how does a Night Court lady find our humble island so far?"

Nesi's expression remains carefully neutral. "It's interesting. There's a peculiar feeling to this place. A heaviness in the air. Do you feel it?" She looks at us both as we continue our walk.

Jalnor's step falters momentarily, his jovial expression shifting to something more serious. "Aye, that there is. Visitors often mention it, though those of us born here don't notice." He casts a knowing look my way. "Though recently it has started to feel heavier to even us locals. Some say it's old magic, sleeping beneath the hills." At the mention of it, I feel the weight settle on my shoulders—heavier now than I remember. It hadn't been noticeable when I lived here, but the longer I stayed away, the more present it became whenever I returned. And now, with Jalnor pointing it out, it feels even more pronounced.

I frown at this new information, however. "What do you mean, 'old magic'? You never mentioned that in your letters."

"Didn't think it worth mentioning," Jalnor shrugs, his massive shoulders rising and falling like small mountains. "It's always been here, hasn't it? Though I'll admit, it's been a bit more concerning lately."

Nesi and I exchange a quick glance. This could be relevant to the rebel activity she's investigating.

"Here we are," Jalnor announces as we crest a small rise. Below us sits a charming stone cottage, smoke curling from its chimney. Behind it stretches a large meadow, beyond which I can see the main house and the outbuildings of Jalnor's meadery. "Nothing fancy, but it's clean and private. No one will bother you here."

"It's perfect," I assure him, genuinely grateful for his thoughtfulness.

As we approach the cottage, Jalnor's voice drops lower. "Now, are you going to tell me what brings the King's right hand and a Night Court lady to our quiet island? Must be important to drag you back after all these years."

Nesi tenses beside me at his directness, her posture shifting subtly into something more alert, more guarded.

"We'll explain everything," I promise, placing a reassuring hand on Jalnor's massive arm. "But first, I could use a drink of that famous mead, and perhaps something to eat? It's been a long journey."

Jalnor's serious expression melts back into his customary grin. "Now that's the Milori I remember! Always thinking with your stomach!" He laughs, the sound booming across the meadow. "Come inside, then. I've got food prepared and plenty to drink."

As we follow him toward the cottage, I notice Nesi studying the easy familiarity between us. For a brief moment, something almost wistful crosses her face—so quickly I might have imagined it—before her composed mask returns.

"Your friend seems trustworthy," she says quietly as Jalnor moves ahead to open the door.

"I'd trust him with my life," I confirm without hesitation. "He knows this island better than anyone. If there's something strange happening here, Jalnor will help us uncover it."

She nods, apparently satisfied with this assessment. "Good. Because I'm beginning to think there's more to this island than either of us anticipated."

Looking across the familiar landscape that once was home, feeling that subtle heaviness in the air that I'd always attributed to my own discomfort rather than anything external, I can only agree. Something about Manthana has changed.

Chapter 8
Milori

The cottage Jalnor has provided is simple and isolated, perfect for what we need. A fire already crackles in the hearth, its golden light dancing across the simple wooden furniture. The main room serves as both kitchen and living area, with two small bedrooms tucked behind a partial wall. It's the kind of place that feels instantly welcoming, especially after days at sea.

"Make yourselves comfortable," Jalnor announces, bustling about with surprising grace for a man of his size. He retrieves a jug of mead from the shelf and three wooden cups from a cabinet. "This batch is something special. It's honeycomb steeped with moonberries and a hint of clove. Won at the spring festival this year."

I settle into one of the chairs at the small table, gesturing for Nesi to join us. She hesitates, her instincts clearly urging her to remain standing, alert and ready. But after a moment, she takes the seat across from me, though I notice she positions herself with a clear view of both the door and windows. Old habits, I suppose.

"This is a nice place, Jal," I tell him as he pours the amber liquid into our cups. "Though I'm surprised you're not living in your father's house now that the meadery is yours."

Jalnor hands me a cup with a grin. "Oh, I am. But I keep this cottage for guests, or when I need some peace from all the workers. Ever since I took over it feels like I am always needed. Sometimes it's nice to just be alone, you know?" I nod my head because I do know what it's like to live on this island with everyone in your business all the time.

He passes a cup to Nesi with a respectful nod before raising his own. "To old friends and new allies. May your time on Manthana be fruitful—whatever you're searching for."

We drink, and the mead is exceptional. It's just the right balance of sweetness, with a depth of flavour that lingers and warms all the way down. I can't help the appreciative sound that escapes me, earning a proud smile from Jalnor.

"By the sun, Jal, this is magnificent. If the palace knew what they were missing, you'd have the royal contract in an instant." The pride I have for my friend is immense.

"And have to deal with court politics? No thank you." He laughs, dropping his massive frame into a chair that creaks under his weight. "I'm content with my simple island life. Not everyone dreams of the big city like you did."

"I didn't dream of the city," I correct him, the memory sharp despite the years. "I dreamed of somewhere I could be accepted and not accidentally burn down half the village. Mother had no idea what to do with me. Her light magic was nothing like my fire. Easiest thing was to send me to the capital to get trained." I take another swig of my drink as memories from centuries ago flood my mind.

"I was only thirty when she sent me away, barely more than a child by Fae standards. She said I needed proper instruction from those with similar powers, that I'd never learn control on an island where no one understood what I could do." I take another deep swallow of mead, the sweetness doing little to mask the bitterness that lingers after all these years. "Two hundred years later, and I'm still not sure if she sent me away for my benefit or because she was more concerned about how much time it would take from her study."

The room falls quiet. Jalnor stares into his cup, likely remembering the day I left. To my surprise, it's Nesi who breaks the silence.

"Interesting that she would send you away rather than teach you herself," she says, her dark eyes calculating. "Noble Fae typically guard their children's education closely, especially those with significant power." She tilts her head slightly, studying me with renewed interest. "And yet she chose to remain here, on this unremarkable island with its peculiar heaviness. I wonder what she found so compelling about Manthana that it took precedence over her own son's development."

She doesn't say what we're both thinking—that my mother's choices were strange, almost too deliberate, given what we're investigating.

Jalnor sets his cup down with deliberate care. "Your mother always was a mystery, Mil. Even to those of us who grew up here." He glances between us, his grin breaking through the lingering weight of our conversation. "Well, this got heavy rather quickly! Perhaps the lady would enjoy hearing about the time Milori accidentally set the village elder's prized goat on fire?"

"Jalnor, don't you dare—" I begin, but Jalnor is already leaning forward, eyes gleaming with mischief.

"You see, my lady, it wasn't just that his powers were strong. They were unpredictable in a way that frightened people. Take the famous Harvest Festival incident, when we were about fourteen years old..."

I groan, recognizing where this is heading. "Must we really revisit my childhood failings?"

"So there we were, fourteen years old and full of ourselves. The elders had finally agreed to let Milori participate in the festival after three years of him being relegated to watching from a distance because of the, ah, burning field incident." He winks at me before continuing. "The festival includes a torch-lighting ceremony, very dramatic. Each of the village elders lights a ceremonial brazier, and then the youngest eligible citizen gets to light the final one."

I groan, already knowing where this is heading. "Must we really?"

"Yes, we must," Jalnor insists, clearly enjoying himself. "So they call young Milori forward, and he's so nervous his hands are literally smoking. Not ideal when you've got fire powers you can't fully control. The Elder hands him this tiny ceremonial torch, and Milori reaches for the final brazier—"

"And I sneezed," I finish hopelessly. "Just as I was about to light it."

Jalnor slaps his knee, laughter booming. "Fire everywhere! The ceremonial banner goes up in flames, three elders lose their eyebrows, and poor Farrim's prize rooster gets so startled it flies directly into the central bonfire!"

"The smell of burning feathers lingered for days," I admit, unable to keep from smiling despite the embarrassing memory. "I wasn't allowed near another festival for five years."

To my surprise, Nesi's lips curl into a subtle smile. It transforms her face, softening the sharp edges of her carefully maintained composure. The smile vanishes almost as quickly as it appeared, and she takes another sip of mead, retreating behind her well-constructed walls.

"Well," Jalnor says, raising his cup again, "to the troublemakers. Always keeping life interesting."

We drink, and Jalnor dives into more childhood tales—embarrassing ones (mostly mine), heroic ones (mostly exaggerated), and a few that are simply nostalgic. The mead flows freely, and even Nesi gradually relaxes, her posture becoming less rigid as the evening progresses. Though she remains largely silent, her occasional wry comments reveal a sharp wit beneath her controlled exterior.

"And then there was the time Milori decided he could fly before his wings had fully developed," Jalnor continues, wiping tears of mirth from his eyes. "He jumped off the boat house roof and landed right in Widow Torrin's prize rose bushes. She chased him halfway across the village with her gardening shears!"

"In my defence," I protest through my laughter, "most noble Fae develop their wings much earlier. How was I to know mine would be delayed?"

"Perhaps because your father very specifically told you they wouldn't manifest until you were at least twenty?" Jalnor counters.

"Details, details." I wave dismissively, then I lean forward with a conspiratorial smile. "But fair is fair. Remember that brilliant idea you had about stealing Old Ferren's boat because you were convinced there was treasure hidden on Serpent's Isle?"

Jalnor's face flushes bright red. "Now wait just a moment—"

"Oh no," I continue, delighted by his discomfort. "You insisted the moon would guide you to the treasure. You even made that ridiculous map, remember? Stained with tea and burned around the edges to make it look ancient."

"I was very convincing!" Jalnor protests, pointing at me with his cup. "You believed it was real!"

"Until you got us both lost at sea for three days," I remind him. "We drifted so far off course we ended up on the wrong side of the island entirely. Your father had half the village out searching for us.And when they found us," I tell Nesi, who's watching our exchange with quiet amusement, "this great oaf tried to convince them we'd been kidnapped by sea sprites rather than admit he couldn't read a navigation chart!"

Jalnor groans, covering his face with one massive hand. "We were banned from every boat on the island for five years. My father made me clean fish barrels for an entire summer as punishment."

"And you smelled like it for twice as long," I add, ducking as he tosses a piece of bread at my head.

We dissolve into laughter, the kind that makes your sides ache and brings tears to your eyes. I catch Nesi watching us, a genuine smile on her face. For a moment, her carefully maintained walls seem to lower letting the moment sink in.

It strikes me how different this is from the laughter I share with my friends at court. Those moments with Timas, Emilia, Garrick, and Alette are precious, of course. They're moments of genuine connection amid the suffocating politics. But there's something uniquely freeing about the simple joy of childhood stories told over good mead, no responsibilities weighing on my shoulders, and no one expecting anything from Captain Milori, the King's right hand.

With Jalnor's booming laugh filling the cottage and Nesi's unexpected presence beside me, I feel a version of myself surfacing that I thought had been lost decades ago—the boy who existed before duty and power complicated everything.

***

As the night deepens, Jalnor rises to add more wood to the fire, his movements slightly less coordinated after several servings of his strongest mead. As the fresh logs catch flame, casting long shadows across the room, his expression shifts from joy to something more thoughtful.

"You know," he says, settling back into his chair with a creak of wood, "all this reminiscing is well and good, but there are some happenings around the island you should know about." His voice drops lower, the storyteller's cadence replaced by something more cautious. "Things have been tense lately."

Nesi straightens slightly in her seat, her attention sharpening as if a switch has been flipped. The relaxed posture she'd gradually adopted throughout the evening vanishes in an instant. "Tense how?" she asks, her voice carefully neutral despite the intensity in her eyes.

Jalnor rubs his beard thoughtfully. "It started a few months back when some newcomers arrived. A group of them, led by a fellow named Derrin. They were pleasant enough. Said they were looking to establish a trading post here."

"That's not unusual," I observe. "Manthana has always welcomed traders."

"True," Jalnor agrees, "but what was strange was how quickly everyone accepted them. Manthana folk are traditionally wary of outsiders—no offence, my lady," he adds with a nod to Nesi, who simply inclines her head in acknowledgment. "But these newcomers, they were welcomed with open arms. Almost overnight, they had a place in the community, invitations to private gatherings, access to the council meetings."

A prickle of unease crawls up my spine. "That is unusual."

"It gets stranger," Jalnor continues, lowering his voice despite us being alone in the cottage. "Over the past few weeks, the island's atmosphere has shifted. People who've known each other all their lives now exchange suspicious glances. Conversations stop when certain folks walk by. There've been arguments in the council about resource allocation and trading rights, things that were never contentious before."

Nesi leans forward slightly. "And these newcomers? Where do they spend their time?"

"That's just it—they're everywhere and nowhere. They maintain a presence in the village, but they're often gone for days at a time. 'Exploring the island,' they say." Jalnor takes a swig of his mead before continuing. "But the places they're rumoured to explore are areas most locals avoid."

"The temples," I guess, remembering our earlier conversation. "The ones where that heaviness in the air is strongest."

"Exactly." Jalnor nods grimly. "The old ruins on the western cliffs. The cave system beneath the central hills. Places our grandparents warned us never to go."

Nesi and I exchange a quick glance. This aligns perfectly with what we're here to investigate.

"Have they approached you?" Nesi asks Jalnor. "Tried to recruit you?"

Jalnor shakes his head. "Not directly. Though they're good customers at the meadery. Always asking questions about island history, old legends, family lineages. Particularly interested in the noble families who've settled here over the centuries." His gaze shifts to me meaningfully. "Families like yours."

My stomach tightens. "Have my parents been bothered?"

"Not bothered, exactly." Jalnor refills our cups, his movements more deliberate now. "But your mother has been different lately. More concerned than usual."

"My mother is always concerned," I mutter.

"True enough," Jalnor acknowledges with a sad smile. "But this is different. She's been making more frequent trips and no one seems to know where she goes. Even your father seems worried about her absences."

This catches my attention. My father worried? He's never questioned my mother's comings and goings, always accepting her mysterious research without complaint. If he's concerned now, something truly must be amiss.

"I saw her just three days ago," Jalnor continues, "heading toward the cliffs at dawn with a satchel full of books. She looked frazzled. Not at all like her usual composed self."

"Did you speak with her?" I ask, trying to imagine my elegant, always-controlled mother looking anything close to frazzled.

"I tried to." Jalnor shrugs his massive shoulders. "She barely acknowledged me. Said something about 'seals' and 'bindings' before hurrying off. Didn't make much sense to me."

Nesi's eyes narrow slightly. "Seals and bindings? Those are terms used in ancient containment magic."

Jalnor and I turn to her in surprise.

"What would my mother know about containment magic?" I ask, though even as the question leaves my lips, an uncomfortable suspicion forms and the pieces all start to fall into place.

"I couldn't say," Nesi replies carefully. "But it might be worth investigating, if these newcomers are showing interest in the same locations she's visiting."

Jalnor drums his fingers on the table, a nervous habit he's held onto from childhood. "There's something else. A gathering is planned for tomorrow night, in the old quarry north of the village. But it's not a local event, it's something these newcomers have organized. They've been quietly inviting certain villagers, the more vocal ones who have been dissatisfied with the current state of things."

"Dissatisfaction?" I prompt.

"Mostly common Fae who resent the noble privileges," Jalnor explains. "Usual stuff. Folks who question why the fates decided only certain bloodlines deserve magic. Others who worry about the Human Queen taking a throne they believe belongs to pure Fae. The usual grumblings you find on any island, but lately, they've grown louder."

Exactly what Nesi described back in Sonas, discontent being stoked and channeled by potential rebel leaders. I glance at her, catching the sharp calculations behind her gaze.

"This gathering," Nesi begins. "Would it be possible to observe it without being detected?"

Jalnor considers this. "Possibly. The quarry has several overlooking ridges that offer decent vantage points. But you'd need to be careful. With how strange things have been, I would assume they will post lookouts."

I shift uncomfortably in my seat. "Perhaps we should gather more information first? We don't know enough about these people or what they're capable of." I glance at Nesi, who shows no emotion, but I already know what she's thinking. A shadow walker won't need ridges or vantage points. She'll simply melt into darkness and observe undetected. And she'll do it with or without my approval. Not that she needs my approval, but this protective feeling is not going to just let me watch her walk into danger.

"We need to see this gathering firsthand," she states, confirming my suspicion. Her tone leaves no room for debate.

"Thank you for sharing this with us," I tell Jalnor.

Jalnor studies us both, his usually jovial expression somber in the firelight. "Whatever you're mixed up in, I hope you know what you're doing. This island has always had its secrets, but lately, it feels like they're stirring. Like something is about to happen and it's going to be bigger than any of us realize."

Outside, the wind picks up, whistling around the eaves of the cottage like a mournful spirit. The flame in the hearth flickers, sending shadows dancing across the walls—well that can't be good.

"We should rest," Nesi says finally, rising from her chair with fluid grace. "Tomorrow will be a busy day."

"Of course." Jalnor stands, towering over both of us. "The bedrooms are prepared. Washroom is through that door." He claps my shoulder, his grip comforting and familiar. "It's good to have you home, Mil, whatever the circumstances."

Home. The word stirs complicated emotions in my chest. Is Manthana still home? Was it ever, truly? No, I don't think so, but it is still where my life started, and for that I will protect it no matter who decides to attack it.

As Nesi disappears into one of the bedrooms and Jalnor prepares to leave, I find myself thinking about what Nesi hasn't told me, and even my own mother's secrets. Apparently the women in my life like to keep secrets. Tomorrow I need to find answers whether they give them to me or not.

Chapter 9

Nesi

The sun rose a couple of hours ago, and I've been awake reviewing Neeve's documents and planning our approach to today's investigation. Sleep came fitfully last night, my mind racing with everything Jalnor shared about the island and these mysterious newcomers. Even if the mission weren't weighing on me, I still wouldn't be able to sleep—not with Milori just a thin wall away, his presence stirring a buzz of excitement and longing.

The quiet clink of cups and the fire being stocked tell me Milori is up and moving around in the main room. I suppose there is no reason to put it off; time to greet my spirit bond and try to ignore the inevitable pull. I tuck the papers back into my bag and rise, straightening my simple dark clothing before stepping out to join him.

"Good morning," he says, looking up with that easy smile that manages to be both charming and genuine. "I hope you slept well?"

"Well enough," I reply, crossing to the small table where he's laid out a simple breakfast of bread, fruit, and what smells like fresh herbal tea. I raise an eyebrow at the spread. "You went to the village already?"

"Jalnor brought these at dawn," he explains, gesturing for me to sit. "Apparently baking helps him think. He's gathering information about tonight's meeting—discreetly, of course."

I take a seat, accepting the cup he offers. The tea is fragrant with hints of mint and something spicier I can't quite place. "We should familiarize ourselves with the village today. Get a sense of these newcomers and the local dynamics."

Milori nods, breaking a piece of bread. "I agree. Though I should warn you, my presence may complicate things. It's been nearly a century, but I wasn't exactly forgotten here."

The way his voice tightens slightly tells me more than his words.

"All the more reason to observe the village reaction," I say practically. "If these rebels are targeting those who feel alienated, seeing how people respond to you might reveal potential sympathizers."

He gives me a wry smile. "So I'm to be bait, then?"

"Not bait," I correct, taking a sip of tea. "A catalyst. Besides, we need to understand what we're dealing with before tonight's gathering."

"Fair enough." We eat in companionable silence before Milori collects the dishes and heads to the door. "Shall we?"

The walk to the village takes longer than I expect. Milori moves at a leisurely pace, pointing out landmarks and sharing bits of history about the island. I listen with half an ear, more focused on scanning our surroundings. The heaviness in the air seems to change as we walk, stronger in some places, almost unnoticeable in others. It's unlike anything I've experienced before. Even in the darkest corners of the Shrouded Forest it was consistently oppressive. This, however, feels like weakening walls.

"You feel it too, don't you?" Milori asks, noticing my attention shift as we pass a particularly dense growth of trees. "The weight in the air."

"Yes." I slow my steps, trying to categorize the sensation. "It's almost like...a presence. As if the island itself is watching. Not so dissimilar to the Shrouded Forest, but oddly alive. Where the forest felt dead, sucking the life from us to survive, this feels aware. Conscious, somehow."

"I always thought it was just me," he admits quietly. "Something I imagined to explain why I never felt comfortable here. But hearing you describe it—maybe there is something more to this place." He pauses for a moment, his lips twisting as if considering his next words.

"What was it like growing up in the forest?"

I take a deep breath before deciding what to say.

"It's hard to explain. When you're born there, you know nothing different. Other than the stories everyone told of what it was like to live outside the forest, we really didn't know or understand that life." I pause, considering how much to share. "My experience was unique, however. I didn't feel the same heavy weight everyone else did while in the forest. I later found out my abilities seem to have some sort of similarity to the forest, which only added to people's fear of me."

"Did that bother you? Being feared?" Milori asks. I study his side profile as we walk. He doesn't look at me, but his question feels genuine, as if the answer will reveal something important to him.

"It did when I was younger," I admit with a shrug. "But I soon accepted that this is what I was. I couldn't change my powers, so I didn't see any reason to dwell on other people's fear."

Milori huffs out a surprised laugh. "How old were you when you decided that?"

He looks at me now, and I just shrug again. "Twenty."

"TWENTY? You were fine with being feared at twenty? I had a complex and an identity crisis at twenty." He mumbles the last bit, and I can't control the smile that takes over my face.

"My mother always said I was a logical child. No sense wishing for something different when there were steps to follow and things to achieve." My voice softens slightly. "Now, that being said, achieving anything in the forest was a feat. After a few decades, Queen Neeve's father had me training and even going out of the forest on reconnaissance as he prepared to attempt a peace treaty with King Timas. That was the first time I had seen the sun or experienced life outside of the forest. It was strange and exhilarating. But I learned early that my abilities helped with observation, and my training was necessary to ensure my safety. The old king didn't abuse my abilities like Oberon, but he saw them as a perfect tool to potentially bring our people out of the darkness."

"So you've always just been looked at as a tool, not a person. Never just Nesi who likes flowers and collecting herbs."

His observation takes me off guard. For a long moment, I'm silent, unable to form a response. I've never really thought about it that way. I've always believed I had a purpose in life, and it brought me contentment. But the longer I'm with Milori, the more I find myself desiring more than just contentment in my job. I want peace in my private life too.

Physically shaking my head, I focus on our walk to the village. One thing at a time, and contemplating my existence is not on the agenda today.

The village comes into view. It's a bustling location, with happy children running around and merchants at their stalls selling wares. It looks like any normal settlement, until people notice us.

Until they notice Milori.

The change is subtle but unmistakable. Conversations falter. Gazes linger then quickly dart away. People adjust their paths to maintain distance from us. Not everyone—some nod respectfully, a few even offer hesitant smiles—but enough to create a palpable tension.

"Not the warmest welcome," I observe.

Milori's smile tightens, though he maintains his confident posture. "Told you so," he murmurs. "Let's head to the central square. The tavern there is where most gossip circulates."

As we walk through the village, I catalogue the reactions, mentally noting which individuals seem most hostile and which merely curious. Several times, I notice people watching us with particular intensity—perhaps the newcomers Jalnor mentioned.

The tavern sits at the heart of the village, a sturdy three-storey building with a weathered sign. Despite the early hour, several patrons already occupy tables, nursing drinks or sharing a morning meal.

"The Barrel and Spear," Milori explains as we approach. "Oldest establishment on the island. If you want to know what's happening on Manthana, this is where you'll hear it."

The moment we step through the door, a hush falls over the room. Every head turns in our direction, expressions ranging from surprise to wary recognition to outright hostility. Milori ignores the reaction, walking confidently to the bar with the ease of someone who belongs, though we both know that's far from the truth.

"Two meads," he tells the barkeeper, an older woman whose eyes widen slightly at the sight of him. "Unless the Fenik brew is still as terrible as I remember."

"Milori," she says, recovering quickly. "Didn't expect to see you back on our shores."

"Hello, Daela." His smile is warm and genuine. "It's been a while."

"A century, more or less." She studies him critically, then glances curiously at me. "And who might your companion be?"

"This is Nesi," he says simply, offering no title or explanation. "We're just passing through, seeing the sights."

Daela snorts, clearly not believing him for a moment, but she doesn't press. "Two meads coming up. Though I warn you, the Fenik brew isn't the same: it's worse." She laughs, turning to fill our order.

Milori motions for us to sit at a table near the bar, a good position to see everything. I position myself with my back to the wall, taking in every detail of the room. Three men at a corner table watch us with particular interest—their clothing distinctly different to that of the locals.

"The trio in the corner," I murmur. "They don't belong here."

Milori doesn't turn to look. "Part of Derrin's group, most likely. The one with the scar across his jaw looks familiar, but I don't know why."

Daela returns with our drinks. "On the house," she says gruffly. "For old times' sake. Though not everyone's as pleased to see you." She nods subtly toward a group of islanders who are openly glaring in our direction.

"Some things never change," Milori says, lifting his cup in acknowledgment. "Though Berrin seems to have grown even more sour with age. Did his face get stuck like that after I left?" Daela laughs as she looks over her shoulder at the table.

The largest of the glaring men—Berrin, presumably—scowls and turns to mutter something to his companions that makes them snicker derisively.

"Ignore them," Daela advises, though there's concern in her eyes. "They've gotten bolder lately, especially with these new traders encouraging them."

"New traders?" I ask, adopting an innocently curious tone that I've perfected over years of intelligence gathering. "Are they bringing in better goods than before?"

Daela leans in slightly, her voice lowering. "Better promises, more like. Talking about how things could change around here. How those with power shouldn't keep it all to themselves, all those people in the capital keeping what all Fae should have." Her pointed glance at Milori makes it clear who "those" refers to.

I feel, rather than see, Milori tense beside me. His easy smile remains fixed in place, but I can sense the effort it takes to maintain it.

"Interesting timing for such talk," I comment lightly. "With relations between the Courts finally improving after centuries of division."

Daela nods, seemingly pleased by my understanding. "That's exactly what I said to Ferrin when he started spouting their nonsense. We've finally got peace, trade is improving. Why rock the boat now?"

A commotion from the corner draws our attention. Berrin and his friends have risen from their table and are now making their way toward us. The tavern goes silent again, tension crackling in the air like the moment before a storm breaks.

"Well, well," Berrin drawls, his voice carrying in the hushed room. "The fire menace returns. Didn't burn down enough of our island the first time around?"

I feel Milori's calm demeanour shift beside me, though his expression remains carefully neutral. "Berrin," he acknowledges with a nod. "Still holding grudges from two centuries ago, I see."

"Some things aren't forgotten," Berrin spits. "Like how your family lords their noble status over honest working folk. Or how you destroyed my father's entire harvest with your uncontrolled magic."

Milori sets down his cup carefully and leans back. "I was a child, Berrin," he sounds exasperated. "I've apologized for that incident more times than I can count, and my family compensated yours generously."

"Money doesn't replace generations of work," one of Berrin's companions chimes in. "Or make up for the fact that some are born with power while others have to scrape by with nothing."

"It's not his fault how the fates distribute magic," Daela interjects, her tone sharp. "And I'll thank you for taking your arguments elsewhere. This is a place for drinking, not brawling."

Berrin ignores her, stepping closer to Milori. "Things are changing around here. Soon, nobles like you won't be able to hide behind your family names or fancy court titles."

"Is that a threat?" Milori's voice is quiet, steady—but there's an unmistakable sharpness beneath it.

"It's a promise," Berrin smirks. "Your kind has kept the rest of us down for too long. The new ways coming will put everyone on equal footing again."

I've heard enough. I stand slowly and walk a step closer to Berrin. Everyone turns to look at me. I am smaller than Milori—and even Berrin—but my unmistakable Night Court look sparks either fear or fury, depending on who stands before me. Today, however, he won't see an exiled Night Court Fae; today, he will glimpse a shadow walker.

"Perhaps you should reconsider your approach," I say softly, my voice calm and measured. The tavern grows unnaturally quiet as I stare down Berrin.

Berrin shifts uncomfortably, the smirk on his face faltering. "This doesn't concern you, Night Court."

"Doesn't it?" I ask, tilting my head to the side. With the smallest movement of my fingers, I call to the shadows. They don't wrap around anyone or make obvious displays, but they shift and flicker at the edge of vision, creating impressions of movement where none exists, suggesting shapes that disappear when looked at directly.

Someone gasps as a shadow briefly resembles a crouched figure before dissolving. Another patron jerks in his seat, swatting at nothing.

"I find threats against Captain Milori quite concerning," I continue, my voice barely above a whisper, yet somehow carrying to every corner of the silent room. "Particularly from someone with no magic at all. What exactly do you plan to do against those with power? Talk them to death?"

Berrin's face flushes with anger, but his eyes dart nervously to the shadows that seem to be playing tricks on everyone's vision.

"My people survived centuries in the Shrouded Forest," I say, moving another step closer. "We learned interesting things there. Skills that kept us alive when the darkness tried to consume our minds. I would be happy to demonstrate what I learned."

The shadows suddenly create the briefest impression of elongated fingers reaching toward Berrin's throat before vanishing. Too many in the tavern are looking off into corners to notice it, though I am sure Milori saw it before it vanished.

"Wh—what are you doing?" he stammers, taking an involuntary step back, eyes wide open with fear.

I smile, showing just a hint of teeth. "Nothing at all. Yet."

One of his friends grabs his arm, clearly unnerved. "Let's go, Berrin. This isn't worth it."

"If you feel so strongly about nobility having too much power," I suggest pleasantly, "perhaps take it up with King Timas directly. I'm sure he'd be fascinated by your opinions."

The shadows pulse once more, creating fleeting impressions of movements all around them, making the men jump.

"We're just here to visit the island," I add, my voice deceptively gentle. "Nothing more. Unless someone forces my hand."

Berrin's face has gone ashen. Without another word, he and his companions retreat to their corner, casting nervous glances over their shoulders, occasionally jumping at perfectly ordinary shadows.

I return to my seat beside Milori with deliberate grace. The shadows settle back to normal, though several patrons continue to look around warily, uncertain of what they just witnessed or if they imagined it all.

Milori turns to me, something like admiration mingled with surprise in his eyes. I meet his gaze steadily, refusing to acknowledge what I've just done as anything unusual. It isn't like me to put on such a display, and I wonder briefly why I felt compelled to intervene. At least that's a lie I am going to tell myself for the time being.

Daela breaks the tense silence with a low whistle. "I don't know what you just did," she says, eyeing me with a mixture of fear and respect, "but I've never seen Berrin back down that quickly. What exactly are you?"

"Just a visitor from the Night Court," I reply coolly, taking a sip of my mead as if nothing unusual has occurred and wincing at the awful taste. She wasn't kidding, it's terrible. "Though I've found rude fools exist in every court."

A few nervous chuckles ripple through the tavern, and gradually, conversations resume, though markedly quieter than before. Derrin and his associates watch us with open intensity, their earlier attempt at subtlety abandoned.

"That was," Milori begins quietly, leaning closer to me, "impressive. And unexpected."

"They were interrupting our information gathering," I say dismissively, though I can feel warmth creeping up my neck at his proximity. "Nothing more."

His lips curve into a knowing smile. "Of course. Purely tactical."

"What else would it be?" I challenge, meeting his gaze.

"I don't know," he says, his voice warm with amusement. "Almost seemed like you were being protective. It was cute."

"I am not cute," I inform him flatly. "And I was not being protective. I was ensuring our mission wasn't compromised by local grievances."

"If you say so." His eyes sparkle with mischief. "Though I must say, watching you put Berrin in his place was thoroughly enjoyable. He's been a thorn in my side since we were children. But I've got myself a Night Court protector! No need to fear now."

I roll my eyes, but something warm unfurls in my chest at his obvious appreciation. This feeling, this connection between us, it grows stronger with each interaction, each shared moment. It's becoming harder to ignore, harder to pretend it's merely an inconvenient physical response as I claimed that first night.

And that is deeply concerning. *Focus Nesi, you have a job to do.* I chastise myself.

Yet as Milori turns to engage Daela in conversation, skillfully extracting information about the newcomers and recent island changes, I find myself wondering what it might be like to follow this connection where it leads. To allow myself the one thing I've secretly longed for all these years: a genuine bond with someone who sees me, all of me, without fear.

The shadows around me stir in response to my thoughts, and I force them into stillness. Not now. Perhaps not ever. The mission must come first.

But for the first time since discovering our connection, I allow myself to consider that there might be an "after," a time when duty no longer stands between us. And that thought, dangerous as it is, brings me more comfort than I care to admit.

Chapter 10

Nesi

I notice Milori rambles when waiting through long silences, an endearing habit I find myself both irritated by and drawn to. We've been hidden in these shadows for hours since sunset, positioned perfectly to observe the meeting. I'm focused on our mission—to infiltrate and discover what's truly happening on this island—but he's launched into an absurdly detailed debate with himself about whether shrivelled grapes should technically be called raisins. His animated whispers fill our hiding spot as I struggle not to silence him with a tendril of shadow, though the thought is tempting. How one person can speak so passionately about dried fruit while we're conducting surveillance is beyond comprehension.

I watch with careful attention as villagers begin to approach the meeting site. They arrive in small clusters, some walking with confidence, others glancing nervously over their shoulders. Most are common Fae from Manthana while others are obviously part of the group holding this meeting.

"Their lookouts are sloppy," Milori mutters, assessing the four sentries stationed around the perimeter with obvious disapproval. Apparently, we have moved on from dried fruit. "Two at the main entrance but none watching the eastern approach? And that one keeps checking the same spot repeatedly, creating a predictable pattern. If I were organizing this, I'd have rotating positions, overlapping fields of vision." He shakes his head. "Amateur work."

I resist the urge to tell him to be quiet. His tactical assessment isn't wrong, and his attention to detail is actually impressive. The shadows conceal us completely, but his restlessness is palpable, like a physical energy radiating from him.

"See how they're positioned? That tall one keeps his back to the forest," he continues, his voice a barely audible whisper against my ear. "I'd never allow such carelessness in my guards. Too many blind spots."

As more people gather, his critiques of the security arrangements gradually fade into silence. I feel the shift in his energy—his focus narrowing, body tensing beside mine. When he speaks again, his voice carries a different weight.

"I still think I should be closer," Milori whispers beside me, his breath creating small clouds in the night air. Despite agreeing to my plan, he's been restless since we arrived, constantly scanning the area with those sharp eyes of his.

I turn to face him, a small smile playing at my lips. "Worried about me, Captain?" I keep my voice gentle, teasing. "I've infiltrated more dangerous gatherings than this. But I appreciate the concern." I'm surprised by my own words, by the warmth in them. Something about his protective instinct touches me in a way I hadn't expected.

He frowns, concern evident in the tightness around his eyes. "And if something goes wrong?"

"Nothing will go wrong." I check my weapons one last time—a slender blade strapped to each forearm, another at my ankle. Not that I expect to need them; the shadows are weapon enough. "I'll observe, gather information, and return. Simple."

"Nothing about this is simple," he mutters, but doesn't argue further. "I'll wait at the fallen oak we passed. It offers a clear view of both the quarry entrance and your most likely exit route." His shift from anxiously waiting to focused on the task is giving me whiplash, or maybe he is just trying to cover it up.

I nod, appreciating his tactical thinking despite my annoyance at his insistence on coming at all. After this morning's incident at the tavern, we'd spent the day gathering more information about these newcomers, confirming what we already suspected—they're recruiting discontented locals, focusing particularly on those with grievances against the noble class. If I was hoping for more helpful information, we didn't get it, so hopefully this will be useful.

"Remember," I say, holding his gaze firmly, "no matter what you see or hear, maintain your position unless I signal. We can't risk a fight with so many innocents, and we don't even know how many people here have powers."

"Unless you're in actual danger," he amends, that stubborn set to his jaw telling me this point isn't negotiable.

I resist the urge to roll my eyes. "Fine. Unless I'm in actual danger, which I won't be, because no one will see me."

He studies me for a moment, then reaches out, his fingers brushing my arm so lightly I might have imagined it. "Be careful, Nesi."

Something about the way he says my name—soft, almost reverent—makes my heart beat faster. I pull away, uncomfortable with the depth of emotion his simple touch evokes.

"I'm always careful," I reply, already calling the shadows to me. They respond eagerly, wrapping around my form like old friends. "Wait an hour, then go to the oak."

Without waiting for his response, I slip away, becoming one with the darkness that pools between trees and stones. Moving like this—not quite invisible, but merged with shadow—is as natural to me as breathing. The night embraces me, guiding my steps as I descend toward the quarry.

I pass the first lookout easily—a nervous young Fae clutching a staff like it might protect him from whatever lurks in the darkness. If he only knew how close that darkness actually was. The second lookout is more alert, her eyes constantly scanning her surroundings, but she too fails to notice me gliding past.

As I approach a third lookout post, I slow, catching fragments of conversation between two men.

"—still say we should've cancelled," one mutters, shifting uneasily. "After what happened this morning—"

"What, you afraid of some Night Court woman?" the other scoffs, though his voice lacks conviction.

"You didn't see what she did," the first replies, lowering his voice further. "The shadows... they moved. People were seeing things that weren't there. Berrin said it felt like ice crawling through his veins."

A small smile curves my lips. Good. Fear is useful; it makes people careless.

"Lord Soren says she's dangerous but not to worry. He'll handle her if she interferes."

I freeze at the name, a chill courses through me and a flood of memories race to my mind. The look of disinterest, a smirk of delight at the person's terror, his cold dead eyes. Soren. He watched as I used my abilities to terrorize and force people to Oberon's will. The guilt in the pit of my stomach twists as I remember how I was used. I can't focus on that right now. Pushing the thoughts away, I focus again, this time with more steel than before. If he is actually here, I will need to be on guard.

The path down is simple to navigate as I focus on one thing, getting to a good position to watch this all unfold. He is here, and I need to find out what he is doing. At least fifty fae have gathered in the bowl-shaped depression, standing in small clusters around torches driven into the ground. Most appear to be locals, though I spot several unfamiliar faces who must be part of Soren's group.

A makeshift platform has been constructed at one end of the quarry, currently empty. The crowd buzzes with anticipation, conversations overlapping as the noise echoes off the walls of the quarry. A physical hum of eagerness can be felt, everyone waiting for this meeting to start.

I position myself in the deepest shadows at the edge of the gathering, where I can observe without risk of detection. Even if someone looked directly at me, they'd see nothing but a slightly deeper patch of darkness.

A hush falls over the crowd as a figure steps onto the platform—tall, lean, with sharp features that have hardly changed in the year since I last saw him. Soren. My blood runs cold at the sight of him, and a wave of angry heat floods my system in response. This despicable man stands tall and proud where he should be bound and tossed in a dungeon or, even better, killed for what he did to me and others.

"Friends," Soren calls, his voice carrying easily across the quarry. "Thank you for coming tonight."

He looks different from when I knew him as Oberon's adviser—less polished, his once-immaculate appearance now deliberately roughened, no doubt to play to the revolutionary leader rather than the courtiers he used to answer to. But his eyes haven't changed: cold, dead, emotionless eyes that seek only power for himself.

"Many of you know me as Derrin, a simple trader seeking opportunity. Tonight, I reveal my true identity." He straightens, authority radiating from his posture. "I am Lord Soren, once advisor to King Oberon of the Night Court."

Murmurs ripple through the crowd. An interesting move to share he is from the Night Court when even here people still are unsure how to treat us after so many years in exile.

"I come not as a noble imposing his will, but as a messenger of change." His voice rises, passionate and compelling. "For too long, our people—both Night and Day Court—have been divided, not just by geography or political stances but by an artificial system that grants power to a select few while the rest struggle."

Heads nod and whispers of agreement pass through the crowd. The sentiment resonates with many here, particularly those who've lived in the shadow of noble privileges their entire lives.

"This wasn't always so," Soren continues, pacing the platform, every bit the inspiring leader. "There was a time when all Fae had equal opportunity, where everyone could challenge for the good of the people and not be subjugated by the wealthy and the magically gifted."

The crowd murmurs, confusion and intrigue spreading through their ranks. This isn't what we are taught as Fae. The history of our courts divided has been like this for millennia, and there is little known information about what the courts looked like before—only that we used to be one court.

"The truth has been hidden from you!" Soren's voice rises with indignation. "The nobles created the current system by stealing power that should have belonged to all! And I have discovered something remarkable—the key to restoring equality lies hidden here, on Manthana itself." My heart begins to beat heavily in my chest.

Gasps ripple through the gathering. The locals exchange bewildered glances.

"An ancient artifact of immense power lives here on this island," Soren declares dramatically, "a Phoenix! It was created during the Great Divide and has been concealed here for millennia. This artifact has the ability to give power! To share it with all fae! No longer will the nobles inherit their powers, but it can be freely given by the use of this artifact!"

Phoenix. The mention of the bird takes my breath away. The bound bird in Neeve's documents—could this be what he speaks of? If so, this is far more serious than we anticipated.

"When found, this artifact will give us the power to right these wrongs!" Soren's eyes gleam with a fervour that I recognize as fake justice. "This explains why this island has always felt different to visitors—heavier, charged with something you locals barely notice. It's the artifact's power, calling out to be discovered!"

The crowd appears stunned. For most, this is clearly the first they've heard of any magical artifact hidden on their island, let alone one that supposedly controls the distribution of magic throughout Fae society.

"Together, we will find it and use it to restore justice!" Soren concludes with a flourish.

Confused but excited cheers erupt, though not unanimously. Several faces show doubt, even fear. One man near the front steps forward, his voice carrying clearly.

"How can this be true?" he calls, bewilderment evident in his tone. "I've lived here my entire life—three centuries—and never heard tales of any such artifact."

Soren's expression darkens momentarily before smoothing into concerned understanding. "The knowledge was deliberately suppressed. Those who knew of it were silenced generations ago." He sounds sad, but I know this is just a mask.

"But this makes no sense," a woman argues, stepping forward to stand beside the first speaker. "If such a powerful artifact existed, why would it be hidden here of all places? Why not somewhere more protected?"

I can see Soren calculating, adjusting his approach to handle this unexpected resistance. "Your skepticism is natural," he replies, his voice gentle yet somehow menacing. "The nobles have worked hard to ensure this knowledge remained buried. But I assure you, I've studied ancient texts that confirm everything I've told you."

More villagers move forward, their voices rising in confusion and protest. "This sounds dangerous!" "We need more proof!" "Isn't this dangerous?" "We should tell the King."

Soren raises a hand, and suddenly four figures materialize from the edges of the crowd—large, intimidating Fae with cold eyes and hands resting on weapons. They move with practised efficiency, seizing the most vocal questioners.

"Unfortunately, some are too frightened to embrace change," Soren says, his voice carrying clearly over the sudden commotion. "We cannot let the doubters jeopardize our path to freedom! They will be kept safe until our work is done, for their own protection." Highly unlikely.

I watch in silent horror as the dissenters are dragged away, kicking and screaming. The remaining crowd shifts uncomfortably, but no one else dares speak out. The feel in the quarry shifts from curiosity to fear and anticipation again. Some of the people in attendance look hungry for change while others are cowed into submitting to Soren's plan.

Much like the document, the true understanding of what this artifact is is not known; Soren is giving half-truths, but if they are even remotely true, we are in trouble and Neeve needs to know. But these people are just pawns to Soren; he cares not for them or their well-being, which means whatever he is about to ask them to do will be for his benefit, not theirs.

"Now," Soren continues as if nothing untoward has occurred, "we need volunteers to help search specific locations. The Phoenix is hidden somewhere on this island, likely guarded by those who benefit from keeping it contained."

He begins listing areas—the western temples, the central caves, the northern cliffs—assigning groups to each. I commit the locations to memory, noting which seem to be priorities.

"Remember," he concludes, "we seek liberation for all Fae. Once the Phoenix is freed, I can give the powers to all! The days of noble privilege are ending!"

The crowd cheers more enthusiastically now, the dissenters' removal having silenced any remaining doubt. Soren steps down from the platform, immediately surrounded by what appear to be his lieutenants—the same men I noticed watching us in the tavern earlier and a few more.

This is my chance to get closer, to hear what they discuss away from the crowd.

The villagers file out of the quarry, leaving behind the secret meeting they just joined, while I move carefully along the quarry's edge, staying within the deepest shadows, drawing closer to where Soren now stands.

"—search parties ready by dawn," he's saying to a dark-haired Fae with a scarred face. "Focus on the western ruins first. The bindings will be strongest where the mystical presence is heaviest."

"And the local nobles?" another asks. "The fire-wielder who arrived yesterday—"

"Will be dealt with," Soren cuts him off sharply. "As will his Night Court companion. I have special plans for her."

A chill runs through me at his words. Does he know I'm here? Or is he simply aware that a Night Court Fae arrived with Milori?

I edge closer, straining to hear more.

"She's powerful," the scarred one says. "Some kind of dark magic. Terrified Berrin's whole group without lifting a finger."

Soren laughs, a sound devoid of humour. "Oh, I'm well acquainted with Nesi's talents. She was one of Oberon's most effective weapons—until the King killed the rightful heir and she joined forces with Neeve."

My blood freezes. He knows.

"She's likely somewhere in this very quarry," Soren continues, his voice dropping to a near whisper. "Watching. Listening. Aren't you, little shadow?"

Before I can react, Soren makes a sharp gesture. Suddenly, a blinding light erupts from his palm, flooding the entire area with harsh illumination. The shadows I've been hiding in vanish instantly, leaving me exposed.

Chapter 11

Nesi

I remain perfectly still, hoping against hope that the sudden brightness has temporarily blinded them. But Soren's eyes find mine unerringly, a cold smile spreading across his face.

"There you are," he says softly. "My most promising student returned to me at last."

I don't waste breath denying it. Instead, I drop into a defensive stance, calling what shadows remain to me, but they're weak, dispersed by the unnatural light Soren continues to emit.

"Seize her," Soren commands, and his men move with alarming speed.

I draw my blades, but I'm outnumbered and cut off from my strongest power. Four against one, with Soren himself the greatest threat. This is precisely the sort of situation I promised Milori I wouldn't get into.

The first attacker reaches me, swinging a heavy club. I duck beneath it, slashing across his thigh with my blade. He howls in pain but doesn't fall. The second and third converge from either side, attempting to flank me.

Though Soren's light neutralizes the shadows directly around me, I can still sense those at the edges of the quarry, beyond his reach. With a flicker of concentration, I pull at them, moulding the distant darkness into menacing forms. Some faceless figures that walk menacingly towards us, some even with long claws that dig into the ground and climb the quarry walls.

"Behind you!" one of my attackers shouts in panic, momentarily distracted by a shadow-form that seems to lunge at his back. I take the opportunity to roll to the side and swipe my blade at one of the attacker's legs, forcing him to his knees in pain. More people come streaming into the quarry at the noise; this is exactly what Milori didn't want to happen.

"Stay focused!" Soren barks. "They're illusions! Her shadows can't reach you in my light!"

His words fall on deaf ears as another fae woman screams as a shadow chases her towards the quarry's edge. Getting onto the other side of two armed fae, I try to reach the darker parts of the quarry, but Soren knows better than to let me get to where I need to be. His magic light heating up all around us, the only natural combat to the darkness I have been gifted.

With every kick and slash of my blade, I make small wins against Soren's group, but it's not enough. The distant shadows continue, giant serpents that slither across the ground and winged creatures that dive from above.

One of Soren's men drops his weapon, backing away in terror as a shadow-form appears to consume another fighter whole before their eyes.

"They're not real!" Soren shouts, his voice cracking with frustration. "It's an illusion! Keep your eyes on her!"

But Soren remains at a distance, that harsh light still pouring from his palm, systematically stripping away any shadow I might use for concealment or attack. Despite the psychological advantage my distant illusions provide, I remain physically vulnerable in the circle of his light.

I find myself wondering where Milori is. The thought isn't about his ability to defend himself—he's more than capable—but about my spirit bond's safety. This sudden protective instinct surprises me, this fierce concern for someone I've known for mere days. Yet the mere thought of him being harmed makes me want to tear this quarry apart stone by stone.

A blow catches my shoulder, sending searing pain down my arm. In the shock of it, I miss the dagger aimed at my temple. I duck, but too late—the blade still leaves a burning gash across my forehead. Blood trickles into my eye as I stagger back, trying to regain my bearings.

I don't get the chance. A boot drives into my ribs with stunning force. Something cracks inside me as I crash onto my back, the world spinning briefly before my eyes.

"Don't kill her," Soren calls out coldly. "Neeve would pay handsomely for her return. Or perhaps Oberon's supporters would prefer to exact revenge for her betrayal."

I grit my teeth, pushing myself up from the ground as three more attackers round on me. The reality is stark. I'm severely outnumbered, and without my shadows, without my greatest weapon, my odds diminish with each passing second.

The realization hits me: Milori may be my only hope. If he's escaped, if he can fight another day...Milori. To think I never even tried to see where our connection might lead. They say in your dying moments, you always wonder about the paths not taken.

A blade nicks my cheek. Warm blood trickles down my face, and I return the favour, ducking under an attack and driving my dagger into an attacker's stomach. Another strike hits my knee, nearly buckling it beneath me. I've managed to incapacitate two attackers, but the remaining five press closer, their coordinated movements leaving me fewer options with each passing second.

I failed. The fear of failure has been my constant companion my entire life, and now I've failed. Failed Neeve. Failed my mission.

Failed Milori.

"Stop." Soren steps forward, satisfaction gleaming in his eyes. "Always so stubborn, Nesi. It would have been better if you'd simply remained loyal to our Court."

"Our Court?" I spit blood onto the ground. "You betrayed our Court the moment you decided to follow Oberon's madness."

His face hardens, that pleasant mask slipping to reveal the cruelty beneath. "Restrain her. We'll decide her fate later."

As his men move to grab me, the night sky suddenly ignites with blinding orange and yellow light. It's not the cold illumination of Soren's palm, but something wild and alive. A screech pierces the air, primal and powerful.

Everyone freezes, heads tilting skyward. Through the haze of pain, I follow their gaze, disbelief washing over me at the sight.

A massive bird of pure fire circles above us, its wingspan blocking out the stars, its feathers burning gold and crimson and amber. It dives toward the quarry, and the men surrounding me scatter in terror.

Soren stands his ground, face contorted with rage and something else—recognition, perhaps even fear. "The Phoenix manifestation," he hisses. "But how—"

The fiery bird swoops directly at him, forcing him to dive aside, his light spell extinguished. Shadows instantly flood back into the quarry, reaching for me like concerned friends. I pull them to me, drawing strength from their familiar touch even in my weakened state.

The Phoenix circles back, landing between me and my attackers with wings spread wide. The heat from its flames should be unbearable, yet it doesn't burn me. Instead, it embraces me like a caress. That now-familiar electric sensation I feel whenever Milori is near pulses through me as the warmth envelops me, almost as if checking that I'm safe.

Then a figure lands beside the magnificent creature, and my breath catches. His wings are stretched wide, his entire body wreathed in blue flames so intense I wonder how he isn't consumed by them. Power radiates from him in waves I can almost see, raw, ancient, and breathtaking.

Milori. My spirit bond.

I stare in awe, unable to look away even as the battle rages around us.

"Touch her again," he says, his voice deadly quiet yet somehow carrying over the crackling flames, "and the Phoenix won't be the only thing burning tonight." A shiver runs through my body at his threat. Why did I think he would leave? Of course he would be here to save me. A mix of emotion floods my system, embarrassment for getting into this situation, but mostly care and affection for him being here.

Soren's men back away, terror pronounced in their faces. They've likely never witnessed power of this magnitude—I've never seen this type of power. But Milori, the charming, fun and happy man now stands exuding strength that I would not want to fight.

Soren barely maintains his composure as he stares down the firebird before him. "Captain Milori," he says, offering a mocking bow. "Or should I say, Master of the Phoenix? How fascinating. I wonder if you even understand what you are."

"I understand enough to know you're not leaving this quarry with her," Milori replies, the Phoenix screeching in agreement, its fiery form growing even larger.

I slowly limp to Milori's side, shadows swirling around me, lending me strength to stand beside my spirit bond. Together we face Soren, my darkness and Milori's flames creating a formidable sight—a combination of power I doubt anyone has witnessed before.

Soren assesses the situation with calculating eyes. "It would seem you have won this round." His gaze shifts to me, cold and promising. "We will meet again, I'm sure."

As he begins backing away, Milori shifts into an offensive stance, his entire body tensing like a predator about to strike.

"You're not going anywhere," Milori growls, the Phoenix manifestation surging forward with a screech of fury. Flames erupt from his hands as he lunges toward Soren, clearly intent on ending this threat here and now.

Soren's eyes widen momentarily before he throws something to the ground—a small crystalline object that shatters and releases a blinding flash of cold white light. The Phoenix's flames collide with this light, creating an explosive burst that sends everyone staggering backward.

When my vision clears, I see Milori picking himself up from where he was thrown, his expression twisted with frustration and rage. Soren is already at the far edge of the quarry, his silhouette barely visible.

"We'll meet again soon, Phoenix Master," Soren calls back, his voice carrying on the night air.

Milori sends another blast of fire hurtling toward him, but Soren has already disappeared into the darkness with his men. The remaining followers scattered as soon as the Phoenix appeared, fleeing into the night without a backward glance.

I collapse to the ground, no longer able to maintain my stance. The fight drains from Milori instantly. He rushes to my side, all that terrifying power replaced with naked fear and concern as he kneels beside me.

"You're hurt," he says, worry lacing his voice. It's not a question but a statement of fact as his eyes take in the blood streaking my face, the protective way I cradle my side, and the unnatural angle of my shoulder.

"I'll live," I reply, though my body vehemently disagrees. My ribs scream with each breath, my vision occasionally blurs, and I'm fairly certain my shoulder is dislocated. The adrenaline is wearing off, allowing pain to assert itself with brutal clarity. "I could have taken them." I try for a joke but Milori's face doesn't crack. I can't blame him. This isn't exactly how I saw tonight going.

"Sure you could," he says dryly, but there's no judgment in his eyes, only deep concern. "That's why you were on your knees surrounded by enemies, bleeding from multiple wounds."

I try to sit up, trying to take a full breath, but it nearly makes me fall over. Milori catches me immediately, his arm gentle around my waist. The warmth from his touch seeps into my battered body, strangely comforting.

"Easy," he murmurs, his voice soft. "You've lost blood, and that shoulder needs attention."

I should be annoyed by his interference, by the risk he took to save me, but I'm not. Instead, I find myself overwhelmed with a complex emotion I'm not ready to name.

"Thank you," I say quietly, the words stiff and unfamiliar on my tongue. "For not listening to me about staying hidden." He looks at me, his green eyes a comfort.

"I shouldn't have waited as long as I did. I just didn't want you to think I didn't believe in you, but I was an idiot. Don't ever think I will wait that long again." I can't help but chuckle even though it makes me wince in pain.

"Fair enough," I say, gripping his shirt tight with my good hand as a new wave of pain pulses through me.

"You need a healer," Milori says, his jaw set in a way that suggests he won't be taking no for an answer.

"We need to go somewhere safe. Who knows who is a part of Soren's group. The cottage first," I counter, unwilling to risk exposure by seeking out the village healer. "Jalnor might have supplies we can use, and I have some supplies I always carry with me."

Milori reluctantly nods, then without warning, scoops me into his arms in one fluid motion. I'm about to protest when pain shoots through my ribs, stealing both my breath and argument.

"This will be faster," he says as his wings unfold from his back. "Hold on."

I do as instructed while he lifts us into the air. I lean my head against his shoulder, relishing the strength of the man carrying me. Is this what it's like to have someone care for you?

"So...a phoenix, eh?" Even against the wind, he hears my words.

"It's a surprise to me too," he replies, eyes focused on the sky ahead as we pass over Manthana, heading back to the cottage. I hum in reply. I've never seen anyone able to summon something so magnificent before. I didn't even know we could.

It feels like mere moments before Milori begins our descent, weaving between trees. I can't help but wince and hold my breath as we manoeuvre through the branches.

"Are you alright?" he asks, his voice close to my ear.

I nod, not trusting myself to speak. The truth is, I'm not alright—not because of the flight, but because of how right it feels to be held like this. How, for perhaps the first time in my entire life, I'm allowing someone else to carry me, both literally and figuratively.

Milori's landing is surprisingly gentle as he touches down right in front of the cottage door. Somehow he manages to open it and walk in without issue.

"I can walk now," I say half-heartedly, knowing full well I can't. The fight has drained from me, leaving only pain in its wake.

"Of course you can," he replies with that charming smile of his, "but then I wouldn't get to hold you. And seeing as you nearly gave me a heart attack tonight, give me this, would you?" He frames it as if it's for his benefit, rather than because I desperately need help, which I appreciate even though I know it's a lie.

I've spent centuries believing that dependency equals vulnerability, that needing others is a weakness I cannot afford. Yet

Milori risked everything to come to my aid, and instead of feeling diminished by his help, I feel...empowered. As if together, we are stronger, and that thought scares me more than I want to talk about right now.

He navigates through the main room to deposit me gently on the bed. The loss of his warmth is immediate and unwelcome, though I'd never admit it aloud.

As he moves away to gather healing supplies, I watch him, this Fae who challenged everything I thought I knew about myself and others. Who refused to let me face danger alone, despite my explicit instructions. Who now tends to my wounds with gentle care and affection.

Maybe doing everything alone isn't necessary after all. Maybe, just maybe, there's strength in allowing someone else close enough to help carry the burden.

The thought should terrify me, but as I watch Milori rummage through the cottage, I find a strange peace in it.

"There is some in my bag," I say, nodding at the bag on the floor. He retrieves it, pulling out the supplies I packed and the documents I haphazardly stuffed inside before we left. My heart pounds as he unfolds a paper, already partially open. It's the image of the bound bird—the Phoenix—that I've memorized by now.

A battle of instincts rages within me, an urge to stand my ground, bound by duty to my Queen, clashes with the guilt of keeping this from him. The guilt weighs heavier with each passing second of his silence.

He sets the paper down without comment and walks back to me. The lack of reaction unnerves me more than anger would have. He places the supplies on the table beside the bed before focusing on my injured arm, his face giving away nothing of his thoughts.

"This will hurt," he warns, hands hovering over my dislocated shoulder.

"I can handle it," I reply, meeting his gaze.

A hint of a smile forms on his lips. "I know you can." The simple acknowledgment of my strength, even in this moment of vulnerability, warms something deep inside me. "But you don't have to handle it alone. Not anymore."

His words hit me hard, and then he pulls on my arm, placing my shoulder back into its socket. The pain halts my thoughts completely as I breathe through it, gritting my teeth against the sharp agony.

When I open my eyes again, Milori is getting bandages out and applying salve to my arm, preparing to wrap the wounds. He dabs a cloth in water to clean the blood from my face with surprising gentleness.

"So do you want to tell me why there's an image of a phoenix on that paper?" He doesn't look at me, just remains focused on tending my wounds.

"Neeve believed that Soren was on this island to find a powerful artifact that he believes will give him power if he finds it," I explain. "My job was to confirm this information and report back to Neeve." I deliver this without preamble because at this point, Milori is in this with me, no matter what.

"Didn't think to share that at the beginning?" He grabs more salve and dabs the wounds on my head before moving to the cuts on my side.

"I was instructed to inform King Timas what was confirmed, not what was speculated by my Queen." I don't mean for it to sound defensive, but I was following orders. I won't apologize for that. Milori merely hums in response, the same reaction and it still continues to unsettle me.

"Why aren't you angry?" I hate how nervous I sound, but I can't help it.

"You were doing your job. I would have done the same thing if Timas had asked me." He looks at me then, and relief floods my system. Traitor. I want to stay strong and be the shadow walker Neeve needs me to be, but Milori's willing acceptance does things to me I can't describe.

"Want to tell me about the phoenix manifestation?" I ask in response. He lets out a huff at my question.

"Wish I knew. One moment I was at the top of the quarry looking down at you fighting, barely controlling myself to wait for your signal." He raises a brow at me. "Which you didn't give, by the way. The next, I see one of the attackers cut you and I just...saw red. My powers coursed so violently through my body I felt the phoenix literally rip from me. I've never done that before, but now I can feel it, just sitting at the edge of my senses, ready for me to call it again." He cuts at my dress to reveal the wound on my side. His hand hovers over it, a look of deep concern and anger crossing his face.

"I should have killed them all," he says, barely above a whisper.

"It's better you didn't. We don't know what we're dealing with, and until we do, we need to keep them alive or capture them. If what Soren said is partly true, this artifact could change the lives of every Fae person. We need answers." I try to reassure him, but he doesn't seem convinced.

He works methodically to tend to my injuries as I adjust myself, sleep pulling at my consciousness.

"I wonder why Soren called you a Phoenix master," I mumble as my eyelids grow heavy.

"I don't know, but we can worry about that tomorrow. You need to sleep. Rest, Nesi. I'll be here when you wake up."

"You better." I don't know if I say it in my head or aloud, but I swear I feel a gentle pressure on my forehead and a whispered "always" as darkness consumes me.

Chapter 12

Milori

The numbness creeping down my arm forces me to shift. Sleeping on the floor seemed like a good idea at the time. Even though there is a thin wall between Nesi's bed and mine, I couldn't pull myself away from her, the bond screaming at me to stay close to my injured spirit bond.

Nesi.

I sit up straight, wincing at the stiffness in my neck, as I frantically look around the room. It's still a couple hours before dawn, but I feel eyes on me. Looking over at Nesi's bed, I catch her watchful gaze.

"The floor must be painful," she observes, her voice raspier than usual from sleep or pain—perhaps both.

I run a hand through my hair, likely making it stand up worse than it already is. "Says the woman who took on several armed enemies by herself," I counter, relieved to see some colour has returned to her face. "How are you feeling?"

"Better." She shifts slightly, testing her injuries, and I can tell from the careful way she moves that better is a generous assessment.

"You don't have to pretend with me, you know," I say, stretching to ease the kinks in my shoulders. "I've seen you bleed. The mystique is already ruined."

A rare smile flickers across her lips, and despite myself, my heart stirs. "I've had worse."

"That's not actually reassuring," I point out, moving to sit on the edge of the bed. "In fact, it makes me want to hurt the person who gave you worse." I gesture toward her bandaged shoulder. "May I?"

She nods, and I gently begin unwrapping the dressing to check the wound beneath. The proximity to her is dizzying, subtle notes of night jasmine linger in the air. She smells heavenly, which is a problem when I'm trying to focus on tending her wounds.

"Thank you," she says, her voice so quiet I almost miss it. "Not just for last night, but for..." she hesitates, struggling to find the words. "For staying. Here. With me."

My fingers pause on her shoulder. "I would sleep on hot coals for you," I tell her, only half-joking. "Though I admit the floor is a close second in terms of discomfort."

She laughs then—an actual laugh that catches us both by surprise. "Hot coals wouldn't bother you," she points out. "You wield fire."

"Well, they aren't a mattress filled with goose feathers. Though the heat wouldn't bother me, the bumpy edges are no treat to lay on, I'll tell you that."

"A lot of experience sleeping on coal?" She says on a laugh. My lip tips up as a memory comes to mind.

"Timas dared me to do it when we were much younger, you know, when we weren't as mature as we are now." This really makes her laugh, full body laugh. The sound is overwhelming in how much joy it brings me. The fact I made her laugh heals a part of me I didn't realize needed healing. "He was convinced it would burn me because the fire isn't my own and doesn't come from inside of me. Jokes on him—I not only slept on hot coals, but it didn't burn me! Just made severe indentations that took months to go away."

I finish wrapping up her shoulder again before taking in her beautiful dark eyes. "But if sleeping on coals doesn't show you how much I would endure for you, I could stand guard in a blizzard. Attend five consecutive royal diplomatic functions. Or listen to Garrick explain the proper way to polish a sword for the forty-seventh time."

Her smile lights up all her features, transforming her usual stoic expression into one of pure joy. I vow to try and keep a smile on her face as long as I breathe.

"Such sacrifices," she says dryly, but her eyes hold a warmth I've never seen before.

I move to check the gash on her temple, which requires me to lean closer, bringing our faces mere inches apart. Her breathing hitches, though whether from pain or our proximity, I can't tell.

"How does it look?" she asks, her voice softer than usual.

"Like you were hit in the head with something heavy," I reply with no hesitation. "But it's healing. You'll live to terrify more tavern bullies."

She rolls her eyes, but doesn't pull away from my touch as I gently apply more salve. "They deserved it."

"They absolutely did," I agree, unable to keep the smile from my voice. "Your shadows were quite effective. I particularly enjoyed when that one fellow thought he saw something behind him and nearly dumped his porridge on his friend. A nice little farewell before we left the tavern."

"He called you a fire menace," she says, something protective flashing in her eyes.

"I've been called worse," I assure her.

We fall silent as I continue to change her bandages, the quiet between us comfortable rather than strained. It's strange how natural this feels—caring for her, being close to her. It's the first time since we met that she hasn't been actively trying to get away from me. I'm afraid to push too far but hope gets the better of me.

"It's different, isn't it?" I say finally, securing a fresh bandage on her temple. "From what you expected."

"What is?"

"This." I gesture vaguely between us. "The spirit bond. Me."

She considers this, her gaze steady on mine. "Yes," she admits finally. "You're not what I expected."

"Disappointingly so?" I ask, trying to keep my tone light despite the sudden tightness in my chest.

"No," she says quietly. "Just...different. I always believed spirit bonds were the most precious gift the old magic could bestow. Like most Fae, I dreamed of finding mine someday."

I sit back slightly, surprised by her admission. "You did?"

She nods, a fleeting vulnerability crossing her face. "In the Shrouded Forest, during those long centuries of exile, young Night Court Fae would whisper about spirit bonds by the hidden fires. It gave us hope that the old magic hadn't abandoned us completely."

She looks away, the moon casting a silver glow on her face. "But I learned that duty and loyalty are luxuries my people cannot afford to compromise. The Night Court needs those willing to fight for its future. Not tyrants like Oberon, or manipulators like Soren, but those who serve. Leaders like Neeve."

"Your service to your queen is admirable," I choose my words with care.

She looks back at me. "It's necessary," she counters, a fervent conviction in her voice. "After everything my people endured, everything Neeve sacrificed to free us...if I allow myself to be distracted, even by a spirit bond, I fear she'll struggle. And the Night Court has struggled enough."

I take a deep breath, gathering my courage. It's time for honesty, plain and unvarnished. "Nesi, I need you to understand something."

Her eyes search mine, wary but attentive.

"Being strong—truly strong—doesn't mean being alone." I choose my words with unusual care. "You can serve your queen, fulfill your duty, and still find room for love. The two aren't mutually exclusive."

She doesn't say anything, but she listens to me as I continue. "Your loyalty to Neeve is something I admire, not something I want to diminish. But you don't have to carry this burden alone anymore, Nesi. I'm here."

"It's not that simple," she argues, though with less conviction than I expect. "My duties to the Night Court—"

"We'll figure it out together," I counter gently. "If you need me to prove how serious I am about this, I will. I'd leave the Day Court and join Neeve's service if that's what it takes."

Her eyes widen in surprise. "You'd leave Timas? After centuries of friendship?"

"If necessary," I nod, then add with a hint of humour, "Or I could ask him to appoint me as official liaison to the Night Court for the next century or so. He owes me a favour anyway."

That draws a startled laugh from her. "You'd do that? Uproot your entire life?"

"In a heartbeat," I tell her, and the conviction in my voice surprises even me. I lean a bit closer, tucking a piece of stray hair behind her ear. "I'm not asking you to abandon your responsibilities. I would never do that. But I am asking you to let me stand beside you while you fulfill them."

Her expression softens, vulnerability showing through the cracks in her carefully maintained composure. She lifts her hand to my chest, and my heart pounds against my chest. "What if Neeve needs me completely devoted to her cause?"

"Then we'll serve her cause together," I say simply. "The Courts are united now. Your queen's struggles are my king's struggles. And I'd rather face those struggles with you than apart."

She looks at me then, really looks at me, as if seeing something she never thought she would see. "Why?" she asks finally. "Why would you go to such lengths? No one has ever..."

It breaks my heart that she can't fathom someone valuing her enough to rearrange their life for her. It speaks volumes about the isolation she's lived with, the walls she's built around herself. I place my hand along her neck, rubbing the side of her face with my thumb.

"Because you're worth it," I tell her, the truth of it resonating in my bones. "Because in all my centuries, I've never met anyone like you. Because when I'm with you, even when you're being impossibly stubborn and refusing to admit you need help, I feel more myself than I ever have before."

I lean forward, slowly enough to give her time to turn away if she wishes, but she doesn't.

"May I kiss you?" The words hang between us as her eyes flicker from my lips to my eyes and back again.

"Please."

I lean in as her eyes flutter closed. When our lips meet, a shockwave of exhilaration courses through me. The bond pulses intensely between us as I deepen the kiss. My hand moves to cradle the back of her head while the other gently frames her face. For a moment, everything else fades away. There's only this feeling of rightness, as if we're finally where we're meant to be.

I reluctantly pull back after a moment not wanting to push her too far, resting my forehead against hers. Her hands grip my shirt, and she's as breathless as I am.

"Wow," she says softly.

I exhale with a gentle laugh. "That's an understatement." It doesn't begin to describe what she does to me. She has ruined me for anyone else, her very presence now the reason I breathe.

Her lips curve into a small smile. "You'd really ask Timas to make you a liaison?"

"I'd start drafting the request tonight if you wanted," I assure her. "Though he'd never let me hear the end of it. He knows how much I hate paperwork."

Something shimmers in her eyes. "I don't know how to do this," she admits softly. "Serve my queen and have this too."

"Neither do I," I confess. "I've been stumbling through this from the start. But I think that's the point. No relationship is meant to be easy. It's meant to stretch you and have you grow together to become one. You don't have to choose between duty and happiness, Nesi. And you definitely don't have to do this alone anymore."

Her hand finds mine, fingers intertwining. "Together," she echoes, testing the word like an unfamiliar language.

The moment stretches between us, a quiet acceptance of where our bond can go, of where it will go, until she yawns. I lean forward and place a gentle kiss on her forehead as I stand to adjust her blankets.

"Rest," I murmur. "You need to heal, and we have much to discuss about what we learned last night."

She nods, but reaches out to hold my hand. "Stay," she says, and it's unclear if she means just for now or forever.

"I'm not going anywhere," I assure her, my voice softening. "You've got me for life, my little phantom. I never want to miss seeing you terrify unsuspecting tavern patrons with your shadow creatures."

She laughs, the sound like music to my ears, even as her cheeks flush pink. The sight of that blush—evidence that I can affect this powerful shadow walker—warms me more than any fire I've ever conjured.

She shifts slightly, making room beside her on the bed. "Not what I meant, but I appreciate your love for my shadow creatures." She smiles warmly at me. "Here. Stay here. Not on the floor," she clarifies, a hint of amusement in her voice. "You look ridiculous sleeping there, and your groaning when you wake up is distracting."

"I do not groan," I protest, though we both know it's a lie.

"Like a wounded bear," she counters.

I shift the pillow to help her settle, then ease onto the edge of the bed. "Just for a little while," I say as she yawns again.

She leans into my shoulder, and I shift my arm to let her rest against my chest. As her breathing deepens toward sleep, I allow myself a moment of pure contentment. There will be challenges ahead, of course there will be, but for now, in this moment, I relish Nesi, her presence, and the strength she gives me to be just me.

For an hour I hold her, but my mind races with questions. I need to visit my parents, and the sooner I do that, the sooner I can come back to be with her. Something tells me my mother has many answers to my questions, and I am determined to find them out.

When I'm certain Nesi is deeply asleep, her breathing slow and even, I carefully extricate myself from her side. She stirs as I lay her gently on the bed, but she doesn't wake. I take a moment to tuck the blanket around her, my chest tightening at the sight of her laying there peacefully.

"I'll be back soon," I whisper, though she can't hear me. I brush my fingers over her hair, savouring the silken feel of those navy blue strands.

The cottage brightens as sunlight begins to spill through the windows. I gather a few essentials and head for the door, pausing to glance back at the room where Nesi rests peacefully. This isn't how I imagined my love story would unfold. I'd expected someone to fall instantly for my charms, not this gradual earning of trust from a woman who guards her heart as fiercely as she wields her shadows. But I wouldn't change a thing.

Her strength gives me stability I didn't know I needed. Perhaps that's what we can be for each other—strong where the other falters, steady where the other wavers. Together, we might become the formidable pair we're meant to be.

As I step outside, the crisp morning air fills my lungs. The sky is painted in pink and gold, welcoming the sun to a new day. I adjust my jacket and walk with purpose toward Jalnor's house. The meadow is covered in dew, and the smell of fire coming from the house is a welcome one.

My thoughts race with questions to ask my mother, and the sinking feeling that everything I know is about to change. If what we know about this artifact is true, and my mother knew about it all along...I'm not sure how I'll react. But I need to focus. I am the King's Captain, and my duty to protect him, the Fae people, and that beautiful sleeping shadow in the cottage is more important than the turmoil of what my mother has kept from me.

Jalnor's house comes into view, a comforting sight despite everything. Before I even reach the door, it swings open to reveal my old friend, a steaming mug in his hand waiting for me.

"I was wondering when you'd show up," he says by way of greeting. "Heard about the commotion at the quarry last night. Half the island's talking about the firebird that appeared."

I wince at that. "Yeah, that was an accident." His eyebrows shoot up, but his smile remains as he steps to the side to let me in.

"Well, this oughta be interesting." He says, and I take the mug he offers me. "Come on, breakfast is almost ready." He walks into the warm space filled with worn furniture and the same decorations his parents had when they were living here. For a moment, I'm a boy again, seeking refuge here after another difficult day of being the island oddity.

"Where's your Night Court friend?" Jalnor asks, moving to the hearth where a pot of porridge simmers. "Don't tell me you've already managed to drive her away with your snoring."

"She's resting," I reply, as I take a seat. "There was trouble last night. She was injured."

Jalnor straightens immediately, his face darkening with a protective anger I recognize all too well. He was always there, shielding me when the locals would terrorize me as a child. For all his jovial nature, he's fiercely loyal when it counts.

"Badly?" he asks, and his genuine concern for my spirit bond makes me grateful he's here through all this mess.

"Bad enough," I admit, pushing my hand through my hair. "I've done what I could with the limited supplies in the cottage, but she has at least one cracked rib. She needs a proper healer, but she's refusing to risk drawing attention. I'll need to find better medication somewhere on the island."

He crosses his massive arms over his chest, his expression hardening. "Who did it?" It's not a question but a demand, his voice taking on that menacing tone that always makes me smile despite myself. Jalnor may be built like a mountain, but he's without any magic, although it never stopped him from trying to fight my battles.

"Soren and his group. You'd know him as Derrin." I let out a weary sigh. "He's been using that alias since arriving here, but he's too strong for you, my friend. He wields light magic." I pause, the memory of last night's confrontation still raw. "And apparently he's equipped with specialized vials designed to neutralize even me and my new...phoenix companion."

Jalnor studies me for a long moment before turning to scoop two generous portions of porridge from the pot. He sets a steaming bowl in front of me without comment, then plants his elbows on the table, his gaze filled with determination.

"So what do you need me to do?" he asks.

By the sun, I've missed his unwavering support and the way he jumps in without hesitation. I take a spoonful of porridge to give myself a moment before answering with the words I never thought I'd say.

"I need to visit my parents."

Jalnor nods knowingly, shoving a spoonful of porridge into his mouth. "Time for a family reunion? Not going to nit-pick your timing, but there needs to be a reason for that." He's not wrong.

I take a long sip of tea before responding. "It's not about reconciliation, Jal. I'm going there as Captain of the Guard. Mother might know what Soren is after, and if my gut means anything, she knows exactly why."

"Doesn't matter who you think you're showing up as. When you get to their door, you'll still feel like the son who was set aside." His words hit with uncomfortable precision. "But I understand. So again, what do you need from me?"

I hate when he's right, but I focus on why I came this morning. "I need you to go to the cottage and stay with Nesi until she wakes up. When she does, tell her I went to see my parents and will be back soon."

I can't help but glare as Jalnor's face morphs into that teasing expression I know all too well.

"The fearsome Captain Milori, worried about a woman who can terrify half the village with a glance? She must be special." He's poking for information, and at this point, I don't care. She means the world to me, and I'd shout it from the top of the mountain if I had to.

"She is," I say.

His expression softens. "Spirit bond?"

I'm surprised for a moment, though I don't know why. Jalnor has always been observant.

I nod. "Yes. How long have you known?" The question falls out as I take another bite of my porridge.

"Since you showed up. Never seen you act like that with any woman, and I knew when you did, she had to be your spirit bond. You weren't going to settle for less." I laugh at his observation because I don't think I could have settled if I wanted to.

"So she has finally started to accept it too, then? Life-threatening situations tend to do that to people." That gets me laughing, but I shake my head, he's right but the situation still precarious.

"I don't know, but something has changed enough that she's let her walls down and let me in."

"Poor woman doesn't know what she's doing. I'll let her know to reinstate those walls to protect her from your new firebird." I throw a cloth sitting on the table, and he catches it, laughing. "I'm kidding, but you're gonna need to tell me about this bird. From what I hear, it could be seen from the other side of the island, and you're saying you made that?" He looks at me, perplexed.

"Yes, I'll explain later. I want to get on the road. I'm gonna walk, give myself time to think and digest everything that's happened and what I'm gonna say to Mother." Jalnor nods his head and stands, grabbing a basket of what looks to be more medical supplies.

"Alright, I'll go be with your spirit bond, make sure she doesn't do anything crazy." He laughs, and I stand, taking one more mouthful of porridge.

"I owe you," I say to him as he comes to stand beside me.

"I'll add it to your tab. Now off with ya. Get the unpleasant family reunion over with. I'll make up a stew for lunch—you used to enjoy that after the more stressful interactions with your mother." We walk to his door and step outside, the sun slowly rising in the sky.

"Thank you again," I put as much sincerity as I can into my voice.

"Of course! Now go! Just gotta figure out how to keep a shadow walker from leaving the cottage before you get back." He mutters to himself as he heads towards the cottage, while I take the other path north of the village in the direction of my parents house.

A couple hours' walk is just what I need to get my head clear, I hope.

Chapter 13

Milori

Could I have flown to get to my parents' house quicker? Yes. But that means I would have been at their house sooner, and I'm still not sure I'm ready for this conversation. Each crunch of gravel beneath my boots sends memories surging through my mind. Strange how the familiar scent of the sea and the drifting smells of the forest can immediately transport me back centuries, to a childhood of never quite belonging. The wound from my visit last month still feels raw—rushing here after years away, heart in my throat at the news of Mother's illness, only to find an empty study and Father's awkward explanations.

Her research had called her away, he'd said. Even when supposedly at death's door, her mysterious work took precedence. Though I still don't know what illness it is, that was never explained to me, not that I stuck around long enough to ask. But Father's face as he made excuses for her, that practiced smile that never reached his eyes, lingers in my mind. The worry in his eyes had been real, which is why I know mother is not well. Despite everything, however, he adores her completely and would wither without her. That's what cut deepest—not her missing my rare visit but watching Father defend her choices while silently falling apart.

I'd boarded the same ship that brought me, vowing it would be my last journey to Manthana for a very long time. Irrational? Maybe.

The house comes into view as I crest the final hill. It's larger than most on the island, built from pale stone with elegant lines that seem at odds with the simple buildings in the village below. The windows are stained glass with decorative images much like the ones you would find in Sonas, but out here it just looks obnoxious. This also did not help me fit in while living here. I'm sure it was Mother's way of holding onto where she came from, but it put even more of a divide between us and the islanders.

Smoke curls from the chimney, and I can detect the faint scent of cooking even from this distance. Despite everything, my stomach rumbles. It's been hours since I last ate, and regardless of the tension between us, my father's cooking was always exceptional.

I pause at the stone walkway that leads up to the door, taking a steadying breath. That did nothing. I just need to keep my head when I walk in there. I'm not the dutiful son, but the King's Captain coming to investigate a potential threat.

The lawn is filled with fresh fruit and vegetables, my father's favourite spot to be. Before marrying my mother, he was a farmer, but she wanted something else—a home by the ocean, not a life on a farm. So they built this house, yet he never let go of gardening, weaving it into the land around them.

The perfectly clean white door looms ahead, but before I can knock, the door swings open, revealing my father. He looks exactly as he did a month ago—tall and lean like me, but with the weathered face of someone who spends his days outdoors rather than in palace halls. His hair is greying at the edges and his smile lines are deep. The shocked green eyes that take me in are the same ones I see in the mirror. I am my father's son.

"Milori?" he says, disbelief evident. "Twice in one month? I never thought—"

"Hello, Father," I reply, cutting him off. "Is Mother actually home this time? Or has she conveniently disappeared again?" I shouldn't be so bitter, but I am struggling to control myself at this point.

He has the grace to look uncomfortable. "She is. And she's..." he hesitates, seeming to choose his words carefully. "She's been in quite a state these past few days. This will do her good." His optimism is misplaced.

"Or will it?" I can't keep the edge from my voice. "Last I checked, mother has her own ideas of what is good for her. I am not entirely sure my presence will be much of an influence in her life."

"It's complicated, son." He runs a hand through his hair—a familiar gesture. "Your mother has her reasons. She always has."

"I'm sure she does." I step past him into the house I once called home. "But this isn't a social visit. I'm here on behalf of the King."

His eyes widen at that, but he merely nods and closes the door behind me. "You're still welcome here," he says quietly. "Always."

The sincerity in his voice catches me off guard, momentarily dousing my anger. Despite my mother's emotional absence throughout my life, my father has always tried his best to bridge the gap she created. It wasn't his fault it was never enough.

Father hurries off down the hall as I trail at a distance.

"Lavera!" my father calls. "We have a visitor!"

I hear movement from the study—my mother's domain that I was rarely permitted to enter as a child. A moment later, she appears in the doorway, looking distinctly frazzled, a word I would never normally associate with my perfectly composed mother.

Her appearance startles me. Like my father, she has aged, though less noticeably thanks to her noble blood. But it's not the few silver strands in her dark hair or the fine lines around her eyes that surprise me. It's her dishevelled state—ink smudges on her fingers, hair escaping its usual elegant bun, a general air of distraction that seems entirely out of character.

Her eyes widen when she sees me, emotions crossing her face too quickly to catalogue.

"Milori?" she breathes, frozen in the doorway.

"Mother," I nod, maintaining a formal distance.

My father clears his throat, clearly uncomfortable with the tension. "I was just making breakfast. Have you eaten, son?"

"Not in a while," I admit, grateful for the diversion.

"Then sit, sit!" he insists, bustling toward the kitchen. "We had heard there were some guests who landed yesterday, but well, we never imagined it would have been you! Why didn't you come sooner? Griddle cakes alright?" He talks so fast you might miss what he said, but it's his way of trying to ease the awkwardness around us.

Walking into the kitchen I pull out a chair and take a seat, I watch as mother debates her next move. "It was a long day travelling, so we stayed with Jalnor." I say to keep the silence from consuming us.

"We?" Mother's head tips as she pulls the chair out to sit down. Of course that piqued her interest.

"My companion and I," I say, giving nothing away. For some reason, I'm not sure I want them to know about Nesi. I don't care whether they like her, but exposing her to them without knowing what they know feels like an unnecessary risk right now."

"We would have been happy to come and pick you up. You could have stayed here," Father grins as he places a plate of griddles and fresh honey down in front of me.

"This isn't a social visit. As I mentioned before, I'm here on behalf of the King." The room, though not loud before, becomes eerily quiet.

"Wh-Why would the King send you here? There is nothing particularly interesting about the island," Mother rushes the words out, and I turn my gaze on her.

"To pretend you are unaware of the comings and goings of this island is ludicrous, Mother. Do not take me for a fool you can convince the sky is yellow." My words come out quick and sharp, and mother flinches at them while father rushes to her side.

"You may be the King's Captain, but I am still your mother," she says with a stern voice that reminds me of my childhood.

"Indeed you are. Which is why I will give you one chance to tell me exactly what you know. What do you know about an artifact on this island?" The only sign she knows anything is a flicker in her eye and my father's anxious movements.

"I don't know what you are talking about." She straightens in her chair, as if preparing for a fight. I shake my head in disbelief.

"You know I have spent most of my years chalking up your absence and odd behaviour to that of a scholar who needs to find answers, but now something tells me that isn't the case. You know a lot more about what is going on on this island than you are letting on." Father shifts uncomfortably beside her, but mother says nothing. "Fine, what do you know about the phoenix master?" Her jaw tenses and a flicker of uncertain plays in her eyes, the title does more to break her mask than I thought possible.

"Who told you about that?" she whispers, as if speaking the words aloud would make them more real.

"A dangerous man who is planning to wreak havoc on the fae people," I say through clenched teeth.

She shakes her head. "No, it's not possible. They can't possibly know anything." She mumbles to herself and looks at my father.

"What's not possible? A threat to this island or this phoenix master?"

"You don't understand, Milori, and it is best you leave this alone. Nothing good will come of it." Mother places her hands in her lap, looking as noble as she can, and I can't sit anymore.

"Leave this alone? I do not answer to you. I answer to my King, and this situation you claim I should leave alone has already caused harm to multiple people from this island! Including my spirit bond!" I heave out a breath.

"Spirit bond?" My father asks. Well, I may have overshared there. I close my eyes and take a deep breath before returning my gaze to my parents.

"That doesn't matter. What does matter is the man behind the rebel group terrorizing the people of the Day and Night court is here looking for an artifact, and he claims I am a phoenix master. Now tell me what you know." I am able to say it without the rage that sits inside me. This must break something in my perfect noble mother, as her face falls.

"Milori, it's not so simple. I can't just tell you what I know." She stands now on shaky legs. "This is bigger than you or me. This could change everything for the entire fae people." Her voice shakes with fear as father holds her hand tight.

"My darling, I think we should tell him," my father murmurs, and my eyes sharpen on them both.

"Tell me what?" Mother looks torn, but she must decide it's worth it to tell me because her shoulders drop as she heads towards the office. I stand in the kitchen for a moment before following behind her, feeling like this is just the beginning of all the revelations.

Stepping into her office feels unnatural, as if I might be scolded at any moment. Growing up, this room was a locked mystery—I was never allowed inside. Now, surrounded by endless rows of books, parchment, and old images, it feels surreal, like stepping into a space frozen in time. Mother stands at the center, hands folded in front of her, while I try to absorb everything around me. The images and writings scattered throughout offer no immediate answers.

"I am a Guardian of the Keepers—a group of noble women sworn to protect." she says finally, her voice formal. "My duty—my sacred oath—is to protect the artifact hidden on this island."

"The Phoenix?" I ask.

"The Mummified Phoenix," she corrects. "One of several elemental beings bound during the Great Division."

My father takes a seat in the corner, watching us with worried eyes. This is not something new for him, that is clear, but this is a new side of my mother I know nothing about, and I can't help but remain guarded.

"I don't understand," I admit.

My mother grabs a box off the shelf that is carved with ancient symbols, some of which look like the symbols and writings on the papers Nesi has. She opens the box, revealing a small red crystal that glows faintly. "Long ago, before the Courts were divided, magic worked differently among our people. It wasn't inherited through noble bloodlines, it was bestowed by ancient elemental beings who chose worthy wielders regardless of birth."

I stare at her, trying to process this information. "Chosen? Not born?"

"Exactly." She lifts the crystal, which pulses faintly like a heartbeat. "The Phoenix was one such being—a divine elemental that chose those who would wield fire magic. The Shadow Leviathan chose shadow-walkers. The Storm Drake chose lightning-wielders. And so on."

"What happened to them?" My voice is strained with a growing anger.

Her expression darkens. "War happened. Chaos swept through our people. As the divine elementals freely bestowed powers upon more and more Fae, bitter conflicts arose over leadership and governance. Magic was no longer rare. It was becoming commonplace, granted to anyone and everyone with no thought to who was receiving it." Her voice grows tight. "Factions formed. Blood soaked our lands. Eventually, the most powerful families—the ancestors of today's nobility—devised a solution. The elementals had to be contained, their influence restricted. Their indiscriminate gifting of power was tearing our society apart."

"They bound the elemental beings," I guess, pieces falling into place. "To control who received magic."

She nods. "The Phoenix was mummified, prevented from its natural cycle of death and rebirth. Other beings were similarly contained. Their power was redirected to flow only through certain bloodlines—the noble families who led the binding ritual."

My heart pounds in my chest and my face grows warmer, anger bubbling up inside of me. "So the entire system, the division between noble and common Fae, the concentration of power, it's all artificial? A construct created to maintain control?"

"It was necessary," my mother insists. "The alternative was endless war. The bindings brought peace and stability."

"To whom? And at what cost?" I demand. "How many generations of Fae have lived without access to abilities that should have been theirs by merit, not birth?"

"That's why the Keepers exist," she continues, ignoring my question. "To protect the bindings, to ensure they remain intact. Each bound being has Guardians assigned to watch over it. I was sent here to guard the Phoenix."

The implications hit me like a physical blow. "That's why you married Father? As a...a cover?"

Her eyes soften as she glances at my father, who meets her gaze steadily. "No. I married your father because I love him. But yes, I was assigned to Manthana because of the Phoenix. Select women from noble households were taught of the truth and were raised knowing they would become guardians. I am but one among many."

My head spins with every piece of new information she reveals.

"And me?" I can barely get the words out. "What am I in all this?"

She hesitates, then says, "You are what the Keepers call a 'master'—one who would have been chosen by the Phoenix had it remained unbound, and one who would lead and teach those fire wielders when they were gifted their abilities. However, even with the bindings in place, the Phoenix can sometimes reach out to those it would have selected naturally. Your unusually strong fire abilities have often made me wonder, but you have never manifested the phoenix, which is essential to being a master."

"Until last night," I say, and I watch as a part of my mother crumbles.

"It's my fault. I shouldn't have visited the artifact when I was pregnant. The Keepers told us not to. The keepers will not take kindly to this." She looks over at my father, seeking support likely, but it just angers me further.

"That's what you are concerned about? If what you say is true, I would have been chosen if it had been free! And your only concern is these Keepers? What kind of mother are you?" The response flies out, unchecked.

"I am not just a mother, Milori, I am a dedicated member of the Day Court doing what I have been instructed to do to protect the fae people!" She turns on me, anger rising in her.

"No, you protect the interest of wealthy and powerful nobles, not the fae people, and you certainly don't protect the interest of the Day Court, or else Timas would have known about this. And because of your secrets, Soren is planning on waking the phoenix, and who knows what he will do when he gets a hold of it."

"No! Milori, he can't! This Soren person doesn't understand what would happen if the Phoenix were unbound. If he believes he can control it, use its power for himself, he is sorely mistaken. The Phoenix chooses its wielders. It can't be commanded or controlled. If improperly awakened, it would cause mass destruction before selecting new worthy wielders across Fae society." Her voice wobbles with emotion.

"And if properly awakened?" I press.

She hesitates. "Theoretically, it would peacefully reclaim its purpose, selecting worthy fire-wielders regardless of birth. But the process would strip power from many current noble families, creating enormous political instability. And it could trigger the awakening of other bound beings, completely transforming our society. You can't consider this!"

I pace the room, struggling to process everything. "So this entire time, you've been guarding an artifact that maintains an unjust system. One that divides not just the Courts, but all Fae people into those with power and those without."

"It's more complex than that," she insists.

"Is it?" I challenge. "Because from where I stand, it seems pretty simple. Over a millennia ago, a group of powerful families decided to monopolize magic for themselves and their descendants. They called it peace, but it was really about control."

"You don't understand the consequences—"

"I understand perfectly," I cut her off. "I've seen those consequences first hand. I've watched common fae resent nobles for privileges they did nothing to earn. I've seen talented, worthy individuals passed over because they lacked the right bloodline. Even I experienced it myself—never quite noble enough for court life despite my abilities."

"Milori," my father says gently, getting up from his chair. "Your mother has dedicated her life to preventing catastrophe. Do not act so quickly when you do not understand the whole."

"Maybe catastrophe is what we need," I reply, my voice hard. "Maybe this system needs to be torn down and rebuilt."

My mother steps forward, her face paling. "You cannot mean that. The Phoenix cannot be unbound without proper preparation, proper ritual. The wards are already failing. I should have paid more attention to this Soren. If he gets a hold of it, it would trigger a disaster that could destroy both Courts."

"I'm not talking about letting Soren have it," I clarify. "But this secret can't stay buried any longer. The fae deserve to know the truth. Timas deserves to know what he is dealing with! This history was not the keepers' right to bury and reveal to a select few. This is for all fae to know. They deserve a choice in their future."

"The Keepers will never allow it," she says firmly. "They are already making preparations to protect the Phoenix. They will not allow anyone to unbind it."

I meet her gaze directly. "Then I'm sorry, but I'll have to act without their permission."

"Milori, please," she steps toward me, genuine fear in her eyes. "You don't understand what you're saying. The Phoenix is dangerous. It—"

"Where is it?" I ask. "Where on the island is it hidden?"

She shakes her head. "I can't tell you that. My oath—"

"Then I'll find it myself," I snap, turning toward the door. "And unlike you, I won't keep secrets from those who deserve to know the truth. Soren is already searching. It's only a matter of time before he finds it. At least I understand what's at stake. And if you are more concerned about these keepers than your King, I pity you. Timas would die to protect the fae people, and he has people like me who would do the same." I turn, heading out of the study and toward the front door.

"Son," my father calls as I reach the door. "Please, let's talk about this. Your mother has given an oath."

I pause, looking back at them: my father, kind and supportive despite being kept in my mother's shadow; my mother, brilliant and dedicated, but blinded by centuries of Keeper doctrine.

"I have thought about it," I say quietly. "All my life, I've felt like I never quite belonged. Too powerful for island life, wrong background for court. Now I know why. I was chosen by the phoenix to right these wrongs. How many others were to be fire wielders? While many nobles take advantage of this gift. You say you know best, that the keepers know best, but when has one small group ever known best for an entire people?"

The question hangs in the air between us. Then another thought strikes me, one that cuts deeper than ancient artifacts and power struggles.

"After all the lies and secrets, tell me one thing honestly," I demand, my voice barely above a whisper. "Are you actually sick? Was that part true, at least?"

My mother's eyes fall to the floor. "Yes," she admits, the word clearly costing her.

"Will you die from it?"

A long pause. "Eventually, yes."

Something breaks inside me—rage and grief tangling together. "And still, you chase after your precious artifact. You've thrown away your family for an organization that only cares about maintaining power." I glance at my father, whose face has gone ashen. "And he adores you. He would fall apart without you. Yet you spend your remaining time with ancient bindings instead of him."

She reaches toward me, her hand trembling. "Milori—"

"I pity you," I say, the words falling like stones between us. "You can always make the right choice. Find me if you change your mind."

I unfurl my wings and take to the sky. Nesi needs to know about this, Timas too. This is far bigger than we thought, and somehow, far more personal than I ever could have imagined.

Chapter 14

Nesi

A jolt of pain runs up my side as I try to turn over, the feeling fading away as I come back from sleep. For a brief moment I forget where I am, and then I think of Milori, last night, Soren, and that forces me upright, which I instantly regret as more pain shoots up my side.

My eyes are heavy, but I force them open to take in the bright sun that now fills the room and immediately startle at the sight of Jalnor sitting in the chair across the room. He looks up from the book in his hands, a smile breaking across his bearded face. "Ah, the shadow walker returns to the land of the living. How are you feeling?"

I push myself upright, wincing as my body catalogs the previous night's injuries. My ribs still hurt, my shoulder throbs, and my head feels as if someone has taken a mallet to it. I will endure the pain, however. "Where's Milori?" I ask, ignoring his question.

"Good morning to you too," Jalnor chuckles, setting aside his book. "Here I thought I would get a simple hello to start with."

I narrow my eyes at him, but his good-natured expression doesn't falter. "Apologies. Good morning, Jalnor. I'm feeling like I fought several armed men and lost. Now where is Milori?"

"He's gone to see his parents," Jalnor says, rising to pour water from a pitcher into a cup. "He asked me to tell you he'll be back soon with stronger medicine for those injuries." He brings the water to me, his movements surprisingly gentle for someone his size. He just barely fits in the room despite the fact he built the cottage for himself. "And he said not to let you leave while he's gone, though I told him I'm not foolish enough to think I could stop you if you truly decided to go."

Jalnor is correct in that assessment. Accepting the water I try to run through this new information. A bubble of anxiety blooms in my chest at the thought of Milori going to his parents' house. He has been dreading visiting them since we arrived on the island, and now he is there facing down what is very likely to be a difficult reunion. Without me. A confusing mixture of emotions washes over me: annoyance that he left while I slept, concern about what he might be walking into, and an uncomfortable feeling that I should be there with him as he faces something so challenging.

"When did he leave?" I ask, trying to gauge how long I've been asleep. The sun hangs high in the sky based on the shadows on the ground, it's at least late morning if not nearly lunch time.

"Around dawn." Jalnor settles back in his chair. "He seemed determined. Sounds like the trip to the quarry last night ended

up being far more dangerous than you both originally anticipated and he believes his mother holds some answers to it."

Dangerous is an understatement but perhaps an apt one.
Soren has this island fully infiltrated by his rebel group looking
for this unknown artifact, and then there was the phoenix. The
thought of that bird that stood beside Milori sends a shiver
of amazement through me again. He looked so powerful and
terrifying. It's a sight I won't soon forget.

"I should go after him," I say, throwing back the blanket only
to have Jalnor raise a hand. I raise an eyebrow in question and
baulk at the idea of being told to remain here.

"I don't think that's wise," he says, his tone still friendly but
carrying surprising authority. "For one thing, you're injured
enough that the walk would be painful."

"I could fly." I snap. Milori shouldn't be alone during this
conversation, and though flying would also be very painful, I
have endured a lot worse for things a lot less important.

"For another," he continues, "Milori specifically asked for
time to speak with his parents alone. This conversation is going to be challenging enough. I doubt he wants to introduce
his spirit bond at this particular moment, especially given his
complicated relationship with them."

My breath catches. "You know about—"

"Oh, don't look so surprised," Jalnor chuckles, his eyes crin-
kling at the corners. "I knew the moment you two walked off
that boat. The real mystery was why Milori wasn't shouting it
from the mast that he'd found his other half."

His smile remains kind, but I see the question lingering in his gaze.

"It's complicated," I murmur, turning to stare out the window, unable to meet his eyes as memories of how desperately I tried to keep Milori at arm's length flood back.

"Complicated? Perhaps." Jalnor's voice softens. "But avoidance will only hurt you both in the end."

A lump forms in my throat as I recall last night: Milori risking his life to save me, the protective way he held me after. Something shifted between us, a wall finally crumbling enough for me to glimpse the truth. Perhaps letting him in isn't as dangerous as I'd feared.

Jalnor rises from his chair again and heads to the small kitchen. I can hear him moving things around before he re-emerges with a tray of food that he sets on my lap. A bowl of porridge, fresh cut fruit, and a cup of tea. My stomach rumbles at the sight of it, so I gingerly grab the spoon and eat the warm sweet oats.

"Thank you for this," I say between mouthfuls of food. "But just so we're clear—if he's not back by midday, I'll be going to find him, with or without you."

Jalnor smirks at my declaration, and I can't help but roll my eyes.

"Wouldn't dream of stopping you. If he's not back by then, I'll gladly show you where his parents live."

I finish my breakfast in silence while Jalnor returns to his book. When I'm done, he collects the tray without a word. Sitting in bed feels confining, so I carefully rise to my feet, ignoring the protest of my ribs as I move to the window.

The view reveals rolling hills stretching across Manthana, their gentle slopes catching the morning light. Something about this place feels uncommonly simple—as if life can unfold without the constant calculation and maneuvering that defines court existence. No political games to play, no expectations of fulfilling courtly duties. Just living. I find myself unexpectedly envious.

Jalnor returns to the room, settling back into his chair without breaking the quiet. The question rises to my lips before I can stop it. "Does Milori miss the simple life of the island?"

Jalnor doesn't respond immediately. I turn to find his brow furrowed in thought.

"To say he misses this island would be wholly untrue. He was not happy here," he says finally, his voice thoughtful. "But I believe that given the chance, he would have wanted a simple life with the woman he loves. His desire as a young man was to have a family, to create the family he desperately wanted but never had."

His gaze grows distant with memory. "He would often talk about how many children he'd have. But over the decades, I watched him resign himself to duty, to being King Timas' right hand."

Jalnor's smile turns bittersweet, and something in my chest constricts at the thought of Milori surrendering his dreams for duty. How similar we are—both placing obligation above personal desire for centuries. Yet the difference cuts deep: he readily accepted our bond while I continue to struggle with the idea of letting anything come before my duty to protect the Night Court.

"I can't imagine what it would be like to find my spirit bond," he adds, his voice softening. "Much like Milori, I would likely be ecstatic. But when two people come together, it's never as simple as immediate acceptance. Spirit bonds are rare, and while I'd rejoice at finding my other half, the adjustment wouldn't be easy."

He chuckles, the sound warm with affection. "Relationships require work—at least that's what my mother always says about being bonded to my father." Jalnor leans forward, his expression earnest. "But what's taken root between you and Milori is magical. A sacred connection that transcends the understanding of love that simple Fae like me will likely never experience. What you share is deeper than most can imagine."

His gaze meets mine, and I can feel him assessing me. "I know there's much to consider, with you both serving different courts. But I believe if you truly embraced this bond, you could find a way to be together while still serving your respective monarchs."

His words strike something that's been battling within me since the moment I met Milori. The longer I spend with him, the more clearly I see that pushing away this bond might be my greatest mistake. The walls I've built to protect myself from connection—from vulnerability—suddenly seem less like shelter and more like a prison of my own making.

"What holds you back?" Jalnor asks, his tone gentle rather than accusatory. "Fear? Duty? Something else?"

The question strikes at the heart of my conflict, the battle I've waged since recognizing Milori as my spirit bond.

"Duty," I say finally. "I swore my life to Queen Neeve and the Night Court. My people need me fully focused, fully committed." That familiar weight of responsibility rises in my chest as I think about all the people who are depending on me to do my job.

Jalnor nods knowingly. "And you believe loving someone would make you less effective in service to your queen."

When he phrases it that way, it sounds almost foolish. "I've put duty before all else my entire life," I explain. "Even before..." I hesitate, uncertain how much to reveal about my past.

"Before what?" he prompts.

I take a breath. "Before I was used as a weapon by those who ruled before. My shadow-walking made me valuable to King Oberon. He used me to eliminate threats, gather intelligence, inspire fear. Before that Queen Neeve's father trained me to be strong. I am sure his intention was to ensure I was protected, but it always felt as if I was also just a tool he was sharpening, preparing me for the future somehow."

Jalnor's expression darkens with understanding. "And now you fear being divided in your loyalty to Queen Neeve."

"Not divided," I correct. "Just...less than what she needs me to be. The Night Court is still fragile, still rebuilding. It has barely been a year since leaving the forest. The alliance between the two courts is still new and tenuous. We do not desire another war and we do not desire to be exiled again. Neeve needs me to be focused so our court can thrive."

"And Milori is a distraction?" There's no judgment in his tone, only curiosity.

I think of Milori's face last night as he tended my wounds, the gentleness in his hands stood in stark contrast to his ferocious power at the quarry. "No. He's far more than that. That's what makes it dangerous."

Jalnor nods his head. "Life is too short—even for Fae—to give it entirely to someone who won't value it as a spirit bond would."

"Neeve values me," I protest, unable to keep the fierce protectiveness from my voice. "She saved our people when no one else would. She carried the weight of our entire Court while we struggled to rebuild from nothing. I owe her everything." My back is straight as I stare down Jalnor.

"I believe she does value you as a spymaster. As a loyal subject, absolutely," he agrees. "But not as Milori values you: as a person, complete with strengths and flaws. Not as someone who would give his life for you without hesitation."

His words hit me with unexpected force. Milori would give his life for me. Last night proved that beyond doubt. Neeve, I believe would give her life for the Night Court in an instant, but would she do it just for me? I'm not so sure.

"He stands for you," Jalnor continues. "Not for an ideal or a court or a position. For you, Nesi. Just you."

And that's what I've been struggling with all along. Not fear that love would weaken my service, but the terrifying reality of being seen and chosen for exactly who I am. Of mattering to someone not for what I can do for them, but simply because I exist.

"I'm not suggesting you abandon your queen," he says gently. "Only that perhaps there's room for both in your heart. Duty and love."

I think of what Milori said last night, that being strong doesn't mean being alone. "I've wanted a family too," I admit, the words strange on my tongue. "In the Shrouded Forest, I would imagine having someone who saw me as more than shadows and power. Someone who wasn't afraid."

Jalnor smiles knowingly. "And now you've found him."

"Yes," I say softly, the admission both frightening and freeing.

"Then what are you waiting for?" he asks simply.

For so long, I've defined strength as independence. But perhaps true strength lies in knowing when to stand alone and when to stand with someone else.

"Thank you," I say, meeting his kind gaze, "for your insight. And for caring about him enough to speak plainly to me."

He grins, the seriousness breaking. "Someone has to keep you Night Court folks honest. Too many shadows, not enough direct sunlight." We laugh and for the first time I finally see that perhaps the light isn't so scary after all.

***

The morning stretches into afternoon, and despite Jalnor's attempts at distraction with island stories and cups of herbal tea, my patience wears thin. Milori has been gone for hours, and I've moved from the bed to pacing near the window, each step sending small jolts of pain through my ribs.

"He should have returned by now," I say, not bothering to hide my concern.

Jalnor looks up from the stew he's stirring. "Conversations with his parents rarely go smoothly or quickly. Especially after years of distance. And if the conversation didn't go well, which it quite likely didn't, he will need a bit of time to decompress."

I'm about to say that we should go find him, when a flash of movement outside catches my eye. Relief floods through me as I spot a familiar figure descending from the sky, powerful wings extended before tucking neatly behind him as he lands.

"He's back," I announce, moving toward the door despite the pain.

The cottage door swings open, and Milori steps inside, his face drawn and shoulders tense. His hair is disheveled, even more than usual, as if he's been running his hands through it repeatedly. But the moment his eyes find mine, his expression transforms, tension melting into visible relief.

"You're up," he says, crossing the room in three long strides. His hands hover near my shoulders, not quite touching, eyes scanning my injuries with concern. "You should be resting."

"I'm fine," I insist, though the pain in my side suggests otherwise. I reach for his face, brushing my fingers against his cheek, searching for any sign of what happened. "Are you alright?"

He catches my hand, pressing it to his face with a quiet certainty. His eyes close for just a moment, and in that silence, I understand more than words ever could.

Behind us, Jalnor clears his throat. "I'll give you two some privacy," he offers, moving toward the door.

"No," Milori says, opening his eyes. "Stay. You should hear this too." His voice carries a weight I haven't heard before, and my concern deepens.

"First things first," he says, reaching into his pocket to produce a small vial of bluish liquid. "The village healer owed me a favor. This will heal your ribs within hours." He presses it into my palm, then retrieves a small jar of salve. "And this is for the cuts and scrapes."

I accept both gratefully. "Thank you."

Jalnor motions us to the table where three steaming bowls of stew await. "Eat while you talk. Whatever happened, food will help." I'm not entirely sure that is true but his thoughtfulness is kind.

We settle at the table, and I uncork the vial, downing the contents in one swallow. It tastes of mint and something sharper—a healing herb I am familiar with. Almost immediately, warmth spreads through my chest, easing the pain in my ribs.

Milori takes a deep breath, pushing his stew aside untouched. "What I learned today changes everything," he begins, his voice steady despite the storm I can see brewing behind his eyes. "The Mummified Phoenix isn't just an artifact. It's an ancient elemental being."

He tells us of the divine elementals who once chose magic-wielders, the war that consumed the Fae, and the noble families who bound these beings to control power.

"The entire magical system—bloodline inheritance, the separation of powers between Courts—it's all artificial," he explains, his hands spread on the table before him. "Created to maintain control and ensure stability, but at the cost of fairness and true merit."

I listen, stunned by the scale of this deception. "And your mother? She's part of this?" I can't help the disbelief that colours my voice. I shouldn't be surprised by anyone grabbing for power, but a part of me thought the person who raised Milori must have honour. That she could participate in something like this seems unbelievable.

"A Guardian of the Keepers," he confirms, a bitter edge to his voice. "Sworn to protect the bindings, to maintain the status quo and she isn't the only one. There are many other beings and many other guardians. That's why she was always absent, always researching. She was guarding the Phoenix."

Jalnor sits heavily in his chair. "By the sun," he mutters. "This explains so much about this island. The heaviness visitors feel, it's the bound Phoenix."

"And what Soren called me last night, the phoenix master," Milori continues. "An individual the Phoenix would have chosen to lead and teach other fire wielders." His jaw tightens. "Turns out a fiery bird saw fit to give me stronger powers to make a difference which obviously didn't help me fit in." He clenches his fist, his tone devoid of humour. "The Phoenix has been reaching out to me despite its bindings."

I think of the magnificent firebird that appeared in the quarry. "The manifestation last night—"

"The first time it's ever happened." He meets my eyes. "Mother had hoped I was not a master, but since I manifested the phoenix the sign is clear I am what she feared I could be." The bitterness in his voice is evident, and despite his best effort his body tenses with anger.

Jalnor leans forward. "So what now? If Soren finds this Phoenix—"

"If he attempts to unbind it improperly, it could cause massive destruction," Milori says grimly. "But according to my mother even a proper unbinding would completely transform Fae society. Power would no longer be inherited through bloodlines—it would be granted to those the elementals deem worthy. The potential of power being taken from current noble families is high and that power could be distributed to deserving fae. The power within our society would be irrevocably changed."

The implications stagger me. "The entire noble hierarchy could collapse."

"Or transform into something more just," Milori counters. "But either way, this isn't a decision for the Keepers alone. Timas needs to know. Queen Neeve needs to know."

I nod in agreement. "This affects all Fae. Both Courts."

"I'm sending a signal to Timas tonight," Milori says, rising from his chair. "A fire flame shot into the sky in the deep of night—something we established years ago after an attempt on his life. He'll know to come immediately."

"And I'll send a message orb to Neeve," I add, already thinking through what to tell her. This goes far beyond what either of us anticipated when I left the Night Court.

Jalnor looks between us, his expression grave. "And Soren? He's still out there, still searching."

"With his men, yes," Milori confirms. "And he now knows I'm a Phoenix master, which likely changes his plans. We need to find the Phoenix before he does, but for now we rest and signal the monarchs. We can't fight this on our own, and we should keep our heads down until they arrive."

I rise, the healing potion already working its magic on my ribs. The pain has dulled to a manageable ache. "Then we have work to do."

"I'll put out feelers in town, see who knows anything. Maybe get an idea of where Soren is searching," Jalnor says as he rises and heads toward the cottage door.

Milori catches his arm, their eyes meeting in a way that speaks of years of shared history. "Be careful. I won't forgive myself if anything happened to you."

Jalnor smiles and slaps a hand down on his shoulder. "Wouldn't want that. You already have a complex, feeling responsible for everyone when you shouldn't." They both laugh as Jalnor makes his exit, though the concern in Milori's eyes doesn't fully fade.

Milori's eyes meet mine, and in them I see the same determination I feel. Whatever comes next, we'll face it together. Not just as spirit bonds, but as partners in a cause that could reshape our entire world.

"Prepare to send your message to Neeve," he says. "I'll prepare to signal Timas. And then," his voice hardens with resolve, "we find the Phoenix."

Chapter 15

Milori

The salty wind whips around us as Nesi and I soar high above Manthana. Her dark wings beat steadily beside mine, catching the moonlight in iridescent midnight blue ripples. Despite the healing potion, I notice her wince occasionally when an air current forces her to adjust suddenly. Her injuries still pain her, but I'm not surprised she doesn't complain.

"Are you certain Timas will see this?" Nesi asks, her voice carrying over the wind between us.

"The signal fire is designed to be visible from the mainland," I explain, scanning the horizon for the perfect spot. "The royal observatory maintains a constant watch for it. When they see it, they'll alert Timas immediately."

She nods, her wings adjusting to match my trajectory. "And he'll know it's from you specifically?"

"The pattern is unique to me," I confirm. "Three concentrated bursts, followed by a sustained flame. Timas created the system after an assassination attempt two decades ago. A couple of the noble guards who are fire wielders have similar signals, but this specific sequence was designed for me."

We fly toward the highest point on the island—a jagged peak that towers over the eastern shore. The spot is deserted, far from prying eyes that might spot us from the village.

I land carefully, folding my wings behind me as Nesi touches down beside me with the natural grace that defines her every movement. She rolls her shoulders back, likely an unconscious adjustment to ease the strain of flight on her healing body.

"This should do," I say, moving to the edge of the cliff. The drop is dizzying, straight down to crashing waves hundreds of feet below. The wind sweeps around us and the sound of the waves calm my tumultuous insides.

"Do you need to do anything special?" Nesi asks, watching me intently.

I can't help the small grin that tugs at my lips. Her curious expression makes my heart skip. After years of people fearing my abilities, her fascination feels like a gift.

"No, just stand back." I flex my fingers, feeling the familiar heat building beneath my skin. The gravity of why we're doing this dampens my excitement, but there's still a thrill in showing Nesi what I can do. After all, impressing my spirit bond isn't the worst reason I've ever summoned fire.

The pull on my power feels different now—easier, somehow. Before, it was being held back, though I hadn't realized it. I thought that resistance was just normal. But now it flows freely through my body, the heat building as I channel the fire to my palms. The phoenix sits at the edges of my consciousness, so easily accessible right now, ready to take to the sky if I were to call to it. Having this access to something so powerful is terrifying but also empowering, no wonder I could wield fire better than anyone I know.

Taking a deep breath, I lift my hands toward the sky and release my power in a controlled burst. Golden flames shoot upward in three distinct pillars, one after another, each rising at least a hundred feet into the air before dissipating. After the third, I sustain a continuous stream of fire that illuminates the entire clifftop with its bright glow.

Amazing how freeing it feels to use my powers now.

"That should do it," I say, turning back to Nesi. Her expression makes me pause. She's watching me with a mix of awe and something else I can't quite place. "What?"

"You're beautiful when you use your power," she add's casually, the admission clearly surprising her as much as it does me. "I mean striking. Powerful. Never mind." She huffs and I can't help but laugh.

Warmth spreads through my body as I make my way over to her, taking her hand in mine and relishing how red her face has become. "That's funny. I think the same about you and your shadows."

Her lips curve into a small smile. "We're quite the pair, aren't we? Fire and shadow." She flexes her fingers around mine.

"Like we were made to complement each other," I agree, moving closer to her. "Though I should confess, my attraction to shadows started well before I knew who they belonged to.

Remember those dreams I mentioned? The ones where I was, as I so eloquently put it, 'attracted to actual darkness'?"

A quiet laugh escapes her. "And here I thought you were exaggerating to be charming."

"Not in the slightest," I assure her, remembering how her shadows had coiled around my wrist that night in the crow's nest, a shiver courses through me as I look deep into her beautiful dark eyes. "I was dreaming about your shadows before I even met you. The spirit bond called to me, I suppose. So yes, we're quite the pair. Perfectly paired. Perfectly matched."

I bring our threaded fingers to my mouth, brushing my lips against the back of her hand. Her breath catches—a small sound that thunders in my ears. My heart soars when she doesn't pull away. For once, she's not fighting our connection, and the hope I've been trying to contain blazes to life inside me like my own personal wildfire.

Seconds stretch between us, neither willing to break the spell. When she steps closer, my breath stalls in my chest. I know we should return to the cottage, that danger lurks on this island, but I can't bring myself to rush this moment or trade it for anything. Not even duty.

"We should get back," she whispers, though she makes no move to break our connection. "We need to prepare for Timas' arrival tomorrow."

"Yes," I agree reluctantly. "But first..."

I lean down slowly, giving her every opportunity to pull away, but she doesn't. Instead she follows my descent. Our lips meet, hers so soft and inviting. Her small sigh is all I need to deepen the kiss. This kiss is different from our first—less urgent, more deliberate, yet somehow more intense. The connection between us pulses like a living thing, sending waves of heat through my body that have nothing to do with my fire magic. She presses against me and I wrap my arm around her as she lays her hand on my chest, grabbing at my shirt.

Everything about this moment feels right—no resistance, no turmoil, only the quiet surrender. No rebellion, no bound Phoenix, no tangled family ties—just us. Our bond burns bright as we finally accept one another. I've waited centuries for this woman, for this moment, and now that she's here, I never want to let go.

When we finally part, both of us are breathing hard, she takes a shaky breath that sends a spark of satisfaction through me. Her eyes remain closed for a heartbeat longer than necessary, her lips slightly parted and flushed from our kiss. When she opens them, the raw vulnerability and desire I see there makes my heart stutter.

"I've wanted to do that since the night in the crow's nest," I confess, my voice rough with emotion. "Maybe since the moment I first saw you."

She smiles at me, that rare expression that transforms her entire face. "You've already kissed me."

I laugh, warmth spreading through my chest at her practical nature. "Yes, but not like that. Not with all your walls down—or well, mostly down." Nervousness flutters in my stomach as I wonder if I've misread this, but her smile widens, and just like that, everything feels right.

"I suppose you're right," she admits, though I can still see conflict behind those beautiful dark eyes.

"Now we can go," I say, unable to contain the joy that fills me like sunlight.

She rolls her eyes, but doesn't hide her smile. "You always have to have the last word, don't you?"

"Only when it's worth saying." I steal another quick kiss, delighting in her startled expression before stepping back and unfurling my wings with a flourish.

We share a look, one filled with promise and understanding, before launching into the night sky. I watch the graceful beat of her wings beside me, the way her form cuts through the darkness with natural ease. We've stolen this brief moment for ourselves, but now it's time to face trouble head-on.

***

The island stretches below us, peaceful in the moonlight despite the hidden dangers we know lurk in its shadows. It takes only minutes to return to the cottage, it's hidden away warmth coming into view, the windows glowing from the warm lights within. But as we descend I notice someone sitting on the small bench outside the cottage, at first I search the surrounding areas but the person is hunched over with their hands on their face. This is no nefarious encounter. Then I see who it is.

My father.

We land a short distance from the cottage, our wings folding away as we approach him. He looks up at the sound of our footsteps, his face shifting from sadness to relief.

"Father?" I call, confusion and concern mixing in my chest. "What are you doing here?"

He stands, and I'm struck by how much older he suddenly appears. The lines around his eyes are deeper, and his posture is less certain than it was this morning.

"Milori," he says, his voice rough with emotion. "Thank the sun you're back."

Nesi hangs back, giving us space while remaining close enough to intervene if needed. Though what she thinks my father might do, I can't imagine. He has never been violent a day in his life, I'm not sure he would even know where to start.

"What's wrong?" I ask, moving closer. "Is it Mother?"

He nods, running a hand through his graying hair while casting his gaze across the field, barely visible in the moonlight. "She left."

"Left?" The word comes out sharper than intended. "What do you mean left?"

"After you departed," he explains, his voice heavy, "she was distraught. More upset than I've seen her in decades. She packed some things, said she needed to go to the Keepers immediately."

Anger flashes through me. "So she ran to her precious organization rather than face the truth."

"Milori," my father says, his tone suddenly stern, "your mother is dying."

The words hit like a physical blow, stealing my breath despite the fact I heard them from her own lips this morning. Somehow, hearing it from my father makes it more real, more immediate.

"I know," I manage, my voice tight. "Or did we forget my first visit and her *explanation* this morning." I shouldn't sound so bitter but this has been a taxing experience.

"No," he shakes his head, "you don't understand. It's getting worse. Much worse, no much faster. The binding, it's killing her. All the Guardians eventually succumb to it. The effort of maintaining the magical containment, it drains their life force over time."

I stare at him in disbelief, a sick feeling spreading through my stomach. "How long has she known?"

"Years," he admits, looking away. "At first, it was manageable. Small symptoms like fatigue and the occasional dizzy spell. But lately..." his voice breaks, "lately she can barely stand some days. The pain is constant. She hides it well—she always has—but I see it. Every day, I watch her fade a little more."

The truth crashes over me in waves. My mother's frantic work, her distraction, her disheveled appearance this morning—signs I ignored, or didn't want to pay attention to. I knew she was dying and now I know the reason—sacred duty. Despite her secrecy, despite the betrayal I felt at discovering the Keepers, my heart aches knowing she is suffering. She is still my mother.

"Why didn't she tell me?" I ask, though I already know the answer.

"Would you have wanted to know?" my father asks gently. "Would it have changed anything between you?"

I have no response to that. Would knowing my mother was dying have softened my judgment of her choices? Or would I have seen it as manipulation, another attempt to avoid accountability?

"Of course I would have wanted to know. She is my mother." My voice rises slightly hurt that he would think so little of me that I would not care about her plight. He seems to think about that for a moment before Nesi steps forward to stand by my side.

"Sir," she addresses my father with surprising gentleness, "I'm Nesi of the Night Court. I believe it would be best to continue this conversation inside." She looks at us both before Father takes her in. He focuses on her more fully for the first time, his eyes widening as he takes in her elegant features and everything that she embodies. His gaze shifts between us, and I see the exact moment realization dawns on him, the way his exhaustion momentarily gives way to pure joy.

"By the sun," he breathes, a genuine smile transforming his weary face. "She's your spirit bond. Your companion from earlier today." He clasps his hands together, looking at me with such pride and happiness that for a moment, I forget the gravity of the situation.

"Father," I start, but he's already stepped forward to take Nesi's hand between both of his.

"I'm Farin," he says warmly, offering a respectful bow that seems to surprise her. "When Milori mentioned finding his spirit bond this morning, I never imagined—" his voice catches with emotion, "I never imagined I'd meet you so soon. This is a blessing, even in such difficult times."

"Father, please," I interrupt gently, touched by his reaction but aware of more pressing concerns. "We should continue this inside."

He nods, reluctantly releasing Nesi's hand, though the joy doesn't leave his eyes. "Of course, of course. But once this crisis passes, I want to get to know my new daughter." That physically stops Nesi in her tracks as father continues walking into the cottage. "The fates must favour you both to bring you together now, of all times." I give Nesi a sheepish smile as she comes back to herself and moves closer to my father.

I place a hand on his shoulder, gently guiding him toward the cottage door. The tension in his body is palpable, and I wonder when he last slept properly. "Come inside, Father. Tell us everything."

Once inside, I stoke the fire while Nesi prepares tea. My father sinks into a chair, suddenly looking even more exhausted. The warm glow of the hearth casts deep shadows across his face, emphasizing the worry lines around his eyes.

"The binding is killing her?" I prompt once we're all seated.

Farin nods, cradling the cup Nesi handed him. "All Guardians experience it eventually. The magical containment requires constant attention, a continuous expenditure of their own life force. The longer they serve, the more it takes from them."

"And Mother has been a Guardian for...?"

"Almost three centuries," he replies. "She was assigned to Manthana shortly before we met."

Three hundred years. The thought staggers me. A few decades before she had me. "Did you know? When you married her."

Something like guilt crosses his face. "No. Not at first. But I suspected she was keeping something from me. She would disappear for days, return exhausted, sometimes barely able to walk. After you were born, I confronted her, and she finally told me the truth."

I try to absorb this, to reconcile the mother I thought I knew with this new information. "And you stayed."

"Of course I stayed," he says, as if the alternative is unthinkable. "I loved her. I still do, more than anything in this world. Her commitment, her sacrifice, it only made me admire her more."

"But she put the Keepers above everything," I argue, old hurt rising to the surface. "Above you. Above me."

My father sighs, his expression softening. "Is that so different from what you've done, serving our king? How many years passed between visits home?"

The comparison strikes uncomfortably close. I glance at Nesi, whose eyes meet mine with understanding, but there was a big difference between what I did and what she did.

"No," I say firmly, surprising both my father and myself with my candor. "It is different. What I found at court wasn't duty—it was family. The family I never had here." My father flinches slightly, but I continue, the words I've held back for centuries, finally finding my voice.

"My loyalty to Timas isn't about obligation or some abstract sense of duty. He's my brother in all but blood. Emilia, Garrick, Alette—they became the family that saw me, accepted me, valued me for who I am." I meet my father's gaze directly. "I stopped coming because there was nothing for me here. Just silence and secrets and feeling like I didn't belong. Feeling like I was a burden. So yes, I stayed away. But not for duty. I stayed for self-preservation, for a chance at life."

I reach for Nesi's hand across the table, her dark eyes meeting mine and I hold onto the strength she gives me. "And now I've found my spirit bond—the most sacred connection our kind can experience." I look back at my father who stares at our entwined hands. "And I promise you, I will never put anything above her." I turn to Nesi, letting her see the depth of my commitment in my eyes. "Or any family we might build together."

Looking back at my father, I see his eyes fill with tears. "I failed you," he says quietly. "We both did. Your mother with her secrets and me with my silence."

"You did," I acknowledge, not to hurt him, but because the truth needs saying. For too long I let guilt prevent me from sharing the pain, but I won't hide it anymore. I don't want to be bitter and angry, that will not be a benefit to Nesi as we continue to grow in our relationship. "But that doesn't mean we can't try to be better now. Starting with saving Mother from the fate the Keepers have trapped her in."

"Your mother made choices I didn't always agree with," he continues solemnly. "But she believed she was protecting the world. Protecting you. The day she realized you might be a Phoenix master was the most terrified I've ever seen her."

"Terrified?" I echo. "Of me?"

"For you," he corrects. "If the Keepers had discovered your true nature, they might have taken you away, put you under their control. She did everything in her power to hide your potential, even sending you to court where your abilities would seem less unusual among noble children. But even still you were strong, I believe it was your friendship with Timas that has protected you all these years."

The implications of this hit me hard. "She sent me away to protect me?" My entire world spins. I've always believed she sent me away because she couldn't or wouldn't help me control my powers. I took too much of her time.

"She sent you away because she loved you," my father states with quiet conviction. "Because she saw what the binding was doing to her and she couldn't bear the thought of you suffering. And though she didn't truly know, she wanted to be sure you were safe. She doesn't always express herself well, but she truly does love you, Milori."

The room falls silent except for the crackling of the fire. Nesi's hand squeezes mine as I run through everything he said. How could I not know any of this?

"Is there a cure?" I ask finally. "For what's happening to her?"

My father's expression falls. "None that the Keepers have discovered. Each Guardian eventually succumbs."

"And now she's gone to them," I say, pieces falling into place. "Because she thinks Soren is close to finding the Phoenix. Because she thinks I might help him?"

"She's afraid," Farin admits. "Not just of Soren, but of what you might do. She has dedicated her entire life to protecting this being, she doesn't know any other way."

A terrible thought occurs to me. "The other Guardians—will they try to stop me? To stop us?"

"Almost certainly," he confirms. "The Keepers believe maintaining the bindings is essential to prevent another civil war. They'll do whatever they think necessary to protect the Phoenix."

"Including harming Milori?" Nesi asks sharply, her shadows darkening around her.

My father hesitates, and that's answer enough.

"We need to find Mother," I say, rising from my chair. "Before the Keepers decide to do something drastic to her in an attempt to try to control me."

"Milori," Nesi cautions, "we should wait for Timas. Rushing in without support—"

"Timas won't arrive until tomorrow at the earliest," I interrupt, already pacing. "By then, the Keepers could move the Phoenix, or strengthen its bindings, or—"

"Or set a trap for you," she finishes, her voice firm. "We need to be strategic about this."

I know she's right, but the thought of my mother out there suffering while protecting an artifact that's slowly killing her—it tears at something deep within me. We may have our differences, but she's still my mother.

"Father," I turn to him, "do you know where the Keepers meet? Where they might have taken Mother?"

He shifts uncomfortably in his chair. "I shouldn't. Lavera never told me directly, but..." he pauses. "I followed her once, years ago. I was worried about her health, and she wouldn't tell me where she was going."

"Where?" I press, hope flaring.

"The jagged cliffs on the western side of the island," he says reluctantly. "There's an old graveyard there."

"I know the place." I confirm.

"It's along the cliffs, facing the water. Nearly impossible to reach by foot unless you are an excellent climber."

"But accessible by air," I note out loud.

"Yes," my father confirms. "I couldn't get close enough to see exactly where she went, but she disappeared into a crevice in the rock face."

Nesi exchanges a significant look with me. "One of the locations Soren mentioned at the quarry."

"Which means he might already know," I agree grimly.

My father reaches across the table, grasping my arm. "Milori, promise me you won't do anything rash. Your mother—whatever our disagreements, whatever choices she's made—she does love you. In her own way."

The emotion in his voice is so raw, so genuine, that I feel my anger softening despite myself. "I know, Father."

And strangely, I do know. Perhaps her love has always been tangled up in duty and fear and secrets, but it was always there. The realization doesn't erase the hurt of all those absent years, but it casts them in a different light—one that makes her choices, if not entirely forgivable, at least understandable.

"We'll wait for Timas," I finally decide, though it pains me to say it. "He should arrive by late morning tomorrow. Then we'll go to the western cliffs."

Relief crosses my father's face. "Thank you. I'll come with you. I can show you exactly where I saw her enter."

"I don't think that is necessary. It could be dangerous," I say with concern.

"She's my bondmate," he replies simply, as if that explains everything. And perhaps it does.

I look to Nesi, finding quiet approval in her eyes. "Rest here tonight, Father. We have much to prepare before tomorrow."

He nods, the exhaustion finally showing fully in his slumped shoulders. I realize he's probably been searching for me all day, worried about both his wife and his son.

As I finish preparing the bed for him, I step outside to get some fresh air. The stars shine above, unchanging and eternal, a constant compared to the turmoil inside me. Somewhere on this island, my mother is with the Keepers, perhaps preparing to defend the Phoenix against both Soren and me. Tomorrow we'll find her—and the bound elemental being that has shaped my life in ways I never understood until now.

I close my eyes, reaching within for that new awareness—the presence of the Phoenix that now stirs consciously inside me. It responds immediately, a warm essence that feels both ancient and familiar. Though bound to me, it is its own being, distinct yet inseparable, like a second soul intertwined with mine. It feels right.

Entirely lost in thought, I don't hear anything until Nesi touches my arm, bringing me back to the present. She stands beside me, her face glowing in the moonlight.

"Your father is settled," she says, her soft voice a comfort right now. "He fell asleep almost immediately."

"Thank you," I say, covering her hand with mine. "For everything."

Her eyes search mine. "Are you alright?"

"I don't know," I admit. "Everything I thought I knew about my family, about myself, it's all changed in a single day. And tomorrow..."

"Tomorrow we face whatever comes," she finishes. "Together."

I pull her into my arms, holding her tight to my chest, comforted by her presence. "Together," I agree.

We stand there under the stars, holding each other as the night deepens around us. Tomorrow Timas will arrive, and we'll set out to find the Phoenix before Soren does. And before the Keepers can move it, or do whatever they see fit with it. Before my mother's sacrifice becomes permanent.

I only hope we're not already too late.

Chapter 16

Milori

I don't think staring at the horizon is the best use of my time, but trying to sleep after last night's revelations was nearly impossible. The signal fire would have reached the observatory immediately, which means he should be arriving soon, assuming nothing has detained him. It's taken a great deal of control not to race off and find my mother and deal with the keepers. What they have done still burns under my skin.

"Do you think staring at the sky will help the time pass quicker?" Nesi says as she comes to stand beside me, two steaming cups of tea in her hands. Accepting one gratefully I try to take a deep breath to calm my nerves, the heat from the cup warming my palms.

"Perhaps if I stare very hard it will summon the mighty King quicker." I joke, smirking at Nesi, though the humour is just a way to forget the time.

"Seems to be working." She takes a sip of her tea and I turn to her slowly, shocked.

"Did you just make a joke?" She tries to hide the smile behind her cup but fails extraordinarily.

"I'm not without joy, Milori." She tries to chastise.

"Obviously not, you have me and I am a delight." She laughs loudly which releases the tension inside me.

When she finally regains some control she says, "Indeed," through a smile.

We stand together silently, drinking our tea and watching the sky, the quiet between us peaceful and comfortable, as if we've known each other for years, not mere days.

"When do you think Queen Neeve will receive your message?" I've been wondering how fast she could inform her Queen, but forgot to ask with everything happening.

"Best case scenario she'll be here by tonight. I sent a messenger orb with Jalnor yesterday and gave him a large bag of coins to expedite the process. He assured me he talked the quickest captain into travelling to the Night Court, though the captain seemed concerned with the destination. I think Jalnor was trying to spare my feelings, but it wasn't necessary. I know what reputation we have."

The idea of Jalnor convincing someone to sail to the Night Court makes me laugh.

"Jalnor cares deeply for everyone, but he'll be especially attentive to you because you matter to me. You'll be invited to every party he throws and receive letters for every special occasion. He's rather persistent about keeping his presence in the lives of people he loves."

Nesi gives me a funny look but, before I can question it, the door to the cottage opens.

"Anything?" my father asks, his voice tight with anxiety.

I shake my head. "Not yet." He comes to stand on my other side as we look at the horizon.

"King Timas will come," Jalnor assures him, as he exits the cottage. "His loyalty to Milori is legendary, even on our remote island." And he stands beside Nesi.

My father nods, though the worry doesn't leave his eyes. Last night's conversation shifted something between us—not healing the rift exactly, but creating a bridge where before there was only open space. For the first time in centuries, we spoke honestly about the pain that drove me away. It wasn't an easy conversation, but perhaps it was a necessary one, one I should have had with him many years ago.

"There!" Nesi points to the right, her sharp eyes catching what the rest of us missed. "Coming from the east."

I follow her gaze, relief flooding through me as I spot five winged silhouetted against the morning clouds. The lead figure is unmistakable, his large powerful wings creating distinct patterns even at this distance.

"Timas," I breathe, some of the tension easing even more from my shoulders. "And he's brought reinforcements."

As they draw closer, I realize something odd about their formation. Four noble guards flank Timas while one follows behind...carrying something? Someone? *Please let this be who I think it is.*

"Is that—" I squint, disbelief warring with growing amusement as the group descends toward our meadow.

The largest guard, Solran, carries Garrick, who looks thoroughly disgruntled. I nearly drop the cup in my hand as I bend over laughing harder than I have in days. He looks completely undignified and it is exactly what I needed this morning. Timas lands and the Noble Guard tucks in close behind him.

"By the sun! The great Garrick has lowered himself again to be carried by the superior fae." I walk over to the group as Garrick practically jumps out of Solran's arms, who looks annoyed as well.

"Shut it, peacock." He rolls his shoulders and stretches his neck. "All night. We have been travelling *all night*." Timas rolls his eyes as he strides toward me, his expression far from pleased. "And he has been complaining for most of it," He mumbles, only making my smile grow.

"Came all this way just to see me?" I can't help but tease. He snorts in response.

"Hardly. My sister and beloved Alette forced me to come to ensure you didn't do anything stupid. I told them it was inevitable and after a few flying pots from my sister, here I am." Garrick crosses his arms over his chest while Timas stares at him like he is an idiot.

"Right, because the fit you threw in the throne room about Milori being in great danger had nothing to do with you caring about his well-being," Timas deadpans. Placing my hands on my chest, I bat my eyes.

"You care for me!" I say far more enthusiastically than I need to. Without thinking, Garrick grabs the axe on his belt and tosses it at my head. Used to his particular brand of annoyance, I catch the flying blade easily.

"Garrick, we are in public! Control your brutish outbursts!" My correction falls on deaf ears as he tries to jump away from a shadow figure crawling up beside him. I look back at Nesi who is concentrating on Garrick.

"Nesi, you don't have to scare the little Orc. He's harmless. Besides, he has thrown worse things at my head before."

She doesn't look away from Garrick as she responds. "I am not a fan of flying projectiles coming towards my..." She looks at me now, the color rising in her cheeks. Oh, this is an amazing moment.

"What is happening!" Garrick bounces back into a fighting position as the crawling figure fades away. The Noble Guards are thoroughly on guard now.

"Ah yes, well, my spirit bond is not a fan of you trying to injure me, Garrick. See what you did? Couldn't control yourself as per usual." I toss the axe back and he catches it easily.

"Then don't say stupid things that require an axe to fix. And ..." Garrick looks at Nesi with some reservations. "My apologies, my lady...that you're stuck with this prissy peacock."

"What an entrance!" Jalnor calls from behind us, and I am now very aware that my father and Jalnor are observing this interaction. "I like this guy," Jalnor says, his smile contrasting Garrick's confusion.

"Well, as entertaining as that was, this visit is far from joyous, I'm assuming, to call us in the middle of the night." The gravity of the situation crashes back into me with a roaring vengeance, wiping the smile from my face.

"You're right, my King." My voice turns heavy. He takes me in—the less than put-together Captain of the Guard—and his face goes grim. "First, I should make some introductions. Nesi from the Night Court, Jalnor my dearest friend, and Father, please meet the King of the Day Court, Timas, the Noble Guard, and the ever so delightful Garrick, brother to the Queen."

"Pleased to meet you all, and you again, Nesi," Timas inclines his head in a respectful gesture as he speaks.

"Pleasure to see you again, Your Majesty." Nesi bows.

Father walks up and bows deeply in front of Timas. "Your Majesty. I am humbled to meet you, and I am so grateful you have been such a good friend to my son all these years." He stands, his face full of genuine gratitude.

"Your Majesty." Jalnor bows. "I have heard many stories from Milori." I shoot him a glare—Timas hardly needs another excuse to toss me around, and Jalnor sharing stories is only going to make it worse."

"All good things," I quickly say, flashing him my most charming grin. He lifts an eyebrow, unimpressed—but not truly concerned. He knows I wouldn't let anything damaging slip.

"Please, everyone come inside. I have some food and drink prepared, though forgive me, Your Majesty, it is not to courtly standard." Jalnor says as he puts his hand out to show everyone in.

"We are going to talk about that," Timas whispers to me as he stares me down. Our talk is going to hurt, I can feel it. "Thank you, Jalnor, for your hospitality." And we all head into the cottage.

"Patrol the area and stay alert. There are people on this island who wish us harm," I say to the Noble Guard, and they nod in understanding taking off in various directions.

The cottage is cramped with everyone inside, and the shift in tone has changed drastically from our warm greeting. Somehow Jalnor manages to find enough seats for everyone and my father bustles about, pouring tea for our guests.

"So, explain," Timas says without preamble, and I do.

"So you're telling me there is an ancient being that is being held captive by a secret Fae organization that ensures magical abilities are only inherited by noble families?" Timas questions, his voice carefully controlled despite the shock I can see in his eyes.

"Correct," I acknowledge.

"An entire system based on lies," he says finally, his voice dangerously quiet. "Generations of Fae denied their rightful powers, all to maintain the privilege of a select few."

"The Keepers would argue they prevented another civil war," my father says, not convinced of his own words.

"Perhaps," Timas concedes. "But that decision wasn't theirs alone to make. It should have been brought before the entire Fae council, the people. How has there been no history recorded that even I, the king, know nothing about this?" I can tell he is wrestling through the implications of a secret organization.

"What matters now," Nesi interjects, refocusing our conversation, "is that Soren cannot be allowed to find the Phoenix first. His method of unbinding would cause catastrophic damage, possibly to both Courts." Everyone nods in agreement.

"And yet, can we truly argue for maintaining this unjust system?" Timas asks, the question hanging heavy in the air.

"No," I say firmly. "But neither can we risk Soren's chaotic approach. We need to understand the proper unbinding ritual, if there is one, before making any decisions. Which means we need to find it first."

Garrick, who has been uncharacteristically quiet, finally speaks up. "So our plan is to find this mummified bird before the megalomaniac does, while also avoiding a secret society of noble women who have been maintaining the status quo for millennia?" He grins broadly. "Sounds like fun."

"Your definition of fun remains concerning," I tell him in a flat tone, though his enthusiasm has an oddly reassuring effect. Some things never change, even when the world is being turned upside down.

"We should leave immediately," Timas decides, rising to his feet. "Each moment we delay gives both Soren and the Keepers more time to act."

"I'm coming with you," my father insists, as he stands too. "I can guide you to the exact location."

I start to protest—the danger is too great for him—but the determination in his eyes stops me. This is his chance to help my mother, to finally take action after centuries of silent support. Who am I to deny him that?

"Very well," I agree. "But you stay with the group at all times."

We all file out of the cottage, preparing ourselves for the fight ahead.

"And to think, we came all this way to fight a bunch of Fae noblewomen. We could have done that back home and not endured the flight over here," Garrick mumbles and I cast him a side eye.

"You poor dear. Was your delicate Orc constitution bothered by the short flight? Should they have carried you over their shoulder to spare your tender feelings? Perhaps next time you can be tied up in a rope and dragged through the air. Far more dignifying." I can't resist the familiar banter despite the gravity of our mission. We laugh and plan our mission, speaking in shorthand and referencing old adventures. I catch my father's eye and catch a bittersweet look. Perhaps he sees what I really found in Sonas, the family I never had here.

As the Noble Guard discusses who is carrying Garrick and other minimal decisions, Nesi comes up beside me placing her hand on my arm. When I look into her beautiful face I see a spark of something.

"Is this your life? In Sonas?" Nesi asks, observing our inter-action. I glance at Garrick, who insults Timas with that careful edge—never quite disrespecting the king, yet perfectly willing to call out his sister's bondmate. They glare and laugh, showing a familial love that only time can create. Turning back to her I see the longing in her eyes.

"Yes," is all I can say because this scene must seem odd to her. "Everything alright?" I ask, turning to face her more fully.

"Your family," she says softly. "Not just your father, but Timas and Garrick—the way you are with them." Her words come in fragments, as if she's still piecing together what she sees.

"They're important to me," I acknowledge.

"I see that." She hesitates. "It's different from how things work in the Night Court. There's a warmth here, a casualness that we don't have."

"Well considering you have been fighting for your existence in the Shrouded forest for centuries, it's unsurprising that the Night Court nobility would tend toward the formal," I try to sympathize. "But that doesn't mean there isn't love in the Night Court," I add.

"No, of course there is love," she says, her eyes finding mine. "But it does make me wonder what it would be like to be part of this." She gestures to the group—to Timas consulting with my father, to Garrick and Jalnor comparing weapon preferences, to the easy flow of conversation between people who have just met but are connected through me.

Her voice drops lower, hesitant. "What Jalnor said yesterday morning about Neeve valuing me as her spymaster, but maybe not in the way..." She pauses, choosing her words carefully. "The Night Court values what I can do, the shadows I can command, the information I can gather. But here, with your friends, with you—it feels different. They see *you*, not just what you can do for them."

A fleeting sadness clouds her features. "I've never known what that might be like. Neeve has always shown me some affection, but she has carried a heavy burden, and the affection of family such as this is missing. What would it be like to be valued for myself, not just my abilities?"

The implication takes my breath away. Is she considering life in Sonas?

"Don't think this means you're choosing between your duty and me," I say, taking her hands in mine. "If I need to join the Night Court to be with you, I will. In a heartbeat."

She studies me, that calculating look I've come to adore. "So willing to leave the family you spent centuries building?"

"I'm not leaving them," I correct her gently. "Timas, Emilia, Garrick—all of them will celebrate this. Because after all this time, I've finally found my other half in you. And true family? You don't walk away from them, even if they do have a flair for the dramatic.

A tear spills down her cheek, catching me by surprise. I brush it away with my thumb, my heart hammering against my ribs.

"You are exactly what I didn't know I needed," she whispers.

I don't hold back. I lean in and capture her lips with mine, pouring everything I feel into the kiss—all the certainty, all the promise, all the future I see before us. The bond pulses between us, stronger than ever, and I know with absolute clarity that this is exactly where I'm meant to be.

"They're cute." Jalnor says from behind me, breaking the moment though I don't stray from her gaze.

"Cute! There is nothing cute about the pretty boy finally picking a woman." Garrick's booming voice cuts through the air. "Though it will be immensely enjoyable to watch all those noble ladies who've been vying for his attention for decades keel over when they find out he has a spirit bond."

"You enjoy drama far too much," I throw back, but can't help my smile.

Timas narrows his eyes at me. "Did you know about this before you left Sonas?"

I try to mask my expression, but fail miserably, and Timas shakes his head. "You know Emilia is going to kill you when she finds out you knew before you left and didn't tell her."

He's right, she'll be furious. I glance at Nesi, who watches our exchange with those perceptive eyes. The corner of her mouth twitches upward, clearly enjoying the prospect of me getting in trouble.

"Oh, speaking of my sister." Garrick pulls out a paper from the bag at his waist. "She sent this." He hands me a neatly folded note with her seal on the back.

"Why didn't she ask me to bring it?" Timas asks, his brow furrowing.

"Because you were all busy doing 'King things' as she put it." Garrick smirks as Timas sulks beside him.

I break the seal and unfold the letter. I adore Emilia. She has fae messenger orbs at her disposal but still chooses to write her letters.

Milori,If you manage to get yourself killed before I see you safely back to be the godfather to our child I will personally kill you myself. You promised to spoil them rotten and I plan on holding you to it. This little one deserves to know you. Come home in one piece—all of you. They have been a mess since you left.

With love, Emilia

P.S. Garrick insisted on coming despite his dislike for being cradled like a baby. Try not to tease him too mercilessly.

"Too late for that last part," I murmur, feeling Nesi close beside me as she reads over the letter, her presence warm at my side.

"I think I'm going to like that woman," she says, her voice warm with amusement.

"Time to go," Timas announces, straightening to his full height. "Solran will stay behind with Jalnor to gather loyal villagers. I fear this may take more than we have at our disposal. Garrick, you will go with Ilmon." Ilmon's face blanches, but he nods his agreement with the King.

"I'll take my father," I say, moving to stand beside him. Without noble blood, he has no wings, and since he's determined to come, this way I can keep an eye on him.

Garrick groans audibly, staring down Ilmon with narrowed eyes. "You will keep your hands here and here," he demonstrates, pointing to his back and knees. "And don't you dare think about dropping me. I will take you with me." His voice rumbles like distant thunder, while Ilmon's face transforms from pale to mortified.

Jalnor nearly doubles over laughing. "Have fun," he calls to Garrick, earning a glare I thought was strictly reserved for me. A burst of laughter escapes me, and Garrick's famous scowl swivels in my direction.

"I hate you," he mutters, his massive frame rigid with indignation. "All of you." He stands stiffly in front of Ilmon, looking for all the world like a man preparing for execution rather than flight.

Unfolding my wings I take a deep breath in. Father is very compliant with every instruction I give him as I hold him and take off in the air.

The group of us makes a sight to behold as we fly through the sky. My father clings to me, his arms wrapped securely around my shoulders as he takes in the sprawling expanse of Manthana below.

"Oh my," he breathes, wonder filling his voice as he gazes down at the island.

"Have you ever flown with Mother?" I ask.

A wistful smile crosses his face. "A few times, early in our relationship. But then after a time, she was unable to take to the sky. The amount of energy it took her to maintain the bindings is great. She has not flown in centuries."

The words strike my heart hard. What she has given up to guard the Phoenix is unbelievable, but even more unbelievable is that she has done it willingly.

The cliffs come into view as my father points at an overhang that sits high above the ocean. Whatever waits for us there is about to change our lives forever. I'm grateful for Timas and the others, for the rare moment of ease. But comfort won't save my mother. Won't save the Fae. The real danger is still ahead, and it's time to face it—to do what I was born for.

Chapter 17

Nesi

The western cliffs of Manthana rise before us, jagged stone teeth jutting up from the ocean. Wind gusts against my wings as we approach. Milori flies beside me, his father held securely in his arms, while Timas leads our group. Even from this distance, I can sense something powerful resonating from within the stone, a strange feeling like nothing I have ever felt before.

"There," Farin points to a narrow ledge halfway up the cliff face, barely visible unless you're specifically looking for it. "That's where I saw your mother disappear." His voice is muffled by the wind but it carries easily enough since I am so close to Milori.

Timas signals and we all descend, wings folding away as we land on the precarious outcropping. The ledge is wider than it appeared from a distance, but still uncomfortably narrow. Waves crash against rocks hundreds of feet below, the sound echoing up the cliff face.

"The entrance must be concealed," I observe, studying the seemingly solid rock wall before us. My shadows stir beneath my skin, responding to something beyond the stone.

Milori releases his father, who immediately approaches the cliff face, running his hands along the rough surface. "It was here, I'm certain of it."

While they search, I close my eyes, allowing my senses to extend through the shadows. There's a thinness here, a place where darkness flows differently—not quite a physical opening, but something else. Something magical.

"Here," I say, opening my eyes and pointing to a section of stone that looks ordinary. "There's a passage beyond this wall, hidden by magic."

Garrick snorts skeptically. "And how exactly do we get through solid rock?"

"It's not solid," I explain, summoning a tendril of shadow to probe the barrier. "It's an illusion, but a complex one—tied to blood or essence recognition, most likely."

Timas steps forward, studying the area I've indicated. "Can you breach it?"

"I can try," I say, focusing my power. "But it might be wiser to let me scout ahead first."

Milori's brow furrows with concern. "Alone? That's too dangerous."

"My shadows can move through spaces others can't," I explain, meeting his worried gaze. "And I'm less likely to trigger defences if I'm alone."

Timas considers this for a moment, then nods. "Go. But observe only. Don't engage unless absolutely necessary."

I can see Milori wants to protest, but he knows I'm right. This is what I do, what I've trained for centuries to perfect. I place my hand on his arm, feeling the warmth of his skin beneath my fingers. "I'll be careful."

His hand covers mine. "You better be."

I begin to gather the shadows around me like a cloak, preparing to approach the wall.

"Sweet mercy!" Garrick exclaims, taking an involuntary step backward as darkness begins to swirl around my form. "Is she melting? She's actually melting!"

"Shadow walking," Milori explains with a hint of pride in his voice. "A rare ability, even in the Night Court."

Garrick's face contorts into a mixture of fascination and horror. "That's not natural. She's turning into actual shadows." He grips his axe handle tighter, though not in a threatening way—more like a child clutching a comforting toy.

"Says the man who can bench press a boulder," Milori retorts with a smirk.

I ignore their banter as I approach the wall, pressing my palms against the stone and feeling the resistance of the illusion. Then I let my form dissolve partially, becoming less substantial as I merge with the darkness. It's a sensation I've never been able to adequately describe—like becoming mist while maintaining consciousness, like existing in multiple places at once. I'm solid but malleable. The gift that terrifies all, my ability to disappear.

"That is the most unsettling thing I've ever seen," I hear Garrick mutter behind me as I begin to fade. "And I've watched Timas eat breakfast."

The barrier resists at first, ancient magic pushing against my intrusion. But shadows find their way through even the smallest cracks, and soon I'm slipping through the enchantment, reforming on the other side. The last thing I hear before passing through completely is Garrick asking Milori, "She can pull herself back together, right? That's definitely a thing she can do? If not, unfortunate for you, huh?"

The passage beyond is bathed in an eerie orange glow that resembles fire, but doesn't flicker or waver like natural flame. It emanates from symbols carved into the stone walls, pulsing with a steady rhythm that reminds me of a heartbeat. The tunnel slopes downward, curving deeper into the cliff.

I follow it with care, merging with the shadows to move unnoticed. The magic here is older than anything I've encountered before. It feels alive somehow, aware in a way that makes my skin prickle. I wonder if it is the magic or the Phoenix. The tunnel curves as it descends deeper into the cliff, the orange glow intensifies, and the air grows warmer, drier.

The tunnel opens suddenly into a vast chamber. I pause at the threshold, my breath catching at the sight before me. The circular room is massive, carved directly from the cliff's heart. Glowing red symbols pulse across the floor in intricate patterns, creating a web of light that seems to breathe with power. The walls are lined with alcoves containing ancient texts and artifacts, and seven robed figures stand in formation around the chamber's perimeter—the Keepers, I presume. Deep red robes, accented by long, vivid red sashes. The trim is dark—perhaps black—standing in sharp contrast to the red fabric.

But they aren't what steals my attention. It's what sits at the chamber's centre that draws my gaze and holds it. Atop a raised dais of black stone floats a mummified bird. Old wrappings that look worn and frayed with time. Parts of the bird peek out from the bindings showing feathers torn and old. A pulsing field of orange magic encases it, impossible to touch if I were to guess. Even from this distance, I can see the intricate binding spells that contain it—hundreds of magical threads woven into an impenetrable cage. The Phoenix. It must be.

One of the Keepers, standing closest to the entrance, appears frailer than the others. She leans heavily on a staff, her breathing laboured, but her posture determined. That must be Milori's mother. Based on the information of her being rather ill it would make the most sense.

I've seen enough. Time to report back.

I begin to retreat when a voice cuts through the chamber. "We have a visitor, sisters."

The central figure—taller than the others, with a more elaborate red sash than those worn by her companions—raises her hand, and a wave of power surges through the room.

My shadows are ripped away, forcing me back into solid form and stealing my breath. I drop into a defensive stance, cursing silently at being discovered for a second time in two days. This is a humbling experience I didn't need.

"A shadow walker," the leader observes, her voice cold and measured. "From the Night Court, no doubt. Queen Neeve grows bold, sending her spies directly to our sacred space."

The phrasing catches my attention: *our* sacred space, not *the* sacred space. This subtle distinction confirms what I've suspected since Neeve's hesitation when assigning me this mission. There are multiple sites, multiple bound beings. Her careful wording, her insistence that I gather information rather than take direct action all makes sense now. Neeve knew more than she revealed, as she always does. Her words and reactions are never without purpose.

A familiar doubt settles in my chest. After centuries of service, I still stand at the periphery of her confidence. I push the thought aside. Now is not the time for wounded pride. The woman before me and what she protects take precedence.

"I mean no harm," I say, keeping my voice level even as I calculate potential escape routes. "I'm here at the request of Milori, son of Lavera."

A visible reaction ripples through the Keepers at this. The ill woman I suspected was Milori's mother straightens, despite her obvious pain, and her eyes widen.

"Milori? He's here?" The hope and fear in her voice are equally palpable. Her gaze shifts to the other robed figures giving away how nervous she is.

"He and others wait outside," I confirm, watching the leader carefully. "Including King Timas of the Day Court."

This causes greater alarm among the women. The leader's expression hardens. "So the King himself comes to interfere with matters beyond his understanding." The annoyance and disgust is evident and I wonder if she will talk that way to his face.

"Perhaps it's time he understood," I suggest, keeping my voice calm and measured. "The secrets you've kept affect all Fae. If you're truly concerned about Soren's attempts to unbind the Phoenix, then allies might serve your cause better than more enemies."

I watch her face carefully, noting how my mention of Soren unsettles them. Several women exchange worried glances, their composure slipping just enough to reveal their fear. The leader's eyes dart to her sisters, a silent communication passing between them that tells me more than words could.

Suggesting an alliance with the King isn't entirely honest, but some deceptions are necessary in war. The Phoenix, and all our futures, hang in the balance.

Looking over at a younger woman the leader says, "Bring them in," She nods and moves swiftly toward the entrance. "It seems we have much to discuss."

I remain where I stand, not willing to turn my back on these women. Their power feels different from what I'm accustomed to. Something binds these women together, something very old, it's like a heavy weight only time can truly understand. Very different to the feeling of my own power.

The Keeper returns moments later with our group. Timas enters first, his regal presence filling the chamber, followed by Milori whose eyes land on me, but he doesn't visibly relax until he sees his mother. A mix of emotions seem to whirl in his eyes but he remains on guard in this room surrounded by old magic. The two royal guards enter next, flanking Garrick whose hand rests casually on his axe as he surveys the room with practiced precision. Farin is the last to enter. The moment he sees Lavera, his steps falter, his shoulders going rigid. A flicker of something—relief, fear—shadows his face.

"Lavera," he says, hastening his steps, but the leader raises her hand and an invisible force halts him mid-step. He grunts at the force that holds him but his eyes never waver from Lavera, and I can see the will it is taking for her not to race to his side. A whisper of his name echoes through the chamber.

"You will remain where you are," she commands, and I see the anger flash in Milori's eyes at this treatment of his father.

"Release him now," Milori demands, stepping forward with his hands clenched at his sides. The air around him shimmers with heat, and I notice small flames beginning to dance between his fingers. "He's done nothing but love her while you've been slowly killing her with your sacred duty."

As Milori's anger grows, something unexpected happens. The mummified Phoenix on the dais pulses brighter, the orange magic surrounding it flickering in rhythm with Milori's flames. The symbols on the floor beneath it begin to glow more intensely, responding to his presence.

The leader shifts her attention to Milori, her expression calculating as she notices the Phoenix's reaction. "Control yourself, Captain. Your fire may be impressive in the Day Court, but here, in the heart of our power, it would be unwise to test the limits of your abilities against ours." Her eyes dart between Milori and the increasingly responsive Phoenix.

Milori doesn't back down, the flames growing more intense as the Phoenix's energy seems to reach out toward him in glowing tendrils. "I've spent my entire life controlling myself. Perhaps it's time to see what happens when I stop."

Timas places a restraining hand on Milori's shoulder, though his own expression remains hard as he addresses the leader. "We did not come here seeking conflict, but neither will we tolerate the mistreatment of our people."

Timas steps forward, his power crackling subtly around him as he addresses the leader. "I am Timas, King of the Day Court. I would like to know who addresses me, and by what authority you hold one of my subjects against his will."

The leader straightens, matching his royal bearing with her own authority. "I am Merida, the High Guardian of the Keepers of Unity. We serve a purpose that predates your throne, Your Majesty, and transcends Court boundaries."

"Release my father," Milori demands, his hand flexing at his side.

"Your father is in no danger unless he interferes with our sacred duty," Merida responds coldly. "A duty your mother has honourably fulfilled for centuries."

During this exchange, I begin slowly merging with the shadows again, preparing to position myself strategically around the chamber. But before I can fully disappear, Merida's eyes snap to me.

"Do not attempt to use your shadows here, shadow walker," she says, her face turning red with anger. "Every flicker of movement in this chamber channels through us. There is nowhere you can hide that we cannot sense."

I pause, genuinely surprised. Few can detect my shadows when I'm actively controlling them. This woman's power is considerable, but if she is somehow connected to all elemental beings perhaps she can sense the shadows because of the leviathan.

Timas steps forward again, drawing Merida's attention. "We know about the Phoenix. We know about the binding of elemental beings to control the distribution of power among our people. What I do not understand is by what right your organization made this decision without the knowledge or consent of the Fae council."

"By the right of necessity," Merida retorts. "You cannot comprehend the chaos that would ensue if these beings were freed. The civil war that divided our people would seem like a minor disagreement compared to what would follow."

"You don't know that," Milori argues, his gaze fixed on the mummified Phoenix. "You're maintaining a system built on lies and manipulation, all to keep power in the hands of nobility."

"We maintain peace," the leader counters, turning her attention directly to Timas. "As a king, surely you understand the necessity of order, Your Majesty. Would you risk the lives of thousands, perhaps millions of your subjects, for idealistic notions of fairness? The noble houses have maintained stability for centuries precisely because they are equipped to handle such power responsibly."

Her voice grows more passionate as she continues. "The common Fae lack the training, the lineage, the inherent discipline that comes with noble upbringing. Power seeks worthiness, and the current system ensures it flows to those prepared to wield it. If these beings were freed to choose new masters regardless of Court alignment, regardless of existing alliances or borders—can you imagine the chaos? Untrained commoners suddenly gifted with abilities they cannot control? The resulting conflict would destroy everything both Courts have built."

I observe the subtle shift in her rhetoric, how she appeals to Timas as a fellow authority figure while revealing her deeply ingrained belief in noble superiority. Despite her talk of peace, her true concern seems to be maintaining the power structure that benefits those already in control.

Lavera stands to the side as the conversation of duty continues, but I can see the idealistic view she had for the keepers doesn't align fully. She hasn't spoken, but I can see the conflict raging within her—devotion to her cause warring with love for her family. Her gaze repeatedly moves between her husband, still frozen in place, and her son who stands tall beside his king, and then back to her leader.

In a brief moment of quiet between Timas and Merida, Lavera steps forward, placing herself between the leader and Farin. Her movements are pained but deliberate.

"High Guardian," she addresses her superior, her voice strained but clear. "I have served the Keepers faithfully for centuries. I've given everything to our cause. Perhaps it's time we consider a different approach."

The leader's expression hardens. "This is not the time for doubt, Guardian Lavera."

"But it is the time for wisdom," Lavera counters. "King Timas is no enemy of peace. What if instead of opposing him, we work together? Share our knowledge, find a solution that doesn't require such sacrifice?" She gestures toward the Phoenix. "Perhaps there's a middle path."

"There is no middle path," the leader speaks with authority. "You know this. The bindings must be maintained at all costs."

"At all costs?" Lavera repeats, her voice suddenly stronger. "Even at the cost of our souls? Our families? I've spent my entire life serving the Keepers," she continues, turning to face Milori and Farin. "I believed in our cause, that maintaining the bindings was necessary to prevent catastrophe." She takes a laboured breath. "But I've watched my son suffer for that belief. I've sacrificed my marriage, my family, my very life force to uphold a system I never fully understood."

"Lavera," Merida warns, but Milori's mother continues.

"No. I've earned the right to speak." She straightens despite her obvious pain. "What if we're wrong? What if in our fear of change, we've perpetuated an injustice that was never necessary? The Phoenix chose Milori despite our bindings. It recognized him as worthy when he was barely more than a child. What does that tell us about the wisdom of these beings compared to our own?"

The room falls silent, the implications of her words hanging heavy in the air. The glowing symbols on the floor pulse more rapidly, as if responding to the tension.

"Touching," a familiar voice calls from a shadowed alcove at the far side of the chamber. "Truly, I'm moved by this family reunion and philosophical debate."

My blood runs cold as a figure steps into the light. Soren is tall, elegantly dressed in Night Court fashion. Gone are the rough clothes of the common people. He steps into the light, bearing all the arrogance he can muster. He is no longer pretending to be the saviour of the people.

"But I'm afraid I'll have to cut it short," he continues smoothly. "The Phoenix and I have a long-overdue appointment."

Merida's face drains of colour. "How did you find this place? How did you breach our defences?"

Soren smiles, the expression never reaching his eyes. "You'd be surprised what secrets people will share when properly motivated. Or perhaps you wouldn't. After all, your entire organization is built on keeping secrets, isn't it?"

The Phoenix pulses between them, its orange glow illuminating, while faces set with determination and fear. Milori shifts almost imperceptibly closer to me, his stance protective, ready for whatever comes next. My heart hammers against my chest at the fight that inevitably will consume this chamber. Timas stands tall, regal and unflinching, a true King, ready to fight. Garrick grips his axe tighter.

Behind Soren, his followers wait: Day and Night Court Fae united in their misguided quest, ready to unleash chaos in the name of freedom. Before us, the Keepers stand in their ancient formation.

And in the middle, the bound Phoenix. Whatever happens next will change everything—for Milori, for both Courts, perhaps for all Fae.

The fate of our world hangs in perfect, terrible balance, waiting for the first move that will shatter centuries of careful control. And somehow, I find myself at the centre of it all, bound to a man whose destiny is intertwined with an ancient power beyond my understanding. A man I've come to care for more deeply than I ever thought possible. A man I will protect with my life.

Soren steps forward, his gaze fixed on the mummified Phoenix. "Now," he says, his voice soft but carrying to every corner of the chamber, "shall we begin?"

Chapter 18
Milori

The chamber pulses with ancient magic as Soren steps fully into the light, his followers fanning out behind him. Their faces are a mix of determination and awe as they take in the mummified Phoenix. My blood boils at the sight of him, so smug and self-assured.

"You have no idea what you're meddling with," Merida snaps, her voice sharp with authority. The other Keepers shift into defensive positions around the Phoenix, their red robes rippling with the movement.

Soren's lip curls into a condescending smile. "I understand perfectly well what I'm doing. Far better than you might think, High Guardian." He gestures toward the bound Phoenix. "That magnificent creature was never meant to be imprisoned. Its power is meant to be claimed by those strong enough to take it."

His eyes gleam with naked ambition as he stares at the Phoenix. He truly believes he'll absorb its power once it's freed. The arrogance is staggering.

"Like you?" I challenge, stepping forward. The heat building inside me responds to the Phoenix's pulsing energy, both calling to each other. "You think you're worthy of claiming its power for yourself?"

Out of the corner of my eye I can see Mother's face pale as she watches the reaction between me and the Phoenix, the orange glow strengthening with each word I speak.

"You are deeply misled about the nature of the Phoenix," Merida interjects sharply. "It is not some tame beast waiting to grant power to whoever releases it."

"The Phoenix doesn't choose based on ambition or greed," Though her voice is strained, Mother speaks with clarity. "It seeks those with the capacity to wield fire responsibly, for the greater good."

Soren's followers exchange uncertain glances at this. A murmur ripples through their ranks—the first sign of doubt I've seen from them.

"Lord Soren," a younger woman from Soren's group steps forward hesitantly. "You said we were fighting to restore the natural order. That all Fae should have equal access to power, not just nobles."

"And so you shall," Soren assures her without taking his eyes off the Phoenix. "Once I control the Phoenix's power, I'll ensure it's distributed...appropriately."

Merida lets out a humourless laugh. "You fool. The Phoenix cannot be controlled. Not by me, not by you, not by anyone. It's a primordial being with a will of its own."

She turns to address Soren's followers directly. "Is this what you were promised? That this man would seize an ancient power and then generously share it with you? Look at him." She points at Soren's fine Night Court attire, at his calculating expression. "He has lied to you from the beginning. He doesn't seek equality. He seeks domination."

Timas steps forward, his presence commanding attention even in this charged atmosphere. "The Night Court was exiled for five hundred years," he reminds everyone, his voice carrying to every corner of the chamber. "Soren lost status, power, and likely loved ones during that time. His hatred runs deep."

Some of Soren's Day Court followers shift uncomfortably, looking at their leader with new suspicion.

"This has nothing to do with ancient grudges," Soren insists, though the lie is transparent in his voice. "This is about justice. About restoring what was taken from all Fae."

"Then why not work with us?" I challenge. "If your cause is just, why the secrecy? Why manipulate these people with half-truths?"

I feel a surge of strength as I step closer to the dormant Phoenix. Every time my emotions spike, the binding around it flickers again.

Mother notices. "Milori," she warns, "control yourself."

But Soren sees it too. His eyes gleam with triumph as he looks between me and the Phoenix. "The proof stands before you all," he announces, gesturing toward me. "Behold a true Phoenix master—one whose power the Keepers have tried to suppress."

He turns to his followers, his voice rising with practiced persuasion. "I told you of his connection to the Phoenix, how the Guardians and nobility have hidden the truth even from their own. Captain Milori, son of a Guardian, kept ignorant of his true nature!" His voice echoes dramatically against the stone walls. "More proof of their deception! More evidence that they fear what would happen if we truly understood our own potential!"

Some of his followers nod, their resolve strengthening. Others still look uncertain, their gazes moving between their leader and the bound Phoenix.

"Enough talk," Merida interrupts. "You will leave this sacred chamber immediately, or we will remove you by force."

Soren's expression darkens. "I've come too far to be turned away now. The Phoenix will be freed today, one way or another."

"You don't understand what you're doing," Mother pleads, her voice desperate. "Unbinding the Phoenix improperly will cause devastation beyond imagination. The backlash alone could kill everyone on this island."

This gives some of Soren's followers pause, fear flashing across their faces.

While Soren works to keep his followers' loyalty, Mother's attention has shifted entirely to Father, who remains frozen in Merida's magical grip.

"Release him!" Mother demands, her voice cracking with desperation as she looks at Father.

My heart twists at the raw pain in her voice. For all our complicated history, for all the secrets and absences, the love between my parents has never wavered. Even now, as the world crumbles around us, they reach for each other first.

Merida's attention divides between Soren's threat and Mother's plea, her concentration visibly wavering as she tries to maintain control of the increasingly chaotic situation.

"I'm OK," Father manages through gritted teeth, his eyes locked on Mother's weakened form. "I love you."

The sound of his voice, laden with decades of devotion and silent suffering, strikes something deep within me. This man stood by her through everything, loving her even when he couldn't understand her choices. What I once mistook for weakness was a different kind of strength altogether.

His words do something to Merida. For just a moment, her resolve falters, her expression flickering with unexpected doubt.

In that instant of distraction, Soren strikes.

He throws his hand forward, unleashing a blinding burst of light that momentarily blinds everyone in the chamber. In that instant of confusion, three of his noble followers—the few with elemental powers—strike. Ice shards, swirling wind, and chunks of stone fly toward the Keepers closest to the Phoenix.

"Together!" Merida shouts, and the Keepers move as one, each using their elemental affinities to counter the attacks. A Keeper with ice powers freezes the incoming wind into harmless crystals, while another diverts the flying stones with a wave of her hand. The coordinated defence speaks to centuries of preparation.

Mother races toward Father the moment he's free from Merida's hold, throwing herself in front of him as another attack comes their way. Her red hood falls back, revealing her exhausted face, but her hands ignite with golden flames. Even in her weakened state, she stands firm, her fire powers flaring to life as she becomes a living shield for her husband.

Timas reacts instantly, lightning not just crackling at his fingertips but arcing across his entire body. His eyes turn pitch black, streaks of lightning flashing across them like miniature storms. He unleashes a blinding bolt that splits into multiple tendrils, intercepting attacks aimed at one of the younger Keepers. The impact of his power shakes the very ground beneath us, stone cracking under the pressure of his raw elemental force. His display of power goes beyond what any normal noble should command, making me wonder if he too might be a master of something we don't yet understand.

"Protect the Phoenix!" he commands, his voice carrying unnaturally through the chaos, and Garrick is already moving, his massive axe cleaving through the air with deadly precision, forcing Soren's followers to retreat.

"Back to back, Captain!" Garrick calls to me, his eyes alight with battle fury as he positions himself to guard my flank.

"I've got your right!" I respond automatically, falling into our old combat rhythm. The memory of fighting alongside him this past year—battling to secure peace across the court and mountains—flashes through my mind, grounding me in the moment.

"Remember those three rebel nobles at the human farmstead?" I call over my shoulder, flames spiralling up my arms as I position myself. "Let's make this another clean sweep!"

"Ha!" Garrick barks, his axe already in motion. "I still say we should have killed that last one!" His words are challenging but his eyes hold the trust forged in countless battles.

I see Nesi move into the shadows, appearing and disappearing across the chamber. Two of Soren's followers drop unconscious before they even realize she's behind them.

The chamber erupts into chaos: magic flying in all directions, the ancient symbols on the floor pulsing erratically with each impact. Through it all, the Phoenix glows brighter, its bindings flickering as the battle rages around it.

I fight my way toward my parents, fire streaming from my palms to create a barrier between them and Soren's followers. Mother leans heavily against Father, her strength faltering.

"Get them out of here!" I shout to Ilmon, one of the Noble Guards who's just dispatched an attacker. He nods, moving swiftly to support Mother's other side.

"No," Mother resists, her eyes fixed on the Phoenix. "If Soren breaks the binding improperly—"

An explosion rocks the chamber, sending several fighters to their knees. Through the smoke, I see Soren approaching the dais, something ancient and crystalline in his hand, a ritual knife of some kind, its edge gleaming with blue fire.

"Stop him!" Merida screams, genuine terror in her voice.

I surge forward, flames erupting around me as I race toward Soren. The heat inside me builds to an almost unbearable intensity, the Phoenix responding to my proximity, to my determination.

Nesi appears at my side, shadows coiling around her arms as she throws her power toward Soren, the dark shadows becoming solid and restraining his arms. Fear flashes across his face—he hasn't seen her do this before.

Timas attacks from the other side, lightning arcing toward Soren.

But then—a Keeper moves, too fast, too reckless.

Merida steps forward, her own magic surging to reinforce the Phoenix's shield—but she miscalculates. Her defensive spell collides with Timas' attack, the energies clashing violently in midair. The shockwave staggers them both, forcing Nesi to pull back, her concentration breaking for just a moment.

A moment is all Soren needs.

His free hand rises, and a shield of dark energy absorbs the remnants of their disrupted attack.

"Too late," he says, his voice almost lost in the chaos.

He plunges the ritual knife into the orange webbing surrounding the Phoenix.

The effect is immediate and catastrophic. The orange field surrounding the Phoenix shatters like glass, fragments of ancient magic spraying outward in a deadly shower. The symbols on the floor erupt into blinding light, and a shockwave of pure energy knocks everyone to the ground.

Through the chaos and pain, I glimpse the mummified Phoenix. Its wrappings begin to crumble away, revealing desiccated feathers that suddenly ignite, not with natural fire, but with something more primal, more ancient.

"What have you done?" Merida screams at Soren, who stands transfixed by the spectacle, the ritual knife still clutched in his hand.

"I've freed it," he whispers, awe and hunger mixing in his voice. "Its power is mine to command now."

But the Phoenix doesn't turn to Soren. Instead, it rises from the dais, its burning gaze sweeping over the chamber until it fixes directly on me.

Heat unlike anything I've ever experienced floods through my body. I can't tell if the scream I hear is from me or someone else. My vision blurs, replaced by flames that consume everything. I hear Nesi screaming my name, feel her shadows trying to reach me through the inferno, but it's too late.

The Phoenix—ancient, powerful, and now unbound—surges toward me in a blinding flash of golden light. The last thing I see before the light consumes me is the horror on Soren's face as he realizes his terrible mistake.

Then fire takes me, and the world disappears in brilliant, burning gold.

Chapter 19

Nesi

Golden light floods the chamber. I raise my arm against the blinding illumination, instinct taking over. The shockwave of power throws me against the wall, my breath knocked from my lungs. When I can see again, I freeze.

Milori hovers above the ground, flames consuming him. But they don't burn—they only surround him, flickering like an untouchable shield. His eyes—those sea green eyes that looked at me with such tenderness just hours ago—now blaze with ancient fire. His body remains, but something else looks out from behind his gaze.

The Phoenix.

"Milori!" I scramble to my feet. My shadows rise unbidden, coiling around me. They don't burn away as they should against such heat. Instead, they dance with the flames from a distance, responding to them like old acquaintances.

The fire that would scorch anyone else merely warms my skin. The spirit bond pulses a living connection between us and I feel the ancient power coursing through him. Fear threatens to overwhelm me, but his constant presence stops me from doing anything drastic.

The flames surrounding him pulse in rhythm with his heartbeat. When he opens his mouth to speak, the voice that emerges is his, but it's layered with something ancient and terrifying.

"For over a millennium, I have been bound." The layered voice echoes through the chamber, making the stone vibrate. "Imprisoned by those who feared what true worthiness might reveal about themselves."

He turns, no, the Phoenix turns his body to face Merida and the other Keepers, who have fallen to their knees. With every movement, fire lingers in his wake—ghostly embers painting the air, tracing his path in fleeting, brilliant strokes.

"You call yourselves Keepers of Unity." The contempt in the Phoenix's voice burns as hot as its flames. "Yet what have you kept? Not balance. Not harmony. Only power. Only control."

Merida's face contorts with fear, though she struggles to maintain her dignity. "We prevented chaos. We maintained peace between the Courts."

"Peace built on lies is merely delayed war." Milori's body floats closer to Merida, the heat intensifying until sweat streams down her face. "How many worthy souls have lived and died, never knowing what they might have become? How many innocents suffered because power was granted by birth, not character?"

Across the chamber, Soren's followers scatter, fleeing toward the exit in terror. Only Soren remains, his expression a disturbing mixture of awe and naked hunger as he stares at Milori.

"Yes," he breathes, stepping forward with the ritual knife still clutched in his hand. "Show them the truth of their corruption. Then grant me the power to set things right."

Timas has pulled himself to his feet, lightning still crackling around his hands as he watches the scene unfold. Garrick stands beside him, axe ready but uncertainty clear in his posture—how does one choose to fight an ancient elemental being possessing the body of a friend?

Lavera clings to Farin, her fingers curling into his sleeve, knuckles white. Both of them stare at their son—motionless, tense, as if unsure whether to reach for him or recoil. Their grip on each other tightens, bodies rigid, caught between instinct and uncertainty. The frail Guardian looks even more diminished now, as if the Phoenix's release has drained what little strength she had left.

"Power is not a prize to be claimed." The Phoenix turns Milori toward Soren, and the flames surrounding him intensify. "It is a responsibility to be earned. You seek only to replace one tyrant with another: yourself."

Soren's arrogant expression falters. "I freed you. The power is mine by right of—"

"By right of what?" The Phoenix's laughter flows from Milori's mouth, sending chills down my spine. "You understand nothing of rights. Nothing of worthiness."

Milori's hand, and a column of fire erupts from the floor directly in front of Soren, forcing him to stumble backward. His fine Night Court clothes singe at the edges, his face contorted with shock.

My heart thunders in my chest as I watch Milori—or what was Milori—floating, wreathed in flames. Shadows pulse beneath my skin, responding to my fear. What if he never returns? What if the Phoenix consumes him completely?

Losing him is not an option. He sees beyond the shadows, beyond the barriers I've built, to the person underneath. No one has truly done that before. And now that I finally have him—I can't lose him before I've even had the chance to hold onto him.

"Release him, Ancient One. This vessel is not meant to contain your full power." Merida tries to rise to her feet, her voice shaking but resolute.

"You presume to lecture me on vessels?" The Phoenix's anger makes the chamber tremble, stones falling from the ceiling. "This one was born to carry my flame. His mother knew it and hid him away. She sent him to court where his power might seem less unusual. But you all perpetuated the system that made such deception necessary."

"We sought to protect the world," Merida insists. "To prevent the upheaval that would follow if powers were suddenly redistributed."

"You sought to protect yourselves." The Phoenix's contempt burns in Milori's eyes. "Your privileges and control."

As they argue, I edge closer, my shadows extending toward Milori. The spirit bond between us pulses faintly, still there despite the Phoenix's dominance. I reach for it, pushing my determination through that fragile connection.

I don't need words. I pour my intent through the bond—I will find you—and feel something stir in response. A flicker of Milori, buried beneath ancient fire but not extinguished.

The Phoenix continues its judgment, turning to address all present. "For centuries, I have watched through bound eyes. I have seen nobles who never should have wielded fire burn villages over petty slights. I have seen them incinerate those who questioned their authority. Meanwhile, children with natural affinity for flame died in accidents they could have controlled had they been given their rightful gifts. Healers who could have used gentle heat to save lives instead watched patients die while nobles used their powers for spectacle."

Golden light weaves through the air, revealing images of past injustices—suffering made visible. "Power corrupts most when given to those who hunger for it, rather than those born to bear its responsibility."

The fire surrounding him forms the shape of massive wings, stretching across the chamber. "The time for lies has ended. True balance will be restored. My brothers and sisters will be restored, and bring balance back to these lands."

Soren, seeing his chance for power slipping away, lunges forward with the ritual knife. "If you won't grant me what I'm owed, I'll take it!"

In a blur of motion too fast to track, the Phoenix turns. A concentrated blast of golden fire strikes Soren directly in the chest. His scream reverberates off the stone walls, a raw, primal cry of agony as the ancient flame consumes him from within. His body convulses mid-air, skin blistering and cracking as golden light pours from his eyes and mouth. The ancient knife clatters to the ground as he hits the wall with a sickening crack, sliding down to collapse in a heap, smoke rising from his charred flesh.

"You were never worthy," the Phoenix says coldly. "Your heart knows only hunger, never service."

Soren doesn't move again.

Sensing my chance in this moment of distraction, I call to my shadows, letting them envelop me completely. They intertwine with the flames in a way I've never experienced, neither fighting nor surrendering to each other.I move through the entwined shadows and light toward Milori, my path clear where others would find only consuming fire.

"The cycle begins anew," the Phoenix declares. "I will seek the worthy. I will bestow gifts based on character, not bloodlines. And those who have abused their borrowed power will find themselves diminished."

"And what of the Courts?" Timas asks, his voice steady despite the situation. "What of the peace we've built?"

"Peace built on justice endures," the Phoenix answers. "Peace built on oppression was never peace at all."

I reach the edge of the flames and pause, observing their behaviour. They part slightly as my shadows approach, drawn by the same recognition, the ancient connection between our powers. Inside that inferno is Milori. *My* Milori. And I will not lose him to an ancient being, no matter how just its cause might be.

Taking a breath, I step forward. The flames curl around me rather than burning me, my shadows weaving between them. The heat is intense but not painful, like standing near a hearth rather than within it. The Phoenix recognizes me, or perhaps it recognizes what I am to Milori.

"Milori," I call, my voice strangled by the intensity of the heat. "Milori, come back to me."

The Phoenix pauses, Milori's head turns toward my voice.

"You cannot reach him," the dual voice says, though something in its tone has changed. "He is one with the flame now."

"No." I force myself closer, shadows burning away faster than I can replenish them. "He is one with me."

My voice grows stronger as I continue to move forward. "I know you think you're delivering justice. Maybe you are. But you're doing it through a man who has suffered his entire life because of the very system you're condemning."

The flames around Milori flicker, hesitating.

"If you can access his memories, then you know what they did to him," I press on, wincing as fire sears my exposed skin. "You know how he was isolated, feared for powers he didn't understand. You know that his own mother wouldn't tell him the truth."

The Phoenix remains silent, watching me through Milori's eyes.

"And if you can feel his heart," I say with a quiet resolve. "then you know what he feels for me. What I feel for him."

I reach out, my hand trembling as it approaches the wall of flame surrounding his body. "I will go anywhere with him. Away from the Night Court, away from everything I've known. Because I love him."

The words seem to hang in the heated air between us, words I've never said to anyone, words I wasn't sure I was capable of feeling until I met him.

"Let him choose," I plead. "If he's truly your chosen vessel, then honour his will. Let him decide if this is how he wants your justice delivered."

For a moment, nothing happens. Then, slowly, the flames surrounding him begin to change. They don't diminish, but they shift. The fire parts before me like a curtain, creating a path directly to Milori's suspended form.

I don't hesitate. I walk forward, the flames parting around me like a curtain, fire and shadow dancing together in perfect harmony. When I'm close enough, I place my hand against his cheek. His skin radiates intense warmth beneath my palm. It's not painful, but alive with power.

"Milori," I whisper. "Come back to me."

His eyes, still blazing with ancient fire, meet mine. For an endless moment, I see no recognition there, only the ageless regard of the Phoenix.

Then something shifts.

"Nesi?" His voice emerges, just his voice, confused and pained.

Relief hits me hard, sharp and unexpected. "Yes. I'm here. Come back."

The flames surrounding us pulse once, twice, then begin to separate from Milori's body. The fire gathers above us, taking the form of an immense phoenix, its wings spread wide enough to span the chamber. It lets out a piercing cry that shakes the very foundations of the chamber, a sound of both freedom and warning.

For a moment, it hovers there, its burning gaze sweeping over everyone present. Then with a final shriek that sounds like a promise, it streaks toward the chamber's ceiling and disappears, leaving only a trail of golden embers floating in the air.

Milori's feet touch the ground as the last of the fire leaves him. His sea green eyes return, though flecks of gold remain, dancing like tiny flames in his irises.

His arms wrap around me, pulling me against him as the last of the Phoenix fire subsides. The relief hits me so hard my composure finally cracks. I cling to him, hands fisted in his shirt, my face pressed against his chest. Tears come without permission—the first I've shed in centuries. I feel the ancient presence recede, not disappearing but settling into some deeper place within him.

"You came back," I whisper against his chest, unable to mask the tremor in my voice. "You came back to me."

"Always," he promises, holding me tighter. "Always."

The chamber falls silent around us, no sound but our breathing and the occasional crack of settling stone. Everyone watches, stunned by what they've witnessed. The Phoenix has departed, but its mark remains. I can still see those flecks of gold dancing in Milori's eyes, a connection that will never fully disappear.

He pulls back just enough to look into my eyes, wonder and gratitude written across his face. "You said you loved me," he whispers, as if afraid that speaking the words too loudly might make them untrue.

I nod, a feeling I've never allowed myself before settling in my chest. "I do."

A smile breaks across his face, so bright it rivals the Phoenix flame. "I love you too," he says, pressing his forehead to mine. "More than I thought possible."

For this moment, despite the destruction around us, despite the questions and chaos that await, I let myself feel only the solid reality of him in my arms, alive and himself again. The battles to come can wait. For now, I have called him back from the fire, and he has returned to me.

And in a world filled with so much uncertainty, that is the only truth that matters.

Chapter 20

Miloti

The world slowly comes back into focus as the golden light recedes. My feet touch solid ground again as the Phoenix leaves me. My limbs feel strange, heavy yet somehow weightless, as if I've been unmade and pieced back together with something fundamentally altered. I blink, trying to orient myself in the chamber that now appears in sharp contrast. Everything looks more defined, the shadows the flickering light more vivid.

Without conscious thought, my arms reach for Nesi, pulling her against me. Her hands grip my shirt as she presses her face against my chest. I feel something wet through the fabric: tears. *From Nesi*. The shock of this nearly overwhelms me as I hold her tighter, protecting her as she finally allows herself this vulnerability.

"You came back to me," she whispers against my chest, her voice trembling.

"Always," I promise, cradling her head with one hand. My mind whirls with what happened.

Fire. Not my fire, but hotter and stronger. Flowing through every vein like liquid gold, filling spaces inside me I never knew existed. The Phoenix's consciousness flooding mine, its memories becoming mine, its righteous fury merging with my own. Centuries of watching, bound and powerless, as those who were never meant to wield fire corrupted its gift. Noble houses burning villages over petty disputes. The worthy passed over while the undeserving flourished.

And the Keepers. Always the Keepers with their secretive rituals, maintaining the prison while justifying control with honeyed words about peace and stability. The rage consumed me. It was the Phoenix's rage, absolutely, but also my own that I'd buried for centuries.

I would have surrendered completely. Would have given myself to that ancient will and watched it remake the world through cleansing fire. In those moments suspended between myself and the Phoenix, justice and vengeance seemed one and the same.

Then came Nesi's voice cutting through the roaring flames like a cool night breeze. "Come back to me." Three simple words that the Phoenix's fury couldn't burn away. Three words that offered something fire couldn't: a future. A choice. Love.

"Milori?" Nesi's voice pulls me fully back to reality, her dark eyes searching mine for any sign I'm still myself.

"Always," I say again, my voice rough but steady. "I'll always come back to you."

I breathe in the scent of her hair, allowing myself to simply feel the solid reality of her in my arms. The bond tightens, the tension pressing toward a breaking point—but this time, it feels different. No longer resisting, no longer fighting against itself. Instead, it settles, as if finally accepted. As if Nesi has finally accepted that this is worth holding onto, worth fighting for.

"You brought me back," I brush some hair from her eyes. "When I was nearly lost in the fire, your voice gave me an anchor."

She slowly lifts her face from my chest, damp streaks glistening on her cheeks. Her eyes, usually so guarded, now hold nothing back as she looks up at me. "I couldn't lose you. I can't lose you. You...you—." Her words falter, emotion overwhelming her practiced composure.

I place my hand along her cheek, rubbing it softly with my thumb. "I understand. We can talk later." She relaxes her shoulders, relief flooding her face. She isn't a person who freely shows her emotion, and to do so now is difficult.

Looking past her, I survey the chamber, now in partial ruin. Broken stone litters the floor, scorch marks streaking across ancient walls. Several Keepers remain kneeling, their faces ashen with shock. My gaze catches on Soren's body slumped against the far wall, smoke rising from what remains. The Phoenix's judgment echoes through me—a terrible but necessary justice.

Timas approaches with careful steps, concern etched on his face. "Milori?" he asks. "Is it you?"

"It's me," I confirm with a weak smile, not releasing Nesi. "The Phoenix has gone off to start a rebellion without us. Rude, really, after all we've been through together. Though I can't say

I miss having an ancient, temperamental firebird using my body as its personal puppet."

Relief washes over him. "Thank the sun." His gaze shifts to the empty dais where the mummified Phoenix once rested. "Though I'm not entirely sure what we just witnessed."

"Justice happened," Merida's voice cuts through the chamber, brittle with fury. She rises to her feet, dusting her singed and torn robes. "Or so you would call it. But you have no idea what you've unleashed."

Timas turns to her, his expression hardening. "I know exactly what was unleashed today. The truth." He surveys the Keepers with the cold authority that makes him such an effective king. "A truth your organization has suppressed for centuries."

"We maintained peace," Merida insists, though uncertainty flickers beneath her defiance. "We prevented chaos."

"You maintained a lie," Timas counters with the weight of his crown behind every syllable. "And now you will answer for it."

He gestures to the Noble Guard, who step forward. "Arrest them all," he commands. "They will be questioned thoroughly about the other elemental beings and the full extent of their organization."

Merida laughs, the sound hollow and bitter. "You think chains will make us speak? We have guarded these secrets for millennia, Your Majesty. Do what you will. We serve a higher purpose than any crown."

"We shall see," Timas replies with quiet confidence.

I give Nesi's waist a quick squeeze before reluctantly breaking our embrace to search for my parents. My heart nearly stops when I spot them huddled in a corner, Father supporting Mother's frail form as she leans against him. I cross the chamber in long strides, kneeling beside them on the debris-strewn floor.

"Mother," I take her thin hand, concerned by how cool her skin feels, so different from the warmth I remember from those rare childhood embraces. "Are you all right?"

Her eyes meet mine, widening slightly. "Your eyes," she whispers, lifting a trembling hand to my face. "They've changed."

"Gold flecks," Father whispers. "Like tiny flames dancing in the green."

Mother's lips curve into a smile, surprising me with its warmth. "The Phoenix has marked you," she says, her voice holding wonder rather than the fear I expected. "All these years, I was so afraid of what that might mean. But perhaps my fear blinded me to the true purpose and joy of it." Her eyes shine with something I've rarely seen directed at me: pride. "You were always meant for this. And I am proud of you, Milori."

The words strike me speechless. This simple admission—this pride in who I am rather than fear of what I might become—is something I've waited centuries to hear. I squeeze her hand, fighting a sudden tightness in my throat.

"Thank you," I try to swallow around the emotion rising. "That means more than you know." I take a breath, then add with a hint of my usual lightness, "And I'm still me. The Phoenix didn't take me. And before you ask, yes, being possessed by an ancient fire deity is exactly as uncomfortable as it looks. Not recommended as a vacation experience."

Her smile widens at my attempt at levity, the shadows of centuries of worry beginning to lift from her face.

"Thanks to your spirit bond," Mother acknowledges, her gaze shifting briefly to Nesi who has followed me. "She called you back from the brink. Not many would have had the courage to reach into Phoenix fire."

Nesi says nothing, but her hand touches my shoulder, her presence the strength I need.

"I'm sorry," I tell Mother, the words inadequate for everything they need to convey. "For not understanding. For resenting you when you were trying to protect me."

Her eyes fill with tears. "And I'm sorry for the secrets. For not finding a better way." She takes a laboured breath that catches halfway. "I convinced myself the binding was necessary. That the sacrifice was worth the greater good. But watching you there, seeing what it did to you—" Her voice breaks. "Perhaps we were wrong all along." I make a point not to agree with her. The guilt that has taken root in her face tells me this will be something she will think about for a very long time.

"How do you feel?" I ask, noticing that despite her exhaustion, some colour has returned to her cheeks.

She seems surprised by the question, her expression thoughtful. "Better, actually. Like something that was constantly draining me has stopped." Her hand presses against her chest in wonder.

"The Phoenix," I explain as understanding unfurls within me, knowledge that isn't mine yet somehow is. "When it broke free, it severed the connection that was feeding on your life force. It's given you back some of what the binding took."

Her eyes widen. "But how is that possible?"

"I'm not sure," I answer. "But something tells me that it will no longer be a problem." I glance at Father, whose face shines with hope that's been absent for centuries. "You'll still need time to heal, but maybe someday...maybe someday you can fly with Father again." Mother turns to face my father, a genuine smile brightening her face.

"I would love that," she says softly. "After all these years."

Father's arm tightens around her shoulders, his eyes bright with unshed tears. "Just like when we first met."

The moment stretches between us, decades of hurt not erased, but perhaps beginning to mend. It's a start, more than I'd dared hope for when I first returned to Manthana.

Timas approaches as the Noble Guard lead the Keepers away. Merida walks with her head high, refusing to look back. Whatever secrets she holds, she'll guard them fiercely.

"We should leave this place," Timas says, his gaze sweeping the chamber. "We need to return to the village and determine the state of it."

"And prepare for quite a few explanations," I add, rising to my feet. The thought of returning to normal life after what's happened seems impossible. Nothing will ever be the same again.

"It would be good to weed out any other rebel members, but I will send for more guards to deal with it."

Timas smiles as we head towards the exit. "Good, glad to see the Phoenix didn't take away your ability to do your job."

I laugh, grateful for the normalcy. "My King, may I remind you I can wield a fire phoenix now? I'm not so sure you want to take this on."

We both laugh. "I guess we will be testing out your new powers when we get back," Timas challenges.

"Great, more property damage. You know the staff gets mad at me, not you, when we do that," I grumble.

"As it should be. I am the King, after all," Timas says with his best kingly voice.

As we make our way through the tunnels, Garrick falls into step beside me. "So," he says, concern barely hidden beneath his gruff tone, "you got possessed by an ancient firebird and nearly burned everyone to cinders. How are you feeling?"

"Like I've been used as a teapot by a particularly enthusiastic fire deity," I reply with a wry smile. "My insides are still a bit singed, I think. But at least I got some fancy new eye decoration out of it." I gesture to my eyes.

He nods, clearly relieved, though he tries not to show it. "Good. Emilia would never forgive me if I let anything happen to you. She's counting on you to be there for the baby."

"You sound concerned, Garrick." I lift a corner of my mouth, trying not to tease, but the look on his face stops me.

"I'm not one for flowery words but...we've fought together. You've come to my aid, helped me get out of that disgusting prison...life wouldn't be the same without you," he says begrudgingly.

"Didn't realize you had such a soft heart, Orcy."

He rolls his eyes and looks like he is about to leave, but I stop him. "I'm glad to have you as a brother."

"I'm still the better looking one," I add, and he grins and punches me in the shoulder.

"Seriously! I was just possessed by a fire deity! Punching me? Really?" He laughs and walks ahead of us.

The atmosphere in our group is still strained, but the light conversation helps to release some of the tension. I look over my shoulder to see Nesi following behind. I turn and intertwine our hands as we close in on the exit.

As we emerge onto the cliff face, sunlight washes over us. The day is bright and clear, the sky an endless blue. How strange that the world can look so unchanged when everything has been irrevocably altered.

"The prisoners need to be secured," I say to the Noble Guard. "Take them to the old storehouse near the village square. Jalnor will know the place—solid stone walls, single entrance, easily guarded."

I turn to Ilmon. "Once they're secure, send a message to Captain Ferris. We'll need reinforcements to transport the Keepers back to Sonas for questioning. Also speak to Jalnor. He will connect you with my network on the island." The one I used to keep an eye on my parents. Timas nods in approval as I issue the orders.

"Yes, Sir," Ilmon replies with a sharp bow of the head.

I turn to my parents, Mother still leaning heavily on Father for support. "I'll carry Mother back to the cottage."

"And what about me?" Father asks with a raised eyebrow and a knowing smile. He likes to joke just as much as I do. "I'm not exactly equipped with wings, in case you've forgotten."

Before I can respond with something remarkably witty, Nesi steps forward. "I can carry you, sir."

Father's eyes widen slightly before a mischievous smile touches his lips. "Well now, isn't this something? Carried by my son's spirit bond. Quite the honour."

Mother manages a weak laugh. "Don't drop him, dear. I've grown rather attached to him over the centuries."

"I'll do my best," Nesi replies with that slight quirk of her lips that passes for her version of a smile.

I carefully lift Mother into my arms, surprised by how light she feels. The binding truly took its toll on her. She rests her head against my shoulder with a sigh that might be relief, or exhaustion, or both. "I love you, son. I will work hard to make up for all those missed years," she says as she lets her body relax and she drifts off on my shoulder.

Something tightens in my chest at her words. The simplicity of them. The promise they hold. After centuries of misunder-standing and distance, it seems almost impossible that things could change so completely in a single day. And yet they have.

With the prisoners secured between the guards, we take to the sky. My wings unfurl with a familiar rush of relief. There's nothing quite like the freedom of flight after being trapped underground. I cradle Mother carefully in my arms while Nesi handles Father with surprising gentleness, despite his ongoing commentary about "the privilege of being carried by a shadow walker."

Timas and the Noble Guard form a protective formation around us as we ascend.

Nesi flies beside me, her dark wings catching the sunlight, midnight blue ripples shimmering with an almost mesmerizing beauty. Without a word, she moves closer until our wingtips almost touch with each beat. An intimate gesture I appreciate greatly.

Below us, the island of Manthana spreads out like a painting, a beauty to behold. Somewhere out there, the Phoenix soars free for the first time in centuries, seeking its siblings, setting right ancient wrongs.

As we bank toward the cottage, I catch Nesi watching me, her expression thoughtful.

"Ready for whatever comes next?" I ask her.

A small smile touches her lips. "With you? Yes."

It's a simple answer, but it carries the weight of a promise. Whatever chaos the Phoenix's freedom brings, we'll face it together. For now, that's enough.

Chapter 21

Nesi

The cottage comes into view below us, a small haven of calm in the midst of chaos. I adjust my grip on Farin, who has been surprisingly quiet for the last few minutes of our flight. His earlier commentary about "the honour of being carried by a shadow walker" has given way to thoughtful silence.

"We're nearly there," I tell him as we begin our descent. He nods, eyes fixed on Milori ahead of us, carrying his mother's frail form in his arms.

The gentle slope of the meadow rises to meet us as we land, wings folding away as our feet touch solid ground. Farin stands steady as I release him, then gives me a small bow that catches me off guard.

"You saved my son," he says quietly, genuine emotion shining in his eyes. "Not just from the Phoenix, but from the isolation he's lived with for so long. You've given him something I feared he might never find."

"He saved me as well," I admit, surprising myself with the honesty. "I've spent centuries in service to duty, never allowing myself to want more."

Farin's expression softens, his smile warm and genuine. "Then it seems the fates knew exactly what they were doing when they brought you together." He reaches out tentatively, patting my arm with fatherly affection. "I look forward to having you as part of our family, Nesi. To building those relationships I know Milori has always wanted."

The unexpected kindness makes something twist in my chest. It's been centuries since I've thought of my own parents, lost during the early years of our exile. I'd buried those memories deep, duty providing the perfect shield against grief. Now, standing here with Farin's unconditional acceptance washing over me, those memories surface, not with sharp pain, but with a bittersweet ache.

"I would like that," I say softly, the words coming easier than I expected. "It's been a very long time since I've had a family."

Farin's eyes crinkle with understanding. "Well, you have one now. Whether you're ready for it or not." He winks, then hurries to catch up with Milori, who carries Lavera toward the cottage.

I watch them go, something warm and unfamiliar expanding in my chest. A future with family—with belonging—suddenly seems not just possible, but inevitable. It's terrifying and wonderful all at once.

Movement catches my eye, and I tense immediately. Several figures stand near the cottage entrance—not just Jalnor, but others dressed in the unmistakable dark attire of the Night Court. My body goes rigid as I recognize the tall, statuesque figure at their centre.

Queen Neeve.

The rest of our party notices as well. Timas straightens, his posture shifting subtly to one of diplomatic formality. Garrick rests his hand casually on his axe, while the Noble Guard move into a protective formation around their king. Milori hesitates only briefly before continuing toward the cottage, his mother still cradled in his arms.

"Your message was most compelling, cousin," Neeve calls as we approach, her voice carrying across the meadow. "Though it seems events have progressed considerably since you sent it."

I step forward, moving to stand beside my Queen as protocol dictates. "My Queen," I greet her with a respectful nod, automatically falling into the familiar position slightly behind her right shoulder. "I didn't expect you to arrive so quickly." Despite my formal address, relief washes through me at her presence. With both Courts represented, perhaps we can navigate this upheaval with some semblance of order.

"Some matters require personal attention," she replies, her ice-blue eyes taking in our battered appearance. "I see much has transpired."

The cottage door opens as Milori emerges, the gold flecks dancing as his eyes catch the sunlight. Neeve's gaze shifts to him, studying the changes in him with quiet calculation.

Jalnor steps forward, edging closer to me despite my position beside the Queen. His usual buoyant manner is somewhat subdued as he leans in, clearly intending to whisper but failing spectacularly.

"Your Queen is rather intimidating," he tells me with wide eyes. "She arrived an hour ago with her guard and has been questioning me ever since." His voice carries easily across the small gathering. "I may have developed a mild terror of Night Court nobility."

A laugh escapes me—sharp and unexpected—at his unfiltered honesty. The sound surprises even me. Genuine laughter is not something I've often allowed myself. Milori's eyes brighten at the sound, his lips quirking into that smile that seems reserved just for me. Jalnor glances nervously at Neeve. "No offense meant, Your Majesty. I'm sure you're perfectly lovely when not questioning helpless island dwellers about rebel activities."

I continue to laugh as Neeve raises an eyebrow at Jalnor, making him squirm slightly, but as the laughter fades, the spirit bond pulses stronger within me, drawing me toward Milori with an intensity that's becoming difficult to ignore.

The pull is almost physical, like a tether connecting us across the space between. Without conscious thought, I move away from Neeve's side and move toward Milori, breaking protocol in a single step.

Relief washes through me as I reach Milori's side. His arm slides naturally around my waist, the contact immediately settling the restless energy within me.

"My apologies, My Queen," I say, feeling compelled to explain this breach of etiquette. "Milori is my spirit bond. The connection...it's stronger now after what happened with the Phoenix."

Neeve's eyebrows rise, but rather than reprimand, I see understanding in her expression. "A spirit bond supersedes Court protocol, cousin. It always has."

Comforted by her words, I lean more into Milori who seems to sense I need more contact because he tugs me closer still.

"Jalnor, would you help my father settle my mother?" Milori asks. "She needs to rest."

"Of course," Jalnor says, relief evident as he hurries inside and away from this small group.

Milori turns to Neeve with a respectful nod. "Welcome to Manthana, Your Majesty. I apologize for the state of affairs."

"No apology needed, Captain," she replies. "I sense we have much to discuss."

"If I may begin," Timas says, taking command of the conversation, "the situation has changed dramatically in the past few hours."

As Timas explains what happened in the chamber I watch Neeve's face. She betrays little, but I've served her long enough to recognize the subtle signs of shock in the slight widening of her eyes, the barely perceptible tension in her shoulders.

"The Phoenix is truly free?" she asks when Timas finishes. Her voice remains even, though I can hear the undercurrent of concern.

"Yes," Milori confirms. His hand remains at my waist, warm and steady. "And based on what I experienced during our brief connection, it intends to correct the wrongs of the past."

"Meaning?" Neeve presses.

"Meaning the days of magic being restricted to noble blood-lines may be coming to an end," Milori says carefully. "The Phoenix will seek out those it deems worthy, regardless of birth."

Neeve's expression grows thoughtful. "And the other elemental beings?"

"The Phoenix mentioned brothers and sisters," I add. "It seems likely it will seek them out."

Neeve exhales slowly, as if confirming something she'd already begun to suspect. "So, it's happening," she murmurs, more to herself than to us. "A complete upheaval of our power structure. Centuries of tradition undone in a day."

"Perhaps," Timas acknowledges, "or perhaps simply the beginning of a more just system. One based on merit rather than birth."

The conversation flows around me as they discuss implications, potential consequences, timelines. My attention drifts to Milori, to the subtle changes in him since the Phoenix's possession. He stands taller somehow, more settled in his own skin.

"We should remain on Manthana for another day," Timas decides. "Secure the captured Keepers, manage the local situation. Then return to Sonas to begin formal negotiations on how this affects both Courts."

"A wise approach," Neeve agrees.

As the conversation ends, Neeve catches my eye and tilts her head slightly, beckoning me to her. I nod, excusing myself from Milori's side with a gentle touch to his arm. He gives me a questioning look but doesn't protest as I walk over to Neeve.

The hum of conversation floats around us. Unable to find complete privacy, Neeve settles for a spot a short distance away from the group.

"You've served the Night Court with distinction, Nesi," she begins, her tone formal, but not cold. "Your assessment of this situation and your actions in response have proven invaluable."

"Thank you, My Queen," I respond automatically.

"I've been considering our next steps carefully," she continues. "When we return home, I'll need you to undertake a delicate mission. I have had my eye on another location, perhaps this is another bound elemental. It would be prudent to investigate it."

My heart sinks, though I maintain my composure. The request is reasonable, expected even. It's the kind of mission I've handled dozens of times before. I look over my shoulder at Milori who is talking with Timas and the guard, and I can't bring myself to think about leaving him. Even the idea of him following me to the Night Court still leaves me alone in the shadows.

"I'm sorry," I say quietly, turning to look back at Neeve. The words feeling foreign on my tongue. "I cannot undertake this mission."

Surprise flashes across Neeve's face, a rare crack in her regal facade. "Cannot? Or will not?"

I meet her gaze directly. "Both. I'm choosing Milori."

The admission hangs between us, simple yet monumental. In all my years of service, I've never refused an assignment, never put personal desires above duty to the Court.

"I see." Neeve studies me for a long moment, her expression unreadable. Then, unexpectedly, her features soften. "When I sent you to investigate these rebels, I never anticipated you would find your spirit bond."

"Neither did I," I admit.

"Yet here we are." A small smile touches her lips. "You know, in the Night Court's earliest days, before the exile, finding one's spirit bond was considered the highest blessing a Fae could receive. Greater than any title or power."

I remain silent, uncertain where this is leading.

"During the exile, survival took precedence over such traditions. Even I was willing to give it up for the sake of the court. But we are free now, and you, Nesi, are free to choose. I've always believed that home isn't a place. It's where you find belonging." Her gaze shifts to Milori across the meadow. "You've found your home, haven't you?"

The question catches me off guard. I think of Milori's easy laughter, of his family's warmth at the Day Court, of the way he looks at me as if I'm something precious rather than something to be feared.

"Yes," I answer.

Neeve nods, satisfaction replacing surprise in her expression. "Then I'm glad for you. That's all any Night Court Fae can truly hope for. To find where they belong after centuries of displacement."

Relief floods through me. "You're not angry?"

"Disappointed to lose my best agent? Certainly," she acknowledges. "But angry that my cousin has found happiness? Never." She reaches out to touch my shoulder briefly, a rare gesture of affection. "The Courts are changing, Nesi. Perhaps it's fitting that you help forge this new path, bridging our worlds through your bond."

I hadn't expected this reaction—this blessing—and find myself momentarily speechless.

"Though I do expect you to visit, you can't spend all the holidays in the Day Court." And this makes me laugh. "And perhaps you can assist with occasional matters requiring your particular talents," she adds.

"Of course," I agree, still processing this turn of events.

Neeve moves to join Timas, resuming their discussion of diplomatic strategies while I make my way to Milori's side, sliding my hand into his.

"Everything all right?" he asks quietly.

"Yes," I say, allowing a small smile to surface. "I've told Neeve I'm staying with you."

His eyes widen. "You're—but your position, your duties—"

"Are less important than this," I interrupt, squeezing his hand. "Than us."

His face lights up with pure joy, and my smile follows. "You're choosing me over the Night Court?"

"I'm choosing the family I want over the duty I've known," I clarify, the words feeling right as I speak them. "I want what you have, Milori—that warmth, that belonging. It will take time to adjust to life in the light, so to speak, but I want to be there with you, with your family."

Garrick, who has apparently been eavesdropping without shame, lets out a bark of laughter. "Another defector changing Courts!" he announces to everyone. "And here I thought I was the only one crazy enough to tolerate those sunshine-obsessed peacocks."

"Garrick," Milori warns, though without heat.

"What?" he protests innocently. "I'm just saying misery loves company. Now I won't be the only one suffering through those absurd Day Court ceremonies." He turns to me with a conspiratorial grin. "Don't worry, I'll show you all the best hiding spots when Timas starts his speeches about the 'glorious sun' and its 'life-giving warmth.' I've been mapping them for the past year. It's the only reason I haven't killed anyone yet."

A snort of laughter escapes me before I can suppress it, earning a triumphant grin from Garrick.

"Ha! She laughs at my jokes," he declares, nudging Milori. "We will be great friends."

"Don't encourage him," Milori groans, pulling me closer. "He's insufferable enough as it is."

Jalnor approaches, carrying a tray of refreshments. "I think it's wonderful. Love transcending Court boundaries! It's like something from the old tales." He chuckles and surprisingly the drinks don't spill. "A bonding ceremony!" Jalnor exclaims, his face lighting up. "You'll need my brewery's best ale—I've got barrels of the special reserve that'll make it a celebration to remember." He nods decisively. "There's a perfect spot overlooking the bay where you can see both sunrise and sunset. Strategic location."

"Jalnor," Milori tries to interject, though his eyes sparkle with anticipation at the mention of a bonding ceremony.

"The village has some good musicians," Jalnor continues, already deep in planning mode. "Nothing fancy, but solid. And for the feast—well, we should have dishes from both Courts. Practical, really. Shows unity." He claps Milori on the shoulder. "Don't worry about the details. I've organized island gatherings for decades. This one will be the best yet."

"We haven't even set a date," Milori points out, though he can't hide his smile.

"Details!" Jalnor waves dismissively. "The important thing is to be prepared. This island hasn't seen a proper celebration in decades. I've been waiting for you to give me a good excuse to throw a party!"

I smile at his enthusiasm, no fear or reservation in sight. I am happy and excited to bond with Milori.

As the planning for our departure continues around us, Milori leads me to the other side of the cottage, away from the conversation.

"Are you certain about this?" he asks, his voice low and earnest. "Leaving your Court, your queen. It's no small thing."

I consider his question for a moment. "For centuries, I've lived in the shadows, both literally and figuratively. I want to be valued for more than what I can offer and you offered me something different. A chance to be seen, to belong somewhere not out of duty, but out of choice."

His hand cups my cheek, thumb brushing gently across my skin. "And I'll spend every day making sure you never regret that choice."

"I know you will," I murmur.

His eyes brighten with sudden excitement. "Wait until you meet Emilia and Alette. They're going to adore you." He pauses, considering. "Well, Emilia might be upset with me first for not telling her about you before I left, but after that initial explosion, she'll be thrilled."

The thought of meeting his family warms me.

"And the bonding ceremony," he continues, his enthusiasm building. "We could do it at the palace, but that might be a bit much with all those nobles. Timas could make them all stay home though..." He trails off, noticing my expression. "Too much?"

"Just different," I admit. "I am not overly excited about so many people being there. I know it's traditional for fae to throw a grand feast, but I wonder if you would mind a more intimate ceremony?"

"We can do quiet, though I am not sure how quiet Garrick can be, or Jalnor for that matter, but I will throw them off the cliff if need be. Whatever makes you comfortable, my little phantom." He kisses the top of my head.

"How would you feel about doing it here on Manthana? It could be a good place for new beginnings, especially with your parents. But we don't have to either. Whatever you are most comfortable with," I say, and his expression softens.

"I think that's a great idea. Create new happy memories here and replace the old ones." He leans in to kiss me, the world melting away as our new beginning starts. We stand together away from the group for a long while before obligation beckons us back.

"We should make sure they aren't making any terrible plans without us," Milori says quietly while still holding me.

"I'm sure Jalnor is keeping everyone in line," I say, which makes Milori laugh.

"For all that is good, he has probably told a story about me getting stuck on that rock in the ocean for hours." He shakes his head, and I push back to look at him.

"How did you get stuck there?" I ask.

"Let's just say the water moved in such a way that looked like there was a big monster in the water, and Jalnor, being the helpful friend he was, spent the entire time laughing on the beach."

We both laugh, and I can't help but think about how much I am going to enjoy spending my life with this man.

Chapter 22

Milori

"Are you attempting to communicate with the seagulls, or is there another reason you're gesturing wildly at the horizon?"

I spin around, my arms frozen mid-shake as Jalnor crosses my parents' back garden with two steaming cups of tea, his eyebrow raised in amusement.

"Absolutely," I deadpan. "I've discovered they're excellent listeners. Far less judgmental than certain friends I could name."

Jalnor snorts, handing me a cup. "And here I thought you were just shaking out pre-wedding jitters like everyone else does."

"Just managing excess energy," I admit, accepting the tea. "I'm not nervous about Nesi. That's the one thing I'm completely certain about. But the ceremony, all these people, making sure everything goes perfectly..." I rotate my shoulders, feeling the tension there. "My body apparently needs to move or it might explode."

"Perfectly normal," Jalnor says with a knowing smile. "Even our stoic island elders pace like caged animals before their bonding ceremonies. Though I must say, watching the legendary Captain of the Noble Guard shake out his nerves is a unique pleasure. I should have brought some of my special reserve ale instead of tea."

I can't even focus on the ocean view from my parents' cliff-side home. Restless energy pulses through me, refusing to settle. In just a few hours, I'll be bonded to Nesi—truly bonded. How is anyone supposed to stand still with that knowledge?

Two weeks since the Phoenix burst free, two weeks of endless reports and diplomatic meetings and rebuilding, and somehow this—standing here holding Jalnor's absurdly perfect tea—feels more surreal than any of it. I'm getting bonded. Today. To Nesi. By the sun, I'm actually nervous.

"There you are!" Father steps through the back door, his face brighter than I've seen it in centuries. The worry lines around his eyes have softened, replaced by creases of genuine happiness. "Your mother's just finished arranging the flowers for tonight. Come see."

I follow him inside, warmth spreading through my chest at the sight of our family home transformed. Garlands of local wildflowers and sea lavender hang from the beams, while lanterns wait to be lit for this evening's ceremony. Mother stands in the centre of it all, directing the placement of the final arrangements with more energy than I've seen from her in...well, possibly ever.

"Milori!" She turns at my entrance, rushing over with a lightness in her step that makes her seem decades younger. "What do you think?" She gestures to the decorations with unconcealed pride.

"It's beautiful," I tell her, my voice steady. And it is. Simple, elegant, and utterly perfect for the small, intimate bonding ceremony Nesi and I decided on. Just family and a few close friends, right here overlooking the sea. I can't believe it's all happening today.

Mother beams, her cheeks flushed with health. The past two weeks have transformed her physically. Freed from the binding that drained her life force, she's put on weight, her skin glowing with renewed vitality. The shadows under her eyes have vanished, and her movements no longer carry that painful deliberation I'd grown accustomed to.

"Nesi seemed pleased with the arrangements when she stopped by earlier," Mother says, straightening a vase of flowers on the table. "Though she is rather difficult to read."

Father chuckles. "You can't expect everyone to wear their emotions on their sleeve like our son."

"I do not wear my emotions on my sleeve," I protest half-heartedly. "I simply choose to express them in a healthy, communicative way that happens to involve my face and occasionally my entire body."

"Of course, my darling," Mother pats my arm indulgently. "That's precisely why everyone at court always knows exactly what you're thinking."

"A tactical advantage," I insist. "They think they know what I'm thinking, but really I'm three steps ahead."

Father's lips quirk in a half-smile, caution still evident in his eyes. Even after two weeks, we're all learning how to be around each other without centuries of secrets between us. "Is that so?"

"Absolutely," I say, leaning against the doorframe. "It's a highly sophisticated strategy."

Mother watches this exchange, her hands fidgeting with a flower stem. The silence stretches a moment too long before she says, "I've been noticing it more, you know. The way you handle the court nobles. How you let them see what you want them to see." There's a note of pride in her voice, tentative but genuine. "You've become quite skilled at it."

The compliment catches me off guard. It's such a small thing, but her recognition of who I am now, of the skills I've developed in her absence, feels like a bridge being built between us, one careful stone at a time.

"Thank you," I say, not hiding my surprise.

She nods with a smile, a quiet promise—the start of something new. "I should have seen it earlier. There's much I should have seen."

Father clears his throat, clearly trying to keep the moment from becoming too heavy. "Well, I've always seen that our son has his mother's intelligence and his father's dashing good looks. A fortunate combination."

Mother adjusts another flower arrangement, her movements more deliberate than necessary. Father watches her for a moment, then looks back at me. Something passes between them, one of those silent communications that only come from centuries together.

He takes a deep breath before speaking. "Milori, there's something your mother and I have been wanting to discuss with you."

The sudden shift in his tone makes me straighten. "That sounds ominous."

"Not at all," Mother says quickly. "It's just important."

Father nods, his expression a mix of nervousness and determination. "Speaking of the noble court," he continues, "your mother and I have been discussing our plans for the future."

"Oh?" I raise an eyebrow, curious.

Mother nods, exchanging a look with Father. "We've decided to move to Sonas."

I blink, sure I've misheard. "You're what?"

"Moving to Sonas," Father repeats with a grin. "We've already found a lovely little house near the eastern gardens. Close enough to the palace that you can visit easily, but not so close that we'll be underfoot."

"But... your home, the island—" I stammer, taking a step closer to my parents, struggling to process this unexpected news.

Mother takes my hand in hers. "Manthana holds too many memories of secrets and separation. We've spent centuries apart from you because of my duty, and now that I'm free of it, I don't want to waste another moment." Her eyes shine with unshed tears. "If you'll have us, of course."

"If I'll have you?" I echo incredulously. "Of course I'll have you! But are you sure? This is your home."

Father shakes his head. "Home is where family is, Son. And our family is growing." He winks at me. "Besides, I want to be nearby when those grandchildren start arriving."

"Father!" I nearly choke, smiling from ear to ear. "Nesi and I haven't even completed the bonding ceremony yet. Don't you think you're getting a bit ahead of yourself?"

"Not at all," he says cheerfully. "A man my age has to plan ahead. I'd like to be nimble enough to chase the little ones around the garden."

Mother laughs at my expression. "Don't tease him, Farin. Though," she adds with a mischievous glint in her eye, "I do think you and Nesi would make beautiful children."

"And on that horrifying note, I'm going to check on the wine," I announce, setting down my teacup with exaggerated dignity. Truth be told, the thought of children—of building a family with Nesi—sends a flutter of excitement through me. Not that I'd ever admit it to my suddenly over-excited parents.

As I leave the room, I find myself contemplating what it will be like to have them so close. A new reality. One I'll deal with when the time comes.

Heading toward the cellar, a commotion at the front door draws my attention. Timas and Garrick's voices carry through the house, arguing as they enter.

"I'm telling you, the Summer Palace would have been perfectly suitable," Timas says as I round the corner.

"And I'm telling you that your idea of small and intimate still involves two hundred nobles and enough food to feed a small army," Garrick retorts. He spots me and grins. "There's the man of the hour! Tell this royal pain that you made the right choice having the ceremony here instead of letting him turn it into a state occasion."

"My King," I greet Timas with an exaggerated bow, "while I appreciate your generous offer to host what would undoubtedly have been the social event of the season, I believe my spirit bond would have murdered me in my sleep had I agreed."

Timas laughs, clapping me on the shoulder. "Fair enough. The last thing I want is to start your bonded life with murder."

"Besides," I add, "you'll have plenty of opportunity to throw lavish celebrations once the baby arrives. I expect nothing less than a week-long festival with acrobats, fire dancers, and musicians imported from every corner of the realm."

"Don't give him ideas," Garrick groans. "He's already commissioned a giant sculpture made entirely of sugar. A sugar sculpture! For a baby who won't even be able to see it, let alone appreciate the artistry."

"It's traditional," Timas defends himself. "And Emilia loves the idea."

"Emilia would love anything that annoys her brother," I point out. "It's one of her most endearing qualities."

We laugh, but the moment doesn't last as Timas' expression shifts to one of business.

"We've received reports from the eastern islands," he says, his voice dropping. "Three noble houses have lost their fire abilities entirely."

I nod, unsurprised. "The Phoenix is making good on its promise, then. Only those truly worthy of the flame are keeping their powers."

"It seems to be the cruelest nobles who've been affected," Garrick adds. "Lord Hiran, who burned that farmer's fields last year over a boundary dispute? Can't light a candle now."

"And Lady Melis?" I ask, thinking of the notoriously harsh noblewoman.

"Reduced to begging for demonstrations from her own guards," Timas confirms. "She's threatening to travel to Sonas and demand an audience with me."

I can't help the satisfaction that curls through me. "Let her come. She'll find little sympathy after how she's used her abilities over the centuries."

"As for commoners," Timas continues, "some have begun manifesting fire abilities. A baker's apprentice in the river valley, a blacksmith's daughter in Westering. Small manifestations, nothing like your power, but unmistakable."

"Just as the Phoenix promised," I murmur.

"The Council is in an uproar," Timas sighs. "Half the noble houses are demanding we find a way to reverse what's happening, while the other half are scrambling to prove their worthiness by suddenly becoming paragons of virtue."

Garrick snorts. "Too little, too late for them."

"And the search for the other elemental beings?" I ask, leaning against a barrel. "Any progress?"

Timas shakes his head. "We've followed up on every lead the captured Keepers have provided, but they're remarkably resistant to questioning. What little information we have is fragmentary at best. We know there are at least five more beings but their exact locations remain hidden."

"Neeve's scouts found traces of elemental energy at three sites in the Night Court territories," Garrick adds. "But whatever was there had already been moved. The Keepers must have relocated the beings as soon as the Phoenix escaped."

"They've had contingency plans for centuries," I remind them. "We won't find the others easily."

"Nevertheless, we'll keep searching," Timas says firmly. "If these beings wish to be found, I suspect they'll make their presence known in time. The Phoenix certainly did."

"And what of the Keepers themselves?" I ask, thinking of Merida and her followers, now imprisoned in Sonas's deep cells.

"Uncooperative but secure," Timas answers. "We've separated them to prevent coordination, but they're still managing to maintain their silence. Whatever oaths bind them, they take them seriously."

I nod. "My mother wishes the Keepers had trusted her more—not for power, but simply to help. If they had confided in her, perhaps we wouldn't be grasping at fragments now.

"If it weren't for your mother, we'd know nothing. She has been an unexpected ally," Timas acknowledges. "Her insights into the Keepers' organization have proven invaluable, limited though they may be. The paintings of the red-sashed nobles that hang in the gallery have led to finding more noble women keepers, though I'm sure we are missing many."

A brief silence falls between us, broken only by the distant sound of voices from above. So much has changed, yet here we stand: the three of us together, as we've been through countless challenges before.

"It won't be the same, you know," Garrick says, his gruff voice unusually soft. "Our little group. All these changes..."

"Change isn't always bad," I remind him. "You survived when Timas bonded with Emilia, didn't you? Moving to Sonas, bonding with Alette."

"Barely," he grumbles. "And now you're bonding with a shadow walker, and Timas is about to become a father, and everything's shifting."

"The core remains," Timas says firmly. "Some bonds transcend change."

Garrick nods, then brightens mischievously. "At least I'll have someone to commiserate with now that there is another person not from the Day Court. Nesi understands the burden of dealing with you sunshine-obsessed fae day in and day out."

"You love us," I remind him, and he huffs a disgruntled agreement.

"I should probably get ready," I say, suddenly aware of how quickly time is passing. "Jalnor threatened to dunk me in the ocean himself if I'm not properly dressed when Nesi arrives for the bonding."

"Can't have that," Timas agrees with a smile. "Go on, then. Your king commands you to look presentable for once in your life."

I bow dramatically before heading upstairs, my heart racing with anticipation.

In just a few hours, Nesi will be here, and our new life will begin.

Chapter 23

Nesi

The mirror reflects a stranger.

My hair cascades in waves around my shoulders, woven with intricate braids, and tiny white flowers nestled within them like stars in a night sky. The dress—traditional Night Court formal wear—shimmers with subtle movement, its deep blue fabric absorbing light rather than reflecting it. Silver threads catch what little illumination filters through the windows of Milori's parents' bedroom, creating the impression of distant constellations against the darkness. Sheer silver fabric drapes across my shoulders, flowing down my arms in a way that reminds me of my shadows when they move of their own accord.

I turn slightly, watching how the fabric shifts like liquid night. This ceremonial attire feels both familiar and foreign, like a piece of home I'm taking with me into a new life.

"You look beautiful, cousin."

Neeve stands in the doorway, her posture as regal as always, though something in her expression seems softer today. She crosses the room with measured steps, stopping a respectful distance away.

"Thank you," I reply, smoothing invisible wrinkles from the dress. "I wasn't sure about wearing traditional Night Court attire, but..."

"But it's who you are," Neeve finishes. "No matter where you make your home."

A silence stretches between us, not uncomfortable but heavy with unspoken words. Through the open window, sounds of final preparations drift up from the garden, Jalnor's voice rising above others as he directs the placement of lanterns. Garrick's distinctive laugh punctuates the gentle chaos.

Neeve's reflection joins mine in the mirror, our similar features a reminder of shared blood. She reaches out, adjusting one of the flower-laden braids with unexpected gentleness.

"I owe you an apology, Nesi," she says, her voice lower than usual. Her fingers linger on the intricate braid, a rare moment of physical connection between us.

"You don't—"

"I do." Her ice-blue eyes meet mine in the mirror. "For years, I've valued your skills, your loyalty, your effectiveness. But I failed to show you that I valued you not just as my spymaster or my agent, but as my family."

I turn to face her directly, surprised by the open emotion in her usually guarded expression.

"The Night Court demanded a certain strength from all of us," she continues. "Especially from me. After the exile, after what Oberon did to our people, I couldn't show weakness, not even to those closest to me."

"I never expected anything different," I tell her truthfully. "We all did what was necessary to survive."

"Perhaps. But necessity doesn't excuse everything." She takes a breath, straightening her shoulders. "You were never just a tool to be wielded, Nesi. You are my cousin. My family. And I should have made sure you knew that."

The words sink into places inside me I'd forgotten existed—spaces hollowed out by centuries of duty and isolation. I'd never allowed myself to need this acknowledgment, this recognition of my worth beyond what my shadows could accomplish. Yet hearing it now, on the threshold of my new life, feels like a circle completing.

"I didn't need to hear it," I say softly. "But I'm glad I did."

Neeve nods, her composure returning though her eyes remain warm. "The Day Court will gain a formidable ally in you. And Milori..." a small smile touches her lips, "well, he's gained something far more precious."

A knock at the door interrupts us. Emilia enters first, her growing belly preceding her, followed by Alette. Warmth spreads through my chest at the sight of these women I've come to know over the past two weeks—Milori's family, and soon to be mine as well.

"We're not interrupting, are we?" Emilia asks, though she continues into the room without waiting for an answer. "Oh,

Nesi, you look absolutely stunning!" Warmth spreads through me and a smile follows.

"Truly beautiful," Alette agrees, her quiet voice a contrast to Emilia's exuberance. "The flowers were the perfect choice."

Neeve steps back, her diplomatic mask sliding into place. "I should check that everything is proceeding according to schedule," she says. "The Night Court contingent will want to ensure all protocols are observed."

I recognize her tactical retreat for what it is—giving me space with my new family while maintaining her dignified persona in front of the Day Court women. I catch her hand briefly before she can leave.

"Thank you," I say, meaning it for more than just today.

She squeezes my fingers once, then slips from the room with regal grace.

"Was that actual emotion I saw from the Ice Queen?" Emilia asks, settling onto a chair with a sigh of relief. "I'm impressed. She's always so..." she gestures vaguely, "composed. Even when she tried to steal my bond mate." She mutters, and I can't help but laugh because yes, Neeve did in fact try to propose an alliance through marriage with Timas.

"Emilia," Alette chides gently.

"What? It was a compliment! Mostly." Emilia grins. "I respect her ability to terrify an entire room without raising her voice. It's a skill I'm still working on."

"You're doing quite well," I say. "Garrick mentioned something about flying pots..."

Emilia laughs, the sound bright and infectious. "He exaggerates. It was one pot, and it was more of a gentle toss in his general direction." She adjusts her position, touching her growing belly with a smile. "I felt the baby flutter this morning!"

"They're excited for the ceremony," Alette exclaims, moving to sit beside her.

"Or they're practicing combat moves like their aunt," Emilia counters with a wry smile.

I watch them together—Alette's calm presence balancing Emilia's vibrant energy—and find myself grateful for their acceptance. When we first arrived in Sonas two weeks ago, I'd expected polite distance at best, suspicion at worst. Instead, they'd welcomed me immediately, folding me into their circle as if I'd always belonged there.

"Milori is practically vibrating with anticipation," Emilia says, eyes twinkling. "Timas says he caught him practicing his vows to a potted plant this morning."

"That sounds like him," I concede, my cheeks beginning to hurt with how much I'm smiling. The past two weeks have been a whirlwind of diplomatic meetings, explanations, and adjustments, but through it all, Milori has been my constant, his unwavering support making everything else manageable.

"He loves you so deeply," Alette observes quietly. "I've only known him a short while, but you can tell how much he adores you."

"I've never seen him so..." Emilia wavers her hand like that explains everything.

"So what?" I ask, genuinely curious.

"At peace," she says. "He always wore a mask, and now he barely cares to put it on. He is genuinely happy, and him not needing to please all the court is enjoyable to watch, though many nobles would not agree and want the old Milori back." She says, far too pleased.

The words touch something deep within me. *Peace*. Not a concept I've associated with myself before. My shadows have always been tools of war, secrecy, and violence. The idea that I could bring peace to someone else, especially someone as vibrant as Milori, feels like a revelation.

"Are you nervous?" Emilia asks, her expression softening.

I consider the question honestly. "No." And it's true. Among all the uncertainty of recent weeks, this is the one thing that feels absolutely right. "I'm ready."

"Then we shouldn't keep him waiting any longer," Emilia says, somehow springing up from her seat. "You know how dramatic he gets when left to his own devices for too long. He's liable to think a catastrophe has happened and storm up here."

I laugh at the accuracy of her assessment. "We can't have that."

They lead me from the room and down the narrow staircase of the cliff-side home that has somehow become the centrepiece of our new beginning. Outside, the sun hangs low in the sky, painting everything in golden light.

The garden has been transformed. Lanterns hang from trees, waiting to be lit as twilight deepens. Garlands of flowers create a natural archway leading to a circular clearing where more blossoms form a perfect ring. Guests stand in small groups—our closest friends and family. They all turn as I emerge from the house.

Milori stands at the center, encircled by a crown of wildflowers.

He wears formal Day Court attire in deep blue that matches my dress, golden threads catching the light with every breath he takes. His sea-green eyes, now permanently flecked with gold, widen as they find me. The naked adoration in his gaze steals my breath.

A priestess stands beside him, her robes a perfect blend of Day and Night Court colours—a symbolic unity that mirrors our own. As I begin walking toward them, the gathered crowd parts silently, creating a path.

With each step, the spirit bond pulses stronger between us, no longer fighting or straining, but settling into place like the final piece of a long incomplete puzzle. The shadows beneath my skin respond to his proximity, reaching toward him in tendrils; I can't control them and I don't want to. They want Milori and so do I.

When I reach the flower circle, Milori extends his hand. "I didn't think it was possible for you to become more beautiful, but I think it's the fact you are bonding me that makes you far more stunning," he says, and I respond with a laugh.

"Yes, I'm sure that's why." His charming smile melts my usual cool demeanour. Since meeting him and truly accepting this gift, I find myself smiling more willingly and laughing more freely.

The priestess smiles, raising her arms to address the gathering. "We come together as the day meets night, as the light touches darkness, to witness the bonding of two souls already connected by fate's design. A spirit bond is the rarest and most sacred connection our kind can experience. It is a gift from the ancient powers that shaped our world."

As she speaks the ritual words, calling on both sun and stars to witness our vows, I keep my eyes on Milori. The ceremony itself feels like a formality. Our true bonding began days ago on a cliff face surrounded by fire and shadow, when we first acknowledged what we meant to each other.

"The strength of fire," the priestess continues, "and the depth of shadow. Two elements that seem opposed, yet together create a perfect balance. Milori of the Day Court, speak your vow."

Milori takes both my hands in his, his eyes never leaving mine. "Nesi, from the first moment I saw you, something in me recognized something in you. Though I should probably mention that you spent that first moment rejecting me and then practically running away." Soft laughter ripples through the gathered guests, and I feel warmth rise to my cheeks. His smile widens. "But perhaps that makes this moment that much sweeter. Having to prove my love to you has been the greatest gift, because now, without a shadow of a doubt—and you have plenty of those—" another gentle laugh, "I know that what we have is real and earned."

His voice grows stronger, more certain with every word. "I vow to stand beside you, not as your protector but as your partner. I vow to be the sturdy wall you can depend on, to support your ambitions rather than impede them. I vow to love you as you are, shadows and all, for all the days of my very long life. And I vow to build with you the family I could only dream of. A place of belonging where neither of us ever has to be alone again."

His words echo those he spoke on Manthana, the promise he made before we fully understood what lay ahead of us. The priestess turns to me.

"Nesi of the Night Court, speak your vow."

I've never been one for flowery words or grand declarations. But looking into Milori's eyes, the words come naturally. "Milori, you saw me when others looked away. You reached for me when others recoiled. You found beauty in my darkness and gave me a place to belong." My voice remains steady though emotion threatens to overwhelm me. "I vow to walk beside you through light and shadow. I vow to be your sanctuary as you have been mine. I vow to love you, not just for what you give me, but for who you are, for all the days of my very long life."

A single tear tracks down his cheek, and he doesn't bother to hide it. The priestess raises her hands again, her voice rising.

"By the ancient powers that bind our world, by the will of both Courts united, I declare these two souls bonded in the eyes of all Fae." She produces a silken cord—one side golden, one side midnight blue—and wraps it around our joined hands. "What fate has joined, let no power divide."

The cord glows briefly, then dissolves into sparkling dust that settles on our skin before fading away. As it disappears, something shifts within the spirit bond, a final barrier dissolving, leaving nothing but pure connection between us. I gasp at the sensation, and Milori's eyes widen, telling me he feels it too.

"Sealed in magic, bound in love," the priestess announces. "With this kiss, let your bond be complete."

Milori lets one of my hands go as he comes up to cup my cheek, his touch gentle as if I might dissolve like the ceremony cord. "My bond mate," he whispers, the words filled with wonder.

"My bond mate," I reply, the unfamiliar term feeling right on my tongue.

When his lips meet mine, the spirit bond flares brilliantly between us. My shadows surge forward to meet his inner fire, no longer two separate forces but a single, harmonious energy. In that moment, with his arms around me and the sounds of celebration rising from the gathered witnesses, I understand what Alette meant about peace.

This is where I belong. Not in darkness, not in light, but in the perfect balance between the two. With him.

Chapter 24

Milori

T he lanterns glow brighter as night falls, casting golden pools of light across my parents' garden. Laughter and conversation drift through the evening air as our small gathering celebrates under the stars. I can't take my eyes off Nesi. My bond mate. The words still feel new on my tongue, sweet and perfect.

She stands across the garden, speaking with Queen Neeve. Even surrounded by Night Court friends, she draws my gaze like a beacon. Her midnight blue dress shimmers under the lantern light, making her look like she's wrapped in stars. The white flowers woven through her dark hair complete the image.

"You're staring again," Timas says, appearing at my shoulder with two glasses of wine.

I accept one without looking away from Nesi. "Can you blame me?"

"Not at all." He follows my gaze, his expression softening. "You two make quite the pair."

"Like we were made to complement each other," I say, echoing words I once spoke on a cliff face that feels like a lifetime ago.

Timas raises his glass in a silent toast. "To new beginnings. And to finding home in unexpected places."

We drink, the rich flavours of Jalnor's finest vintage spreading warmth through my chest. Beyond Timas' shoulder, I catch sight of Garrick entertaining a group of villagers with what appears to be a dramatic re-enactment of our encounter with the Northern Orc Clan. His exaggerated gestures and booming voice carry across the garden, drawing laughter from his audience.

"Should I be concerned that he's telling everyone I fainted at the first sign of trouble?" I ask, nodding toward Garrick.

Timas glances over his shoulder and smirks. "I believe his exact words were 'screamed like a startled peacock before swooning delicately into my waiting arms.'"

"That's outrageous," I sputter. "I was taken aback for a moment at the sheer amount of orcs on the mountainside! And I certainly didn't swoon into his arms. If anything, he was cowering behind me."

"I'm sure historical accuracy isn't his primary concern,"

"Well, two can play at this game." I hand my wine glass back to Timas. "Excuse me while I go remind everyone about the time Garrick got trapped in that cave because he thought a particularly menacing shadow was actually a terrifying monster."

Timas laughs, shaking his head as I make my way through the crowd. Before I can reach Garrick, however, a hand catches my arm.

"Running off already?" Father asks, his eyes twinkling with mischief. "The bond ceremony was less than an hour ago."

"Just going to correct some historical inaccuracies," I say, throwing a mock glare in Garrick's direction.

Father chuckles, steering me away from my intended target. "Let him have his moment. It's not every day one gets to embarrass the Captain of the Guard at his bonding celebration."

I sigh dramatically but allow myself to be redirected. "Fine, but I'm keeping a ledger of every exaggeration. Payback will be swift and merciless."

"Naturally." Father guides me toward Mother, who sits near the garden wall, deep in conversation with a woman from the village, Quella. The transformation in her still takes my breath away. Her cheeks flush with colour, her eyes bright with life rather than dulled by constant pain. She laughs at something Quella says, the sound carrying clearly across the garden. It's a sound I've heard more in the past two weeks than in centuries before.

"You look happy, son," Father says softly.

"I am." The simple truth of it resonates deep within me. "Happier than I thought possible."

"Good." He squeezes my shoulder. "That's all we ever wanted for you, you know. Even when we went about it all wrong."

"I know that now." And I do. The past weeks have brought understanding and great healing. It's a start, a foundation to build upon.

Mother spots us approaching and waves us over. "There's my handsome son," she calls, patting the bench beside her. "Come, sit with us for a moment."

I oblige, settling beside her as Father takes position on her other side. She immediately takes my hand, her fingers warm against mine.

"You performed the ceremony beautifully," she says, pride evident in her voice. "Your bond mate is extraordinary."

"She is," I agree, finding Nesi again. As if sensing my gaze, she looks up, our eyes meeting over the heads of the gathered guests. The spirit bond pulses between us, stronger now after the ceremony—a constant awareness of her presence that feels like coming home.

"The gold in your eyes shines brighter when you look at her," Mother observes. "The Phoenix approves of your choice."

I turn back to her, surprised. "You can tell?"

She nods, something like wonder crossing her face. "It's still strange, seeing you embrace what I feared for so long. But watching you with the Phoenix's power, it suits you. It always did."

"Well, I certainly prefer having it as an ally rather than a roommate," I joke. "Being possessed is vastly overrated."

Mother's expression grows more serious. "There will be challenges ahead, you know. The Phoenix's freedom has only begun to change our world. The other elemental beings..."

"Will be found when they're ready," I finish for her. "And we'll face whatever comes together." I glance at my father. "All of us."

And we take comfort in our new budding family.

"Speaking of changes," she says, "your father and I have a gift for you and Nesi."

Father produces a small wooden box from his pocket, intricate carvings decorating its surface. He hands it to me with a flourish.

"What's this?" I ask, turning the box in my hands.

"Open it," Mother encourages.

Inside, nestled on a bed of midnight blue velvet, lies a key—ancient by the look of it, made of burnished gold with intricate patterns etched into its surface.

"The key to this cottage," Father explains. "Your mother and I want you and Nesi to have it."

I stare at them, momentarily speechless. "But you love this place. And I thought you were moving to Sonas?"

"We are," Mother confirms. "But this has been our home for centuries. It should remain in the family." Her eyes grow misty. "Perhaps someday, you'll bring your children here. Show them where their father grew up."

"Besides," Father adds with a grin, "we need somewhere to escape when court life becomes too tedious. A vacation home, if you will."

"I—" words fail me as emotion tightens my throat. "Thank you. Both of you."

Mother squeezes my hand. "It's the least we can do, after everything."

Before I can respond, a familiar voice calls my name. Jalnor approaches, weaving through the crowd with a bottle of his reserve ale in one hand and two glasses in the other.

"There you are!" he exclaims, stopping before me with a broad smile. "Can't hide from the host of the feast, you know."

"I wouldn't dream of it," I assure him, rising to my feet. "Mother, Father, if you'll excuse me?"

They wave me off with knowing smiles, and I follow Jalnor to a quieter corner of the garden. He pours two glasses of his golden ale with the ceremony the brew deserves, handing one to me with exaggerated formality.

"To my oldest friend," he says, raising his glass. "May your bonded life bring you all the joy you deserve."

We drink, the ale rich and complex on my tongue. "This is exceptional, Jalnor." He hums in agreement.

"So," he says after a moment, his voice taking on a serious tone. "How are you feeling? Really feeling, I mean."

I consider the question, knowing he's not asking about the bonding. "Different," I admit quietly. "The Phoenix left a mark, there's a part of me that wasn't there before, or perhaps was always there but dormant."

Jalnor nods, his expression thoughtful. "I've noticed something similar, actually. Though not nearly as dramatic as your situation, of course."

This catches me off guard. "What do you mean?"

He glances around before leaning closer. "The other day, I was at the brewery. One of the barrels had spoiled. Good ale wasted. I got angry, really angry, which you know isn't like me."

"You? Angry? I don't believe it," I tease, trying to lighten his suddenly serious mood.

He doesn't smile. "The entire room shook, Milori. Bottles rattled off shelves. At first, I thought it was an earthquake, but..." he trails off, looking troubled. "It was me. Somehow, I know it was me."

I stare at him, comprehension dawning. "The Earth Titan," I whisper.

Jalnor shrugs uncomfortably. "Maybe. Or maybe I just had too much of my own product that morning." He forces a laugh, but his eyes remain serious. "Either way, it's unsettling. To suddenly discover you might be something other than what you thought."

I place a hand on his shoulder. "Trust me, I understand that better than most."

"I know you do." He sighs, then brightens with visible effort. "But enough of that on your bonding day! We'll have plenty of time to worry about ancient beings and mysterious powers later."

Before I can press him further, a commotion near the centre of the garden draws our attention. Garrick stands on a bench, his massive frame swaying slightly as he raises a glass high.

"Attention, everyone!" he calls, his voice carrying easily across the space. "I'd like to propose a toast to the happy couple!"

"This should be good," I mutter to Jalnor, who chuckles in agreement.

We make our way closer as Garrick continues, "I've known Milori for what feels like forever. He's saved my life more times than I care to admit, though I've saved his at least twice as often." Scattered laughter ripples through the gathering.

"When I first found out about his spirit bond, I was certain she would take one look at the preening pretty boy and run away." He meets my eyes across the crowd, his expression softening despite his teasing words. Nesi appears at my side as if summoned by his words, her hand slipping into mine with natural ease. The spirit bond hums contentedly at her proximity. "But then I saw them together, and I understood. She was just as delusional." Everyone laughs. "Don't send those shadow things after me again," he quips, looking directly at Nesi.

"No promises," she says loudly to everyone's joy.

"To Milori and Nesi," Garrick raises his glass higher. "May your shadows always keep his ego in check, and may his light always show you the way home."

"To Milori and Nesi!" the crowd echoes, glasses raised toward the darkening sky.

Nesi leans against me, a smile playing at the corners of her mouth. "An unexpectedly sweet toast from someone who threatened to throw an axe at your head when you first introduced us."

"Garrick expresses affection through violence and insults," I explain, pressing a kiss to her temple. "It's part of his charm."

She laughs softly, the sound still rare enough to send a thrill through me. "The Night Court expresses affection through subtle nods and marginally less severe frowns. Perhaps that's why Queen Neeve is having such difficulty with your exuberant friends."

I follow her gaze to where Neeve stands stiffly beside Timas, her expression carefully neutral as he gestures animatedly about something. "She'll adapt. Or flee back to the Night Court in horror. Either way, it's entertaining to watch."

"You have a wicked streak," Nesi observes, but there's warmth in her voice.

"Just one of my many charms." I grin down at her. "Speaking of which, would you like to see another?"

Curiosity flickers in her dark eyes. "What did you have in mind?"

I lean closer, my lips brushing the shell of her ear. "I may have arranged a surprise for later. Away from all these watchful eyes."

"Intriguing." Her shadows ripple subtly beneath her skin, responding to my proximity. "When do we leave?"

"Whenever you're ready," I tell her. "The night is ours, bond mate."

The words sends a fresh wave of joy through me. After centuries of watching others find their perfect match, I've finally found mine. In the most unexpected person imaginable.

"Then perhaps we should begin our farewells," she suggests, her hand tightening around mine. "Before your mother starts hinting about grandchildren again."

I laugh, remembering Mother's not-so-subtle comments earlier. "An excellent point. Though I fear we'll never hear the end of it now that they're moving to Sonas."

"I can handle your mother," Nesi says confidently. "It's Emilia and Jalnor's combined enthusiasm that concerns me."

"Fair enough. Lucky for you Jalnor lives here." I raise our joined hands to my lips, pressing a kiss to her knuckles. "Shall we?"

We make our way through the gathering, accepting congratulations and saying our goodbyes. Emilia embraces me fiercely, whispering threats about taking a long enough vacation before returning to work. Timas clasps my arm in that way of his that manages to convey both kingship and brotherhood simultaneously.

Neeve surprises us both by embracing Nesi—briefly but genuinely—before inclining her head to me with something almost like approval in her eyes.

Finally, we reach my parents. Mother hugs me tightly, whispering, "Be happy, my son. That's all I ever wanted for you."

"I know," I whisper back. "I am."

Father embraces me next, his familiar scent of sea air and pipe smoke enveloping me. "Take care of each other," he says simply.

"We will," I promise.

With final waves to the gathered crowd, Nesi and I unfurl our wings. We launch into the air together, the familiar rush of flight heightened by the spirit bond pulsing between us. Below, our friends and family grow smaller, the lanterns becoming distant stars as we soar higher.

"Where are we going?" Nesi calls over the wind.

"You'll see," I answer with a grin, banking toward the island's northern shore.

We fly in companionable silence, wings beating in perfect rhythm. The island spreads beneath us, dense forests giving way to hidden valleys and secluded coves. I lead us toward a wooded glen I discovered as a child. It was my secret refuge when judgment from the town became too much.

We descend through a break in the canopy, landing softly on mossy ground. Lanterns hang from the surrounding trees, casting warm light across the small clearing. A large tent stands at its centre, crafted from fine fabric in deep purples and golds.

"What is this?" Nesi asks, her eyes wide as she takes in the scene.

"Jalnor's doing," I admit. "I mentioned wanting somewhere private for our first night as bond mates, and he...well, he exceeded expectations, as usual."

Inside the tent, plush cushions and fine linens create a luxurious nest. More lanterns hang from the ceiling, their golden light reflecting off burnished metal surfaces. A small table holds wine, fruits, and cakes for later.

"It's perfect," Nesi says softly, turning to face me.

I take her hands in mine, suddenly overcome by the reality of this moment. "I can't believe we're here," I confess. "After everything that's happened—the Phoenix, the Keepers, all of it—I keep expecting to wake up and find it was all a dream. Or at the very least, you still running away from me."

"I didn't run away, I walked briskly." Her hands tighten around mine. "But it's not a dream. Though I understand the feeling." Her eyes meet mine, dark and beautiful in the lantern light. "I never expected this. Any of this."

"Regrets?" I ask, only half-joking.

She shakes her head, a small smile playing at her lips. "None. Though I am curious about what happens next."

"Well," I say, drawing her closer, "I have some thoughts on that particular subject for tonight, but if you mean in the broader sense..."

"Both." Her smile widens. "But perhaps start with the broader sense."

I laugh, wrapping my arms around her waist. "Ever practical, even on our bonding night." I lean my forehead against hers, considering the question. "I think we return to Sonas. I continue my duties as Captain of the Noble Guard, and you can be the spymaster or a delicate noblewoman, your choice."

"I'll take the spymaster position, please." She chuckles.

"I know a person who can arrange that." I pull her closer, needing to feel her close to me.

"And the other elemental beings?" she asks.

"We find them," I say simply. "Or they find us. Which seems to be happening with Jalnor." Nesi startles, hearing that information. "I'll explain later. But it seems with the phoenix unbound, the others' bindings might be weakening."

"The Shadow Leviathan..." Nesi touches the necklace around her neck her mother gave her.

"Have you felt different?" I ask, and she nods her head.

"Yes, like a stronger pull to find where my shadows keep running off to," she shakes her head in disbelief. "That sounds crazy."

I cup her face. "No, it doesn't. We will search and find out the answers. Together."

She leans into my touch, her eyes drifting closed. "Together," she agrees.

The spirit bond pulses between us, stronger than ever before. It no longer feels like separate forces meeting—my fire, her shadows—but a single, harmonious energy that belongs to both of us.

I lean down, capturing her lips with mine. The kiss starts gentle but quickly deepens, weeks of tension and anticipation igniting between us. Her hands slide into my hair, pulling me closer as shadows dance across her skin, reaching for me with eager tendrils. The fire inside seems to burn bright, and when we pull apart, breaths heavy, I look at the beautiful woman in front of me.

"Your eyes," she whispers. "They're glowing."

"Yours too," I tell her. The darkness of her irises has deepened, subtle shadows moving within them like living things. "Beautiful."

She pulls me down for another kiss, more urgent this time. "I love you," she murmurs against my lips, the words still new and precious between us.

"I love you too," I reply, meaning it more than any words I've ever spoken. "My phantom, my heart, my bond mate."

Outside our tent, the night deepens. Somewhere across the island, celebrations continue. Somewhere beyond Manthana, ancient powers stir, awakening after centuries of slumber. The world is changing around us, power shifting like sand beneath the tides.

But here, in this moment, none of that matters. Here, there is only us: fire and shadow, day and night, two halves of a whole finally united. Whatever tomorrow brings, we'll face it together.

For now, that's all I need to know.

Also by TM Goodkey

The Fae King Series

Fated Mates and Funny Side Characters? Try out this series!

A Spy's Fateful Bond

Bonded By Intrigue

Garrick's Story:

Bonded By Destiny

Milori's Story:

Bonded Across Courts

Acknowledgements

You did it! You made it to the end! I hope you enjoyed the story and if you do I would greatly appreciate a review on any and all platforms you can. As an Indie author reviews help us out so much!

Thank again to, you, for all the support. I wouldn't be able to write like this if it wasn't for the constant support.

Thank you also to my wonderful friend Delanie, you tolerate my whirlwind writing style and edit my books right a long side me, I can't begin to thank you for that.

Please if you like my stories and want to follow along please follow me on IG @tmgoodkey or even sign up for my newsletter.

https://authortmgoodkey.eo.page/newsletter

All my love.

TM

About the author

Making dwarves blush, orcs believe in love, and elves lose their cool - that's what TM Goodkey does best. Living in Ontario, Canada, she's beyond happily married with two beautiful children and a backyard full of chickens (which, according to her kids, definitely count as pets). An avid reader of ALL things magical/fantasy with a side of romance, TM has been a published Indie Author since May of 2024. She writes closed door romantasy filled with funny characters, swoony moments, and everything in between.

You can find her here:

Website- www.tmgoodkey.com

Facebook- TM Goodkey Author

Instagram @tmgoodkey